Acclaim for STEVEN MILLHAUSER's

LITTLE KINGDOMS

"Irresistible. . . . Steven Millhauser is, all in all, a wonderfully appropriate writer for our very own fin de siècle."
—*Washington Post*

"Steven Millhauser is one of the best, most exhilarating writers in the United States today." —*Cleveland Plain Dealer*

"As Gothic as Poe and as imaginative as *Fantasia*, Millhauser's deceptive fables are funny and warm. But they're dark as dungeons, too—unsettling and possibly dangerous. He bewitches you." —*Entertainment Weekly*

"[Steven Millhauser] creates a world that is exquisite in its tortures and terrors, a world which only the heightened consciousness of an artist or a dreamer could inhabit."
—William Kennedy, *Washington Post Book World*

"Mr. Millhauser possesses a bountiful imagination, and an ability to catch his perceptions in a bright butterfly net of prose."
—Michiko Kakutani, *The New York Times*

"What a pleasure it is to read a writer this good—Millhauser seems sometimes to return us to the original sources of art, the awe and wonder before the untrustworthy but beautiful force of existence. . . . I love this writer." —Peter Straub

STEVEN MILLHAUSER

LITTLE KINGDOMS

Steven Millhauser received the Pulitzer Prize for *Martin Dressler*. He is a recipient of the Lannan Award and has been honored by the American Academy of Arts and Letters. The author of *Edwin Mullhouse, The Barnum Museum,* and *The Penny Arcade,* among other books, he teaches at Skidmore College and lives with his wife and two children in Saratoga Springs, New York.

LITTLE
KINGDOMS

Three Novellas

STEVEN MILLHAUSER

VINTAGE CONTEMPORARIES

Vintage Books

A Division of Random House, Inc.

New York

FIRST VINTAGE CONTEMPORARIES EDITION, FEBRUARY 1998

Copyright © 1993 by Steven Millhauser

"Catalogue of the Exhibition" previously appeared in *Salmagundi* Issue #92. "The Princess, the Dwarf, and the Dungeon" previously appeared in *Antaeus* Issue #70.

Millhauser, Steven.
Little kingdoms : three novellas / Steven Millhauser.
p. cm.
Contents: The little kingdom of J. Franklin Payne — The princess, the dwarf, and the dungeon — Catalogue of the exhibition: the art of Edmund Moorash (1810–1846).
ISBN 0–375–70143–5
I. Title
[PS3563.I422A6   1998]
813'.54—dc21   97–34396
CIP

Random House Web address: http://www.randomhouse.com/

Printed in the United States of America
10 9 8 7 6 5 4 3 2 1

To Jonathan and Anna

CONTENTS

The Little Kingdom

of

J. Franklin Payne

ONE

One warm blue night toward the middle of July, in the year 1920, John Franklin Payne, a newspaper cartoonist by trade, looked up from his desk in the third-floor study of his home in Mount Hebron, New York, and saw with surprise that it was three o'clock in the morning. The world was absolutely still. Through the windows the sky was a deep, glowing blue, as if there must be a bright moon somewhere, and Franklin felt a sudden desire to burst through the window into the blue night sky. The desire startled him, for he liked to work alone in his tower study late into the night. The study was warm, uncomfortably warm; despite the new screen in the lower half of the center window, the small room held the heat of the roof.

In the hot stillness Franklin took off his vest and looked again at the glass-cased clock on top of his high-backed desk. The glass door with the brass handle, the lacy clock-hands, the exposed cogwheels, the big metal key lying under the swinging pendulum, all this seemed strange and unseen before, though the clock had stood on the mantelpiece of his parents' home in Ohio since his earliest childhood; and the familiar, strange clock, the glowing sky, the mysterious hour, all seemed connected with something inside him that was about to burst. As he stared at the pendulum he began to notice that the stillness of the hour was really a secret riot of sound: the dark tick of the clock, like drops of water dripping from an eave, the shrill of crickets beyond the screen, and under it all, clearer and clearer, the gentle rasp of his wife's breathing as it came through the open window of the second-floor bedroom. He had told Cora he would be done in an hour or so, but the six-panel strip had proved unexpectedly stubborn. And then he had laid aside his drawing board, that smooth-worn dark board with a faint shine that reminded him of the shine of a well-handled pipe, and with a sense of excitement he had brought out the packet of carefully trimmed rice paper, set up his other board with its glass window, pulled over his jar of Venus pencils and a fresh bottle of black drawing ink, and set to work on his secret, exhilarating project.

What to do? If he went down to his bedroom next to Cora's on the second floor, and fell asleep instantly, he would get only two and a half hours of sleep before the rattle of milk bottles in the wire box on the front porch announced his five-thirty rising. But Franklin was too excited to sleep. He was excited by the glowing blue sky, by the clamorous silence, by his lamplit tower room high above the rest of the house, by the sense that he was creating a world far more enchanting than the world of his comic strips, which had already brought him a certain notoriety. He was bursting with energy. He thought how nice it would be to creep downstairs and slip into bed with Cora—but she would be angry if he woke her. For though Cora was given to passionate whims of her own, she did not like to be surprised. Franklin remembered that a colleague was coming up for a visit on Saturday, and he had a sudden misgiving about Max: suppose Cora—but there was no use worrying about it now. He decided to work straight through the night. Immediately he decided not to. His eyes ached, his temples throbbed, his hand had become slightly unsteady—the last drawing had almost been spoiled.

Franklin numbered the piece of rice paper carefully in the lower right-hand corner and added it to the pile of thirty-two new drawings, each of which had been traced over the preceding drawing and exactly resembled it except for a small departure. Each of the separate drawings still had to be gone over in ink and then mounted on a piece of cardboard in order to be examined in his viewing machine. He now had 1,826 India-ink drawings, which had taken him almost three months to complete. At sixteen frames per second he would need nearly 4,000 drawings for a four-minute animated cartoon.

Franklin pushed back his chair carefully, for Cora complained that she could hear his chair scrape even though her room was not directly below the tower study, and walked over to the center window. He had inserted the adjustable screen only three weeks ago, after a hard-shelled insect had come in at night through the raised sash and struck his drawing hand like a piece of flying tin. Down below, the shadow of the house fell halfway across the sloping lawn. He saw plainly the elongated tower with the pointed roof, from which he was looking down into the yard, and for a moment he had the odd sensation that he was down there, strewn across the lawn—at any moment his shadow-form would emerge from the shadow-tower and pass into the brightness of the moon. Under one of the high old maples a child's table, set with cups and saucers and teapot, lay half in light and half in shade: one chair, pulled back slightly, glowed almost white, while the other chair lay in black shadow. The brilliant spout of the teapot looked like the raised trunk of an elephant. He would have to remind Stella to bring in her toys before dark—or maybe the dolls had come out to have a tea party under the summer moon. In his childhood home in Plains Farms, Ohio, he had heard things come alive at night: dolls woke from their daylight spell, teapots poured tea, dishes came down from their cupboards and walked about the house, clowns in jigsaw puzzles rose up and danced, the little boy in the wallpaper caught a fish with his yellow fishing pole. Franklin had lain very still, listening to the secret life in the house, and twenty years later he had put it all in a Sunday color strip—but in the last panel the boy had wakened from his dream. And one summer night in Ohio, Franklin himself had sat up in bed and pushed aside the curtain and the stiff, heavy shade to stare at the brilliant backyard. He had longed to pass through the window into the dark enchantment of the summer night; and in the morning when he opened his eyes he found he had fallen asleep with his head against the window frame. Franklin was restless. The tower study was unbearably hot. All at once he had a marvelous idea.

With a thrust of his palms he pushed up the half-open lower sash. The adjustable screen, framed in maple, fit snugly against the vertical parting-strips that ran the length of the window frame and separated the upper and lower sashes. He released the stiff spring, carefully removed the screen, and placed it on the floor against the side of his desk. Then with dream-ease he stepped out into the blue summer night.

A narrow roofslope lay directly beneath the window. On his knees, backward, Franklin made his way to the edge. There, as if he knew what he was doing, he slid over the roof edge and swung down; for a moment he hung wildly before dropping to the wide and nearly flat roof of the front porch.

He was standing beside the tall window of his own bedroom, directly beneath his tower study. The shade was pulled down all the way, as if he were inside, fast asleep. And for a moment he imagined himself lying fast asleep in his bed, dreaming this other Franklin, who had stepped out of a tower into the sky. Franklin strode past the window, noticing himself passing jauntily in the dark pane of the upper sash—and how easy it was to walk this way, along the shingles of a roof, with one's hands in one's pockets at the magic hour of three in the morning; he felt like kicking up his heels. But he slowed as he drew near Cora's window.

Through the adjustable screen he saw Cora lying on her back with her unbound hair strewn over the pillow. He could make out the proud line of her forehead and thought he could see, escaping from her thick pale tumble of hair, the bottom of an ear. Franklin felt a little sharp burst of longing, and with a feeling of dream-freedom he released the steel spring that held the screen tight against the window frame. At that moment Cora turned slightly in her sleep, half opened an eye, and seemed to look at him.

"I'm only a dream," Franklin whispered, and held his breath. The eye closed. Franklin adjusted the screen and tiptoed away along the porch roof.

The roof turned with the wraparound porch, and as he stepped around the corner Franklin walked into the brightness of the moon. The moon startled him: it was much larger than it ought to be. It seemed to be growing bigger and bigger—at any moment it would engulf him and he would dissolve in an exhilaration of whiteness. In an old strip he had shown the moon setting on top of a saloon on Vine Street, rolling drunkenly across rooftops, toppling into the Ohio River with a splash. Franklin continued around the corner and came to a moon-flooded window. In the room his three-year-old daughter lay sleeping on her back. One leg rested on top of the covers and one arm was flung back on the pillow and bent over her head, as if she had fallen asleep suddenly in the midst of an ecstatic dance.

Franklin eased out the screen and climbed inside. At the bed he pulled the sheet and bedspread over Stella's legs, removed a lump that turned out to be a white one-eyed bear, and lay down beside Stella with his hands clasped behind his head. "It's a wonderful night," he said. "I think the moon's going to land on the roof in a few minutes. We can climb up on it and have moon pie.

Won't that be fun?" Stella stirred in her sleep and slowly rolled against him. "Shhh, now," Franklin said. "Just another dream." He kissed her forehead and sat up. Creatures with moon-glittering eyes looked at him from shelves and chairs, watched him as they leaned against each other's shoulders. "I'm surprised at you," Franklin said. "This is no time for loafing." He rose from the bed and began gathering up the dolls and animals, which he placed on the floor in two lines facing Stella's bed. In the center of the front row sat a Raggedy Ann doll, a kangaroo, a ballerina in silver slippers, and a donkey with one ear. "Night," Franklin said to no one in particular, then climbed out the window onto the porch roof. The moon had returned to its proper size. Franklin bent into the room and replaced the screen.

He continued to the end of the porch roof, where he came to a projecting bay formed by an empty guest room. Above the bay rose a third-floor gable. The roofline was above his reach, but a brilliant white downspout, gleaming as if the paint were still wet, climbed a corner of the bay. Franklin placed one toe on the louver of a shutter and one toe on a brace of the rainspout, grasped the roof edge, and pulled himself up onto a steep slope.

Slowly, bent over to his fingertips, he made his moonlit way along the peaks and valleys of his jumbled roof, passing through gable-shadows and bursts of brightness. He felt as if he had come down from the moon, an enchanted visitor, to walk on the bumpy top of a town. Once he slipped on a strip of flashing, once he sat straddling a crest of roof, and once he passed a tall, thin chimney that widened at the top and made him think of a pedestal with a missing bust. In a burst of high spirits he imagined chimney statues: a bust of Homer with his bald head gleaming under the moon, a Civil War general with raised sword on a rearing horse, a white marble Venus stepping out of her bath. He had become quite used to his up-and-down journey under the spell of the moon when he found himself in a sudden valley beside a polygonal tower.

Dreamily he made his way down to the skirt of roof beneath the open window and entered his warm study.

Nothing had changed. The mahogany desk-chair with its padded leather seat was turned slightly from the desk, the pendulum swung slowly above the key in the glass-cased clock, a collection of cedarwood penholders standing in a square jar looked like a handful of pick-up-sticks about to fall. On the faded wallpaper with its pattern of repeated haystacks, the little reapers lay asleep with their hats over their eyes. Franklin laid his last drawing on top of the glass rectangle in the sloping animation board. He turned on the light bulb beneath the glass, placed a blank piece of rice paper over the drawing, and lined up the two pieces of glowing paper by matching the crossmarks in the four corners. He tried to recall his mood of moonlit exhilaration, but it all seemed to have happened long ago. Choosing a blunt-tipped Venus pencil from his pencil jar, Franklin began to trace the background for drawing number 1,827 as the first little ache of tiredness rippled along his temples and began to beat softly with the beat of his blood.

TWO

When Franklin summoned up his childhood in Plains Farms, Ohio, he always remembered three things: the warm, sunbaked smell of the tire that hung from the branch of the sweet-gum tree, the opening in the backyard hedge that led out into the tall meadow grass where he was forbidden to go, and the sound of his father's voice counting slowly and gravely in the darkened kitchen as he bent over the piece of magic paper under the light of the enlarger. Franklin loved the darkroom: the four trays on the sink, each with its pair of tongs; the separate smells of the developer, the stop bath, and the hypo; the red light glowing in the darkness; the dark hump of the enlarger on the kitchen table. It was his job to remove a piece of magic paper from one of the yellow-and-black packages and seal the package carefully so that the rest of the paper wouldn't be exposed when his father clicked on the enlarger light. He remembered the feel of the paper: smooth on both sides, but smoother on one side than the other: that was the side that had a shine to it in the dark-red light. His father placed the paper in the metal rectangle with adjustable sides, which somehow reminded Franklin of the funny metal tray the man in the shoe store made him place his foot on, and when everything was ready his father clicked on the enlarger light and began to count. He counted in a slow, grave voice, and as he counted he slowly lowered and raised one hand, with the long finger held out. Franklin could see light shining through the negative, throwing the black-and-white picture onto the glowing paper. The moving hand, marking the rhythm of the numbers, had a red sheen in the red-lit dark. Suddenly the light clocked off. Quickly his father removed the paper and brought it over to the sink, where he slipped it into the developer pan and allowed Franklin to hold it down with the tongs. This was the part Franklin liked best: the paper was blank, but as he watched, tense with expectation, he became aware of a slight motion on the paper, as of something rising to the surface, and from the depths of whiteness the picture would begin to emerge—an edge here, a gray bit there, a ghostly arm reaching out of a shirt sleeve. More and more the darkness rose up out of the white, faster and faster, a great bursting forth of life—and suddenly he saw himself on the living room rug, reaching out to put a piece in his ship puzzle, but already he was lifting an edge of the photograph with the tongs, in order to slip the picture into the second tray, where the developer would be washed off and the picture would stop getting darker. His father had shown him once what happened if you didn't stop the action of the developer: the picture grew darker and darker until it was completely black. Black was nothing, and white was nothing too, but in between—in between was the whole world. After the stop-bath tray came the hypo tray, to fix the picture in place and keep it from changing in light. From there the picture went into the water tray, and then it was laid facedown on a towel to dry. But Franklin's interest had already begun to slacken when the picture rose dripping from the first tray, for the excitement was always in the sudden emergence of life from the whiteness of the paper.

He felt the same excitement when he drew on white paper with crayon or pencil. As far back as he could remember he had liked to make lines on paper, and from the age of five or six he liked to draw everything: the tire swing, the state of Ohio with a cow in it, his mother with her bag of yarn balls and knitting needles, his spoon and fork. In elementary school his teachers praised the drawings and hung them up in the back of the room. He drew pictures of school desks, carefully shaded bottles of ink, colorful cereal boxes with precisely reproduced words and faces, but he also kept returning to old, familiar things, improving them each time, so that his tire swing became mottled with skillfully drawn shadows of leaves and hung from a meticulously rendered rope that showed all of its intertwisted strands, while the state of Ohio, copied from his father's atlas instead of from his childish jigsaw map, showed all the counties, every curve in the Ohio River, and the letters and numbers of the superimposed grid. In the sixth grade he began copying his favorite comic strips from the Cincinnati *Enquirer* and inventing strips of his own.

In high school he was an indifferent student but continued drawing; somewhat to his surprise his sketches took a satirical turn. One summer he wrote away to a correspondence school whose advertisement he had seen on the inside cover of a matchbook. He followed three lessons before giving it up with an inner shrug, but the sense of something to be learned, of rules to be mastered and broken, stayed with him. In his senior year his father told him that he was being sent to a Commercial Academy in Cincinnati, nearly two hours by buckboard and train from Plains Farms, in order to prepare for a career in business. Franklin agreed to go without protest, as he agreed to most things, while inwardly withdrawing to a quiet corner of his mind. In the tall-windowed rooms of the Commercial Academy, with the sound of automobile engines and voices coming from the street below, he took notes faithfully and did his best to pay attention. But he preferred to wander about the exciting city on the river, with its German shopkeepers and crowded sidewalks, its horse-drawn cabs and handsome automobiles, its sudden glimpses of the river, of the suspension bridge with its soaring towers, of the green hills of Kentucky. At the entrance to the suspension bridge stood the sheds of apple and peanut vendors, and Franklin liked to walk across the river with his pockets full of peanuts and sit on a bench in Kentucky and look at the city of Cincinnati rising up at the river's edge. On the broad city streets he liked to look in the plate-glass windows at displays of cameras with black leather bellows and automatic shutters; stem-winding pocket watches with silver-plated cases engraved with train engines or antlered stags; mustached mannequins in striped suits and Panama hats, with walking sticks tucked under their arms; phonographs with shiny brass horns or the new cabinet models in oak and mahogany that concealed the horn and had room for one hundred records; stylish women's boots with glossy patent-leather vamps and creamy calf tops; gleaming white-enameled sinks and bathtubs. He liked the big-city drugstores with their window displays of dental creams, hair pomades, self-stropping safety razors in plush-lined cases, and bottles of perfume with exotic scents: *fleur d'orange*, new-mown hay, night-blooming cereus, ylang-ylang, opoponax, patchouly. His favorite haunt was Vine Street, which ran down to the river at one end and up into the hills at the other and was crowded with shops, hotels, and every variety of saloon, from shabby riverfront grogshops to the palatial cafés in the business district, with their wrought-iron doorways flanked by marble columns, and their interiors of carved mahogany and onyx and great mirrors that reflected bronze statues—and farther away from the river, the comfortable saloons of the German neighborhood, with their sitting rooms and shady outdoor gardens.

It was on Vine Street that Franklin discovered one day a five-story building called Klein's Wonder Palace, an old dime museum that had flourished in the nineties and now, in 1910, housed a movie theater, Madama Zola's palmist parlor, and an array of faded exhibits and aging curiosities, such as a sickly two-headed chicken, a tired-looking counting pig, and a tattooed man so ancient that he continually fell asleep with his head hanging down. Franklin wandered the old halls with delight. He made his way through a dusty mirror maze and followed arrows to a dim-lit room with roped-off alcoves in which he saw Jenny Scott the Armless Wonder, Dee-Dee the Dog-Faced Boy, and the Missing Link. There was an old wax museum showing tableaux of famous murders, an historical collection that included the bloody neckerchief of Abraham Lincoln and George Washington's childhood ax, and a stage for performers where you could see John Blake the Contortionist, who could squeeze through a crack no wider than a finger, or Little Ellie Trinker, who played popular tunes by cracking her bones. In a corner of the surprisingly crowded second floor, not far from the Bearded Lady, Franklin saw a young man with very pale skin who stood at an easel and made startlingly swift and accurate charcoal portraits for twenty-five cents apiece. Franklin fell into conversation with the quick-sketch artist, who said he made a dime for each sketch but was planning to quit at the end of the month to join his brother in a printing plant in Ypsilanti. He showed Franklin, who was amused by quickness but didn't much admire it, a few tricks of the trade. Ten days later Franklin was hired to work three afternoons a week and all day Saturday in Klein's Wonder Palace. He divided his time between the Commercial Academy and the Wonder Palace until, one day a few months later, the manager offered him a full-time job making advertising posters; and Franklin, after thinking it over for a week, withdrew from the Commercial Academy and moved into a small studio at the back of the upper floor of the Wonder Palace.

His advertising posters, in flamboyant colors, at first showed simple portraits of the Bearded Lady, or Jenny Scott the Armless Wonder, or Dee-Dee the Dog-Faced Boy, but soon they began to include perspective backgrounds and small secondary figures, real and fanciful, arranged artfully within the total design. Backgrounds became filled with meticulous detail, the decorative titles began to include minute fantastic creatures with tails and wings; and before six months had passed, Franklin received a raise.

One day after he had been living for nearly a year in the Wonder Palace, Franklin was sketching in his room when there was a knock at the door. "Just a," he said, and looked up from his drawing to see a man in a white linen suit with a red silk handkerchief in his breast pocket and a diamond stickpin in his cravat. The stranger introduced himself as Montgomery Nash, glanced negligently at Franklin's sketches, and offered him a job in the art department of the Cincinnati *Daily Crier.* Franklin's hand paused in midstroke before continuing along the curve of a handsome handlebar mustache. He had heard of Montgomery Nash, the dandyish business manager of the *Daily Crier;* the offer was so tempting, so exactly in line with his secret ambition, that he felt an odd, melancholy desire to refuse it. Instead he began to ask precise questions and to insist clearly on his lack of training, his lack of suitability for the job. Nash gave him a shrewd look, pulled at the brim of his fawn fedora, and told him to report to work the following Monday.

In his office on the sixth floor of the *Daily Crier,* Franklin's favorite piece of furniture was the high-backed oak swivel chair, which allowed him to tilt back and, with a slight pressure of one foot, swing away from his desk to the sunny window with its raised venetian blind. He liked to look across at the commercial building with its arched windows in the upper stories and its ground-floor row of small shops and restaurants, all with fringed awnings and plate-glass windows, before pushing with his foot and swinging back to his drawing board.

At first Franklin drew decorative borders, elaborate titles, and miscellaneous illustrations, while using his spare hours to learn the art of the editorial cartoon; and as his editorial cartoons began to appear regularly, showing France and Germany glaring at each other across a table while a Japanese waiter looked on with a smile, or Civilization, crowned with vine leaves, walking away with bowed head from the bench of Judicial Vice, he tried his hand at occasional gag cartoons, which he drew slowly and in loving detail. The success of these single-panel cartoons, as well as his ability to summon up a wealth of images from his childhood in Plains Farms, from his long walks in Cincinnati, and from his year in the Wonder Palace, led him to try his hand at a comic strip, which he set in a phantasmagoric dime museum on Vine Street. "Dime Museum Dreams," a six-panel black-and-white strip that appeared weekly, was an immediate success. The format was invariable: in the first panel, an unnamed boy was seen holding his mother's hand—nothing was shown of the mother except her hand and forearm—and staring at an exhibit in the dime museum: a bearded lady, or a two-headed chicken, or a man shaped like a pretzel. In the next three panels the freakish creature became more and more frightening—the pretzel man began to wrap himself around the boy's legs, the bearded lady became entirely covered with thick long hair—until in the fifth, climactic panel the height of horror was reached and the boy shrieked out in terror. In the last panel the exhibit had returned to its original shape, while the boy sobbed against his mother's leg and listened to her words of comfort. The success of the strip led Franklin to attempt another; and by the end of his second year at the *Daily Crier,* in the summer of 1913, he was drawing three daily strips and a color strip for the Sunday supplement, in addition to editorial cartoons and spot illustrations.

One afternoon in July, as Franklin stepped out into the reception room of the *Daily Crier* on his way to lunch, he saw a handsome young woman in a straw hat with a bunch of fresh cherries on the brim. Her straight nose, her broad shoulders, the squiggle of pale hair falling along one temple, above all the faint shine on the skin beneath both eyes, all this struck him as vaguely familiar, and with an apology for intruding he asked her whether they had met. Slowly she raised her head and said, with nostrils tight-drawn: "I was under the impression that this was a newspaper office, not a dance hall," and lowered her face decisively. Later he learned from a reporter in the newsroom that the haughty young woman was Cora Vaughn, daughter of Judge James Rowland Vaughn of the City Court; she was a schoolteacher who occasionally stopped by to look through the files in connection with school projects. Franklin, who had never heard of Cora Vaughn, was certain he had seen her somewhere: the quivering nostrils, the slight flush, the cherries trembling on the hat brim, all this made a deep impression on him, and when, the following summer, he sat all night by his father's sickbed in the house in Plains Farms, remembering the tire swing and the grave voice in the darkroom, he suddenly thought of those quivering nostrils, those cherries trembling on the hatbrim. The crisis passed, though the mild apoplectic seizure seemed to have aged his father ten years. Two weeks later Franklin sat in his office, gazing out the window at reflections of passersby in the window of a restaurant and wondering if he could capture the effect in the next installment of his Sunday strip, when he saw Cora Vaughn step into the street. A moment later he saw that it was a different woman—he had been misled by the straw hat—but he remembered where he had first seen the real Cora: he had sketched her portrait in Klein's Wonder Palace.

His courtship of Cora Vaughn was the most difficult thing he had ever set out to do. At first she refused to speak to him when he presented himself at the elementary school after the last bell had rung, and when he began sending her cartoons drawn especially for her, she promptly returned them. In the long winter nights, in the boarding house two blocks from his office, he brooded over Cora Vaughn until she seemed as familiar as his own childhood and at the same time mysterious and ungraspable. One Sunday afternoon when he was walking in Eden Park he saw her skating on the pond; she wore a blue wool coat and a white scarf, plumes of breath streamed out behind her, he felt strangely drowsy and heavy headed yet sharply alert. He turned away and stood looking down at the Ohio River, bordered by greenish ice. He thought of the war in Europe and wondered if the Marne ever iced over in winter. Men his own age were dying in battle every day. When he turned back she was no longer there, and he wondered if he had imagined it all: the white scarf, the plumes of bluish breath, the dark blades of the skates lifting and falling, the distant war. Slowly the ice in the river melted, the magnolias put out their waxy flowers, and one day as he was rounding the corner of Walnut and Sixth he looked up into the smiling face of Cora Vaughn. And all at once, just like that, he was sitting on her warm front porch with the tall pillars, inhaling a heavy odor of lilacs and speaking of the house in Plains Farms and his father's voice in the darkroom. Evening after evening he sat on Judge Vaughn's porch, watching the fireflies come out in the lavender dark and listening to the creak of the porch glider, and one August night in a riot of crickets that reminded him of the meadow behind his house in Plains Farms he proposed to Cora. She looked at him in troubled surprise, as if he had failed to understand something, and refused him brusquely. Suddenly she burst into tears and fled into the parlor.

After three sleepless nights Franklin returned to her street but dared not approach the porch. In the office the next day he found a brief, impatient note from Cora, asking where he had been. That evening she said that although she enjoyed his friendship, she could never marry a man who drew comic strips—the whole idea was unthinkable and impossible. Franklin opened his mouth to defend his trade, suddenly saw himself through her eyes, a ridiculous childish man who made silly pictures, and sank into silence. Cora Vaughn played Schubert sonatas on the piano and liked to talk about the contrasting methods of Delacroix and Ingres—how could she marry someone who thrilled to the life of a seedy dime museum and spent ten hours a day drawing for the funny papers? He thoroughly understood her distaste for what he did, and at the same time he obscurely felt that she herself didn't understand something. She didn't understand that his funny drawings were his path to a necessary place—a place that could never be expressed in words or pictures but that somehow was the vital center of things. He felt a confused pity for Cora Vaughn, and was shocked at his pity. He rose, tried to say something, and left in silence. That night he vowed to forget her and live in solitude; the next day he found an irritable note from Cora in his office, and eight months later they left on their honeymoon for New Orleans.

In Cincinnati Cora found a large house with bay windows and bracketed eaves, four blocks from Judge Vaughn's mansion. Franklin would have liked to live farther from Cora's old neighborhood, for she liked to spend the evenings at her father's house; the judge was a grave but amicable man who seemed slightly puzzled by the presence of his son-in-law in the parlor and sometimes gave the impression that he had forgotten his daughter was a married woman. Franklin loved to watch Cora play the piano: she sat very straight, half closed her eyes, and allowed her head to sway and bow slightly; the mixture of stern control and dreamy abandon filled him with tenderness and longing. Sometimes he felt that he longed for her too much, that he was crude and disgusting in his desire; for he never knew whether Cora would welcome him or turn her face away and complain of tiredness. She had insisted on having her own bedroom, and although Franklin had agreed without protest, the arrangement left him feeling a perpetual guest. Once, in the first weeks of their marriage, Cora had come to him late at night. The sight of her standing by the bed in her pink silk nightgown trimmed with lace and small ribbons, her hair unbound, her eyes looking down at him with a kind of solemn tenderness, filled him with such pride and happiness that he suddenly became afraid, as if he had been given something he did not deserve and would not be allowed to keep.

Their daughter, Stella, was born the following spring. Franklin liked to warm her feet by pulling her tiny socks on, placing his mouth on the sole of a sock, and blowing until his lips felt hot. Sometimes at night he woke up, fearful that she had died in her sleep. Then he would creep into her room and bend down to hear her breathing, and after that he would stare at her a long time before pulling the blanket up to her chin and returning to his room.

He thought about blowing on her feet as he stood one night leaning against the wall of a barracks building in Waco, Texas, and stared up at the blue-black sky. He was dressed in olive drab. The sky reminded him of long boyhood summer evenings—the kind of evening he might never spend with his daughter. The armistice was signed three weeks later, and he was home for Thanksgiving, but for a long time he couldn't get over the feeling that he was somehow responsible for neglecting precious weeks of his daughter's life and that he must now be more attentive to her than ever.

That winter his father died, of a lingering cold that developed into influenza. He had never been the same since his stroke before the war, and Franklin, staring at the gaunt and white-haired man lying in bed with closed eyes, was carried violently back to the other father, the one who had raised and lowered his hand in the darkroom as he gravely counted out the numbers. It was as if this elderly stranger had usurped his father's place and now, in death, was permitting the real father to return. After the funeral Franklin tried to find something of his father's to bring back with him—an ivory-handled penknife, a photograph of the sweet-gum tree—but it all seemed flat and dead, and he returned to Cincinnati empty-handed, but with the real father alive inside him.

When Stella was two years old a syndicate purchased one of Franklin's daily strips. He hurried home to surprise Cora with the news, but found her pacing irritably. Dr. Stanton had just left; Stella was trembling and her temperature had risen to 105. In the next two days, as Stella's life seemed to hang in the balance, and Cora, who needed her sleep, grew more and more irritable, Franklin remembered the picture of Jehovah on the cover of his child's illustrated Bible, and prayed to the bearded man in the robe to save his daughter. The fever lessened, Dr. Stanton said Stella had croup; and as the days passed and life returned to normal, Franklin never found the right moment to announce his news to Cora. One night after Stella was in bed he told Cora in an offhand way that one of his strips had been syndicated. "I'm glad for you, Franklin," she said, "but you know I never understand these things." He waited for her to ask a question, but she said no more, not a word, and he never mentioned it again.

He was given a raise and promoted to assistant director of the art department; and one day a letter came from a New York editor, offering him the position of staff artist in the art department of the New York *World Citizen* at a startling salary.

Cora greeted the news coldly, with quivering nostrils. She said she could no more think of moving to New York City than she could think of moving to the dark side of the moon. Franklin dropped the matter but lay awake at night wondering if he was to spend the rest of his life living four blocks from his distinguished and slightly disapproving father-in-law. He knew the offer was a good one; it would permit him to cut back on editorial cartooning and devote his energy to the daily strips that had begun to attract national attention—and quite apart from all that was the sense of a challenge, an invitation to adventure that he felt it would be harmful to ignore. The idea of moving excited him: New York was the center of the newspaper world. But more than that, he wanted Cora to choose him decisively; after three years of marriage she still half lived in her childhood home.

When, a week later, Franklin announced that he had accepted the job, Cora drew back as if he had struck her in the face. Then she turned on her heel, marched into Stella's room, picked up the sleeping child, and carried her out of the house. Franklin went to his desk and thrust a letter into his pocket before following Cora to her father's house, where he found her weeping in her old room. Downstairs he showed the judge the letter from New York. The judge promised to speak to his daughter; Franklin had known he would recognize a good offer if he saw one.

At the train station Franklin was thrilled by the names of cities on the board above the grated windows of the ticket sellers, the bustle of porters, the squeak of luggage, the rows of high windows in the passenger cars, the big iron wheels of the engine rising higher than Stella's head; but when he looked at Cora in her red velvet hat with the black osprey feather, flinching at the sound of grating steel and hissing steam, and gazing about as if she were looking for someone she had lost, he longed to throw himself at her feet and beg forgiveness for the squeaking bags, the shine of sweat on the cheeks of the Negro porter, the little girl in a kerchief, crying on a brown wooden bench, the sides of the passenger cars rising up like the flanks of a bull.

At first they rented an apartment in a brownstone in Brooklyn Heights, on a shady street lined with maples and sycamores. Franklin walked to the city each morning over the promenade of the noble bridge with its churchlike double arches that seemed to rise higher than skyscrapers, its four suspension cables sweeping up into the sky, its rumble of electric trolleys and elevated trains, its secret evocation of the old bridge over the Ohio. It deeply pleased him that both bridges had been designed by the same engineer, as if his choice had obeyed a hidden design. On Sundays he went for walks with Stella around his new neighborhood, showing her street signs that bore the names of fruits—Pineapple Street, Orange Street, Cranberry Street— and pointing to brilliant glimpses of the river at the sunny ends of shady streets. Sometimes he sat with Cora and Stella on a slatted bench under a tree at the end of Montague Street and pointed at the giant bridge rising over the mansard tower of the old ferry house, at the barges and tugboats passing on the river, at the wharves and shipping factories and tall buildings rising on the other shore. Then he told Stella about his other life, when he sat on a bench in Kentucky and looked across the river at the Cincinnati waterfront. But Cora seemed confused by the new streets, the strange buildings rising across the river, the sound of foghorns at night and of doors shutting in other apartments. Often he would come home from work to find her sitting pensively in her mahogany rocking chair with the lion's head finials, staring through the bow window at the street below; and one day, hearing by chance of a house in a village north of the city, one hour by train from Grand Central Station, he asked Cora whether she would like to move to Mount Hebron. At first sight of the many-gabled old house with the two towering sugar maples flanking the front path, set halfway up the slope of the village on the river, Cora placed a hand on Franklin's forearm and, with the wind blowing back her hair, tightened her grip as if she were climbing a stairway. The house on the hill was a little more than Franklin could readily afford, and a part-time housekeeper proved to be an absolute necessity, but seated in his tower study two floors above the front porch, separated from the ordinary life of the house but feeling that he drew secret strength from the floors below, Franklin worked far into the night, unable to sleep through sheer exhilaration. He had begun work on two new strips that were as unlike each other as possible, and these experiments had led directly to his recent adventure with rice paper.

THREE

The offices of the New York World Citizen occupied four floors and the basement of a commercial building on Thirty-second Street off Sixth Avenue, two blocks from Herald Square. Although the business and executive offices on the fourth floor were arranged in an orderly way, on both sides of dim-lit hallways, the corridors of the floors below had a tendency to go astray, as old walls were knocked down and new ones erected to make space for additional rooms. The second floor, where the art department had its offices, was nicknamed The Warren, for in the course of three separate efforts at expansion the halls had begun to take odd, surprising turns, new rooms had sprung up unexpectedly behind suddenly appearing doors, and one day an old Linotype machine from the composing room in the basement had been discovered in a cramped room between the offices of two political cartoonists; and rumor had it that several members of the department were entombed in rooms accidentally sealed off during a recent bout of construction. The dim, abruptly turning corridors, the maze of brownish offices, the smell of printer's ink and floor wax, the racket of typewriters and ringing telephones in the newsroom on the first floor, and, underneath it all, the rumble of the web-fed rotary presses, all this excited Franklin, who had a small office with half-open, yellowed venetian blinds, a framed and faded newspaper photograph from 1905 showing dignitaries seated at a table in Portsmouth, New Hampshire, at the conclusion of the Russo-Japanese War, and an old rolltop desk entirely covered with cracker boxes, cedarwood penholders, rough-sketched cartoons, and scientific gadgets picked up here and there: a dusty gyroscope, a radiometer with slowly turning black-and-silver vanes, and a model steam engine with a brass boiler, a firebox, a working piston, and a flywheel. The office contained an old mahogany armchair upholstered in a pattern of faded pink cabbage roses, but Franklin preferred to sit at his desk for eight to ten hours a day, composing comic strips and single-panel cartoons on a drawing board that slanted from the desk edge to his lap.

On the morning after his moonlit escapade, shortly before eleven o'clock, as Franklin sat frowning down at his drawing board and slowly stroking his left temple with two fingers of his left hand, there was a sharp, quick rap at the door, which instantly swung open with a clatter of blinds.

"I met a man the other night," Max Horn said, flinging himself into the faded armchair and stretching out his legs, "who asked me whether I considered myself an expressionist. He wasn't kidding. Now what do you say to a guy in a silk tie who wants to know whether you consider yourself an expressionist? I told him I'd started out as an expressionist but dropped it at age sixteen. You look awful, by the way. So he blinks at me through his specs and asks whether I think the comic strip is the art of the future. There's no stopping this gent. I tell him the art of the future is the American billboard. He asks me what exactly I mean by that. I invent a theory on the spot, dragging in cave art and primitive masks. Finally I can't take it anymore and try to beat a retreat. He grabs my arm and hands me his card—J. Bateson: Bathroom Accessories. I saw the light, Franklin. The American bathroom and the avant garde walking hand in hand into the future. Cubist paintings on shower curtains, free verse printed on rolls of toilet paper in violet ink. An expressionist in every tub. I'll be there around one."

"Good," Franklin said. "I'll meet you at the station."

"Later it struck me Bateson might be right. The art of the future is American art, and what is American art? I'll tell you what it is. American art is efficient art—quick art. We're busy, we want something that doesn't take up too much time, something we can throw out. The art of the future is throwaway art: the comic strip, ads for Cracker Jack, the architecture of the tin can."

"You missed your calling, Max."

"You bet your sweet life I did. I should've been an adman. Brush your teeth with Zippo and you'll never grow old. Do you know what my father did for a living? He sold coal. When I was a kid he talked to me about the virtues of anthracite. So what did I do? I took pieces of soft coal and drew pictures on brick walls. Story of my life. The Troll's been hounding me again."

"You know how he is," Franklin said. "He'll get over it."

"Says my work hasn't been up to the mark. I like that: up to the mark. What mark? Whose mark? I'd rather sell bathtubs for J. Bateson. Drawing for the funny papers. Is this a life? I'll see you on Saturday."

When Max left in a rattle of blinds, Franklin lowered his eyes to the slanted drawing board and continued rough-sketching the third panel of a strip, in which a monkey in baggy pants was hanging from the top of the frame.

Because the Cincinnati *Daily Crier* held the copyright to "Dime Museum Dreams," Franklin had been forced to draw the strip for the *World Citizen* under a new title, while the original strip continued appearing in the *Daily Crier* under the original title, though drawn by a different artist. The unsatisfactory new name ("Danny in the Dime Museum"), the sense that he was duplicating a strip appearing elsewhere, the need to distinguish his new strip from his old one while keeping it the same, all this constricted Franklin's imagination and seemed boring and worthless, so that he had begun to introduce new settings while keeping the invariable format: Danny at the Circus, Danny at the Bronx Zoo, Danny in Central Park. But these variations, though at first they amused him, failed to excite his deepest attention, and in searching for new ideas he had suddenly invented two entirely new strips.

The first one, called "Phantom of the City," grew directly out of the unsatisfactory Danny series and permitted Franklin to express his detailed love for his new city while at the same time it gave his imagination fuller rein. The eight-panel strip was less rigid in format than "Danny in the Dime Museum," which ceased appearing within a month, though the new strip followed a definite pattern in its black-and-white daily version and later in Sunday color. The Phantom, a mysterious stranger from a distant city who had ghostlike powers, penetrated a new place in each strip: the halls of Egyptian antiquities in the Metropolitan Museum at midnight, the tunnels under Grand Central Station, a loft in a shirtwaist factory where pale women sat at receding rows of sewing machine tables, the helical stairway leading to the crown of the Statue of Liberty, a smoky Bowery saloon; each time he discovered someone who was suffering and who expressed a wish, which the Phantom instantly granted. What excited Franklin wasn't the crude fairy tale but the elaborately drawn settings for each strip. He visited each place with sketchpad in hand, recording impressions, noting odd perspectives, rapidly copying bridge piers with their patterns of reflected light, cast-iron lampposts decorated with iron leaves, gigantic bells in bell towers, the underside of the Second Avenue el, the ceilings of movie palaces, the structure of elevator cables and subway straps, the views of receding avenues from the top floors of midtown hotels. His hymn to the city, in panels of rich, meticulous detail, combined with a mystery phantom and an invariable happy ending, struck a responsive chord; readers were enchanted, and sales of the *World Citizen* notably increased.

The second strip, which sprang into his mind within days of "Phantom of the City," though it took much longer to assume a workable shape, was so different that Franklin wondered whether he was two people—two people who shared the same house, exchanged amicable remarks at breakfast, and departed down two different streets ending in mist. If the Phantom strip emphasized precision of detail, including carefully drawn perspective views, and required Franklin to walk out into the city with sketchbook in hand, the second strip rejected the very notion of realistic settings and insisted on its own artifice. It took the form of a six-panel Sunday strip called "Figaro's Follies," and week after week it was a variation on a single theme: the frame of the panel was drawn into the adventure of the strip's only character, a sinister but smiling little monkey dressed in baggy pants and a jacket with big buttons. In the first panel of the first strip, Figaro was shown in jail. In the next four panels, the monkey sawed through the frame of the panel and escaped; in the last panel, he stood on top of the cartoon frame. In another strip, Figaro used the frame as a jungle gym; in another, he drew the sides of successive panels closer and closer together, until in the sixth panel he was thin as a pencil. In Franklin's favorite of the series, the monkey opened a door in each panel and entered a new panel with a different shape: the first panel led into a circle, the circle led to a tall, thin tube, the tube opened onto a stairway, the stairway led to a small box, and a door in the box opened to a hot-air balloon with a basket, in which the monkey stood with a spyglass trained on the reader.

Although "Figaro's Follies" was less successful than "Phantom of the City," Franklin knew that each one drew its strength from the other. For when he had labored over the view of a pier of Brooklyn Bridge as seen from a barge passing beneath the bridge, and checked his drawing by standing in a coal barge and observing the structure of shadows and the play of water-reflected light on stone, then he felt the need to escape from the constriction of physical things into a world entirely of his own devising; but when he had entered a world of four black lines, which he broke apart and reassembled in any way he liked, so that his impish monkey seemed the very expression of his longing to break free of some inner constraint, then he felt a craving for the lines and shadows of the actual world, as if the imaginary world threatened to carry him off in a hot-air balloon on a voyage from which he might never return.

Franklin never talked about such passions and contradictions to his colleagues in the art department, a hard-pressed and hardworking group through whom erratic gusts of whimsy blew, and he rarely put such questions even to himself, preferring instead to feel his way with his fingers. Sometimes he had a sense of groping in the dark—and suddenly he would feel something that made him snatch his hand away. With his fellow cartoonists he was content to discuss deadlines, editorial policy, the news of the day; they were busy and friendly and had formed a complicated network of alliances and social habits that made him feel, without rancor or surprise, a little on the outside. The exception was Max Horn, a cartoonist two years older than Franklin who wore stylish hats and white duck pants, smoked small thin cheroots that he tapped flamboyantly in the direction of ashtrays, and gestured emphatically with his long, slender, carefully manicured hands. Horn drew with astonishing swiftness, claimed never to correct his work, and had the ability to imitate any style without having formed a distinct style of his own. He seemed to take an interest in the newcomer from Ohio, a state he said he hadn't heard of—was it west of Brooklyn? He always stopped when he saw Franklin in the halls, firing at him witty remarks, baseball scores, and office gossip, and he took to stopping by Franklin's office once or twice a week, where he would throw himself into the faded armchair, stretch out his legs and cross his ankles, tip back his head, and blow a stream of plump and slowly turning smoke rings that he studied intently for a few moments before scattering his ash and launching into a shrewd analysis of office politics or Franklin's style. Although the visits sometimes interrupted a bout of work, which Franklin had to make up at night in Mount Hebron, he looked forward to the sound of Max Horn's quick, decisive rap on the door. Franklin understood that the flamboyant Horn enjoyed playing to Franklin's presumed innocence, but he recognized that beneath the brashness was a sharp, restless intelligence, as well as a surprisingly clear grasp of Franklin's work. Franklin in turn admired Horn's worldliness, felt the pull of his mocking mind, and enjoyed his own slightly absurd role as greenhorn from the frontier.

At one o'clock on Saturday afternoon, under a brilliant blue sky that held a single white cloud resembling a puff of chimney smoke in a color comic strip, a train trembling with sun and leaf-shade pulled into the small Victorian station one township south of Mount Hebron.

Franklin, who had been standing in the hot shade of the platform for twenty minutes, was startled to see Max coming down the iron steps of the train. It was as if he had expected Max not to show up.

Or no, he explained as they drove in the open Packard along a dirt road bordered by pine woods, that wasn't it exactly. It was as if Max was so much a part of that other world that Franklin hadn't been able to imagine him in this one at all. It happened a lot: you failed to imagine something, and suddenly found yourself amazed, whereas if you'd imagined it to begin with—but here Franklin lost the direction of his thought. He glanced at Max, who seemed not to be paying attention. "Trees," Max said, pointing over the side of the car. "We have them up here," Franklin said. Max continued to stare at the passing woods. "I've read about them," he said after a while, as Franklin turned onto the shady road that ran along the river.

When Max climbed the steps of the unscreened front porch he turned to take in the view, and Franklin turned with him. He tried to see with Max's eyes the front lawn sloping down to the towering maples, the wooden rope-swing hanging from a high branch, the tall hedge bordering the unpaved road, the tree-shaded roofs and backyards below, the riverside street of small stores, and an abandoned knitting mill on the sunny brown river. When he turned back he saw Cora standing in the doorway. Max took off his hat and looked at Franklin as if in surprise.

"Franklin," he said reproachfully, "you should have told me you were married."

Cora looked at Max coolly. "Franklin," she said, "you should have told me you were bringing a friend."

Max burst into high, nervous laughter; and suddenly sweeping out his arm he made a low, graceful bow.

"And you must be Stella," he added at the bottom of his bow, and dropped quickly to a squat. From behind Cora, Stella looked out uncertainly, holding her mother's dress with one fist. "Here," Max said, patting a pocket of his suit jacket. "I think there's something in here." Stella glanced up at her mother, then stepped forward and reached into Max's pocket. She drew out a gray tin mouse and held it upside down by its leather tail. "I couldn't resist," Max said, still crouching at Cora's feet. He took the mouse gently from Stella and wound it up; Stella watched intently as the mouse moved in zigzags along the boards of the porch.

Franklin knew that Max Horn had a quality that for lack of a better word might be called charm, though the word seemed to obscure something more complex and interesting in Max's nature: a combination of energy and sympathy, an energy that continually and subtly adapted itself to the sensed mood of another person. It was less an art than a faculty he exercised helplessly. That afternoon, as something relaxed in Franklin, he realized he had been secretly fearful of Max's making a bad impression on Cora, and he felt grateful to his friend for knowing how to please her, how to draw her into the center of things instead of keeping her on the sidelines as a wife. Max asked her questions about Cincinnati, which he imagined to be a lazy river town where pigs roamed the rutted dirt roads, hay wagons with big wooden wheels drove down Main Street, and women in bustles went to square dances and quilting bees. Cora said that the description was so exact he surely must have been there. Even Stella, shy and wary Stella, clutching her tin mouse but refusing to play with it, succumbed to the stranger after watching him for a long time, and finally permitted herself to be lifted onto Max's shoulders and carried about the yard. Only when Max had let her down did he reach into his other pocket and produce a shiny red apple. "You see," Max said, "we have apples in the city, but they're not exactly like yours." Stella looked at it doubtfully. "Look, I'll show you." Sitting on his heels, Max held the apple carefully at top and bottom and suddenly pulled it into two hollow halves. Inside sat a smaller apple. Then he pulled apart the second apple—and as the apples grew smaller and smaller, Stella stared in enchantment until, opening a little apple the size of an acorn, Max held out to her, on the long palm of his hand, a tiny apple tree.

After dinner, on the dark front porch lit only by the yellow glow of the shade-drawn parlor windows, Max and Franklin and Cora sat talking and drinking lemonade. The porch looked down across the lawn to the looming dark maples, the yellow squares of windows seen through a trembling blackness of leaves, and the wavering lines of light on the black river. Max, opening a slender tin box and removing a cheroot wrapped in crinkly pale-blue tissue paper, said he was no drinker, but he objected to the anti-booze amendment on principle: it was an effort by politicians to prolong the childhood of Americans. Besides, it would never work—anyone could buy medicinal whiskey at the local drugstore with a doctor's prescription. Franklin looked over at Cora, and after a while he went down to the cellar and brought back one of the six bottles of wine they had kept on hand since the amendment had passed. "Ah, you gay dog, you," Max said, and blew a stream of perfect little smoke rings the size of half dollars; and as Franklin poured the wine into the lemonade glasses he felt a gaiety come over things. The festive wine, the warm summer night, the sense of sharing in a secret violation—it was all peaceful and exhilarating, like riding home at night in the buckboard after long Sunday picnics on the river. Cora, who had been laughing at one of Max's stories so that she had to wipe one eye with the back of her fingers, grew suddenly serious and began to speak about her girlhood in Cincinnati: ice-skating on the pond in Eden Park in late afternoons as the yellow sky turned darker and darker, the rows of long icicles hanging from porch eaves, wax angels with glass wings on the Christmas tree and real candles burning on the branches—and when Max asked if it was always winter in Ohio, she looked up in confusion, as if she had sunk into a winter dream, and spoke of long summer evenings composed of two sounds: the notes of mazurkas and nocturnes coming through the open window onto the darkening lawn as her mother sat at the piano after dinner, and the deeply satisfying sound of a jar-top coming down on a jar as another lightning bug was snatched out of the dark. Then she told Max how, when they'd first arrived in Brooklyn Heights, the thing that most made her feel she was in a foreign place was the way people spoke of standing *on* line, instead of *in* line; and people had smiled at each other when she said things like "Golly Moses." Later, when Cora stood up to go to the kitchen, she walked into the arm of the porch glider; and she let the wooden screen door bang loudly when she stepped inside.

When Cora returned, holding a tray of cheese and crackers,

she bumped open the screen door with her hip. The slight im-
modesty of her suddenly outthrust hip, the momentary awk-
wardness of her body, the lamplight from the front hall around
her darkening form as she stepped onto the porch, all this excited Franklin and made him impatient for Max to go up to bed,
or dissolve into mist, but he kept sitting there and sitting there;
and after midnight, when they had all moved into the parlor,
Cora at last rose with a look of weariness and said decisively:
"Now I want you and Max to stay up and talk, you hear?"

Franklin, who had begun to rise, looked for a sign from Cora,
who had already turned away. A warm, drowsy feeling came over
him, as if he had not slept for a long time. "I'll be up in a few
minutes," he said, sinking into the soft armchair; and the yellow lamp shade, the cry of the crickets, the shadowy wallpaper
with its trellises of pink roses, his friend sitting in a chair with
one leg hooked over the arm, all seemed part of some drowsy,
peaceful mystery he was on the verge of understanding. He
looked at Max and felt an odd burst of gratitude that he should
be sitting there, far from the city, in the dead of night, and all
at once he began telling Max about his father's grave voice in
the darkroom, the pictures emerging mysteriously from the paper in the developer tray. He spoke of the dime museum, the
strangeness and odd comfort of it, and about the advertising
posters and how it was all somehow connected with the magic
of the darkroom. Suddenly Franklin felt a wild thrill of exhilaration, mixed with fear, and standing up he said, "I want to show
you something."

The two stairways, each with its landing, seemed much too
long, as if he had taken a wrong turn somewhere, but when he
pushed open a door he saw the familiar study, the jar of penholders on the desk, the glass-cased clock. Max bent intently
over the rice-paper drawings and asked precise questions.
Franklin then showed him a little invention that he had modeled after a penny-arcade mutoscope: a metal cylinder, turned

by a crank, was fitted with slots that held the cardboard-backed drawings. When you turned the crank, the drum of drawings turned. A metal rod was attached in such a way that each drawing struck it and was held for an instant before being released. And in the viewer the pictures moved—at first too quickly before he found the right rhythm of cranking, then flickeringly, waveringly, but unmistakably. In a hall of the dime museum the knife-thrower with his cape and mustache was lifting the little girl with the big, frightened eyes from the circle of spectators. The words HELP!! HELP!! appeared on a title card. Franklin invited Max to look through the viewer, and as he continued turning he saw the pictures moving in his mind: the knife-thrower tied the struggling child to a wheel and with a single sharp finger set the wheel spinning. Reaching back for a row of knives he began flinging them at the blurred wheel as Franklin stopped turning.

"Golly Moses," Max said, shaking his head admiringly as he took the crank and continued to turn.

"That wheel cost me a month of work," Franklin said.

Max looked sharply at him. "You realize you're out of your mind, don't you? A raving madman in a padded cell. You do know that, don't you? You do all the drawings yourself? I know a man who—"

"I'd rather be out of my mind than in my mind," Franklin said, and felt suddenly tired and immensely unhappy and exhilarated all at the same time. If he spent four hours a night six nights a week he ought to be able to finish the drawings by late fall or perhaps December at the latest, assuming that his comic strips didn't spill over into the evenings, which they often did. The animated cartoon was about to enter a new sequence, in a new hall of the dime museum, where the tattoos on the tattooed man came to life and danced a wild dance around the terrified girl, and he would need all his powers of concentration to get the motions exactly right. "You see," he said to Max, who for some reason had climbed onto the desk and then onto the top of the door frame, where he sat crouched like a gnome as dark wings grew from his shoulders; and opening his eyes Franklin could not understand the bright dawnlight pouring through the windows of his bedroom, while somewhere far away a cup was rattling on a dish.

"I understand that the motions have to be exactly right," Max was saying a few days later in the faded armchair in Franklin's office. "You'll grant I'm not precisely an idiot. I'm arguing that you can get them exactly right and also save a devil of a lot of time. You don't want to spend the rest of your life working on a four-minute cartoon, do you? Or do you? This new process—"

"But I don't want to save time," Franklin said irritably, although as he spoke he realized it wasn't entirely the truth. The mechanical retracing of every drawing was utterly exhausting, and if he could draw each stationary background only once, placing over it a transparent sheet of celluloid on which only the moving portions were drawn, then he had no objection to the new technique. But the cartoons he occasionally went to see did not inspire confidence. It seemed to Franklin that the new studio-produced cartoons were all too intent on saving time; the cel system didn't seem to encourage the kinds of detailed background one might have expected, but instead produced simple backgrounds consisting of a few boring props: a horizon line, a rock, a bushy tree. Besides, his own backgrounds were themselves continually changing in small ways—his dime museum was alive in all its parts, and in the climactic sequence an entire hall, with its pillars and archways, was going to come alive. Besides, the cel process was patented and required a license, and the public nature of applying for a license violated his desire for absolute secrecy. Besides, though Max was trying to be helpful, Franklin didn't want to be helped. Besides, he had a splitting headache.

"You own a telephone," Max was saying. "You insist on drawing with a Gillott 290 pen point. To be consistent you ought to bang out messages on a drum and draw cartoons with the sharpened tip of a goose feather. No, don't bother to defend yourself, I don't have time. The Troll's been riding me again. He called me in for a little chat the other day. 'Good work,' says he. 'But look here, Horn—in this corner—is it a dog, or is it a cat?' I look at the corner. It's a cat, with whiskers. I ponder. Scratch my head. Try to see a dog. It's still a cat. Always was a cat. It's pure essence of cat. I look old Alfred straight in the eye. 'I believe it's an elephant, sir.' Really, sometimes I think old puddingface fails to appreciate my sense of humor. If he wants me to draw his damn cats for him then let him pay me a living wage. I'd rather fix drains in Flatbush. Tell your daughter I'm madly in love with her."

Toward the end of the summer Franklin again invited Max to Mount Hebron, this time with a new misgiving: he feared that the second visit could never equal the freshness and surprise of the first. Cora, too, seemed to anticipate disaster. She was restless and fretful, wondered what she could possibly serve for dinner, changed her dress twice before lunch, asked Mrs. Henneman, the housekeeper, to clean the mirrors and polish the silver, and scolded Stella for always being underfoot. Franklin, who had been staying up till midnight to work on his newspaper strips, now saw the weekend as a lost stretch of time for his animated drawings and cursed his bad luck, and Max, and life in general, and above all his exasperating shirt collar, which kept riding up on his neck—and then, as if he had arrived unexpectedly, Max was there, sweeping them all into his gust of talk, rescuing them, it seemed, from a ruined afternoon. Cora had planned a picnic at the top of the wooded slope above Mount Hebron. Sitting in the sun-speckled shade of the picnic table, biting into his cold chicken leg with eyes closed in pleasure, raising his glass of red wine into the brightness of the sun, Max looked down at the town, at the sunny brown river, at the wooded hills of the far shore, and said that his idea of bliss would be to own a piece of land on those hills, across from Mount Hebron. "Matter of fact," Franklin said, stretching out one arm in a long, slow yawn, "there's land for sale. People buy, sometimes build." Cora said there was a real estate agent on River Street and two more in the next township. Max asked if they would accept an IOU, and wondered if a real estate agent could supply him with a wife. After lunch, Max proposed a hike in the woods; and as he led them along leaf-strewn paths he stopped from time to time to point at something and say to Stella, "Is that a lion?" or "Those are very peculiar-looking telephone poles."

That evening, when Cora came down to the front porch after getting Stella ready for bed, Franklin went up to tell her the next installment of a continuing bedtime story about a little girl who discovered in her dark attic a bright country of dolls. When he returned to the porch he sat for a while jiggling an ankle and then rose and said he'd be back in two minutes. Two hours later he returned guiltily from his study and was relieved to find Max talking easily with Cora; and throwing himself down on the cushion of a wicker chair Franklin felt a burst of gratitude to Max for getting on so well with Cora, for being such an easy and undemanding guest.

One afternoon toward the end of September, Franklin was working in his office at the *World Citizen* when Max entered and announced that he had found a distributor. "A what?" Franklin asked, looking up from a page covered with sketches of noses. He was pleased with his latest strip, which in certain ways was the best thing he had ever done, but Kroll had not been enthusiastic. "We've got to have a more appealing hero," he had written in a long memo, "someone the public can take to their hearts," and although Franklin understood exactly what Kroll meant, he was disappointed and even shocked—couldn't Kroll see that what he was doing had an appeal of its own? Kroll liked domestic strips with strongly developed gags, as well as the working-girl strips that had recently come into vogue; he had never really cared for "Figaro's Follies," which he had tolerated solely for the sake of the more popular "Phantom of the City." For that matter the Phantom strip had begun to edge its way toward the fantastic, as Franklin sought out increasingly unlikely though carefully researched and scrupulously rendered settings—the insides of vast sewer pipes, abandoned subway excavations deep under city streets, the hollow caissons buried beneath the bed of the East River under the piers of the Brooklyn Bridge—and as Franklin studied wood engravings in old newspapers that showed the ingenious structure of the caissons, with their limelit shadowy chambers, their air locks and supply shafts, he could tell that Kroll was hoping for a really popular strip of a more familiar kind. The new strip, called "Harvey" and already cast in doubt by Kroll's memo, showed a boy with a pen who drew his own world, which he then entered; the world turned more and more threatening until, at the climactic moment, Harvey took out his pen and devised his own escape.

"A distributor," Max said. "You can have the photography done at Vivograph in that arcade building up on Fifty-third Street and they'll pass it on to their distributor, National Pictures—all very reasonable, very legit. Vivograph will charge you ten percent of whatever they can get from National. They distribute all over the States and in what our sainted editor calls 'Yurp.' "

"I think I know what you're talking about," Franklin said.

Max widened his eyes in feigned astonishment and, looking about at an imaginary audience, said: "You heard what he said, folks. I think it's a remarkable development." He dialed an imaginary telephone. "Hello. Horn here. Listen, he thinks he knows what I—what I—hell. Lousy connection." He hung up.

Franklin, who liked Max's enthusiasm but was also wary of it, began to explain that despite a good recent bout of work he had been forced to spend the last week doing editorial cartoons

for Kroll, who was disappointed in the latest strip and seemed
to take pleasure in loading him with plebeian work, but in the
middle of his explanation he had an idea for a brand-new strip,
which might be just the sort of thing Kroll had in mind. He began sketching rapidly in a blank corner of the page, and when
he looked up he stared in confusion at the pendulum swinging
in the glass case, the wallpaper with its faded haystacks where
drowsy reapers lay with their hats over their eyes.

There now began a long, blissful period of work, when
Franklin was able to throw himself nightly into his dime museum drawings and daily into editorial cartoons and three strips:
a new and uninspired one for Kroll about office life at a magazine publisher, the old Phantom strip with its new decor, and a
recent one that had sprung up in the shadow of "Harvey," about
a boy who stood on his pillow each night and climbed into his
dreams—and beyond the images that flowed from the tip of his
Gillott 290 pen point he would be aware of dimmer images, like
a yellow leaf lying on the porch rail or a black grackle shimmering with purple as it shrieked from a bare maple branch, and
one day he noticed with surprise that long, sharp icicles hung
shining from a roof edge, casting slanted black stripes against
the bright white wood.

One morning in mid-December Franklin laid aside his drawing board, put on his hat and coat, and made his way along the
warren of brown rooms to an old door with a frosted-glass pane,
behind which Max shared an office with a melancholy sports-
page cartoonist called Mort Riegel. Franklin rapped with the
knuckles of two fingers and opened the door. Max, alone with
his feet up on the desk, looked over his shoulder with raised
eyebrows and placed a hand on his chest in a parody of surprise.
"Put on your coat and come with me," Franklin said. "Ask no
questions." He led Max out into the sunny cold day and hailed
a cab, which came to a stop five minutes later before an old arcade building lined with shops. Between a barbershop and a

shoeshine parlor a flight of dark stairs with a loose handrail led up to the offices of the Vivograph Company. "I delivered it nine days ago," Franklin said as he turned a dented doorknob. The Vivograph studio, he had learned, turned out its own biweekly animated shorts, as well as travelogues and educational features, but rented its camera, an antiquated machine that had been supplied with a motor and could be set to shoot one frame at a time, to anyone willing to pay. In a small projection room whose single window was darkened with a crooked venetian blind that let in shafts of dusty light, Franklin and Max sat straddling a pair of folding chairs with their arms resting on the backs as they watched the four minutes and twelve seconds of *Dime Museum Days* by J. Franklin Payne. The title cards (HELP!! HELP!!) struck Franklin as superfluous, the bearded lady sprouting bushels of hair was funnier but less frightening than he had expected, here and there the flickering caused by faulty alignment was irritating, but on the whole it seemed to work: the long perspective shots into the depths of the museum were effective, and the final sequence, in which an entire hall came to life and kept changing into sinister figures who pursued the terrified girl down dream perspectives and nightmare corridors, was very satisfying, despite one or two small details that needed attending to. When it was over he turned to Max to ask about the bearded lady sequence and was surprised to hear applause in the back of the room, which came from the projectionist and two studio employees who had crept in to watch, and when he turned back to Max he was startled to see Max staring at him with a glitter of wild excitement in his eyes.

FOUR

"You've always been impossible," Max said as they walked down the stairs into the arcade, "but this, my friend, takes the all-time impossible cake."

"Oh, you'll see I'm right, you'll see. Walk or cab? Look: that barber's just committed a murder." The barber stood smoothing a white towel over the face of a man who lay with his head tipped far back, his chin pointed at the ceiling. Franklin, who carried the can of film in his coat pocket, was amused by Max's dismay but also disappointed: didn't Max realize that several sequences had to be redrawn entirely? There could be no talk of deals and distribution until the entire thing was fixed up and rephotographed.

"Easy come, easy go," Max said with a shrug. He glanced at a passing girl, who glanced back, and Franklin, who had assumed he'd been speaking of the man in the white towel, suddenly wondered whether Max had meant the girl, or *Dime Museum Days,* or something else entirely.

But he had to admit, as the world vanished behind his study

in swirls of falling snow, that Max might have been right. To the clack of a rented projector Franklin watched his moving pictures night after night on a wall of the tower study while snow fell steadily, and the repeated viewings revealed new flaws. It wasn't simply a matter of occasional irritating technical lapses, as when, for instance, despite his system of crossmarks, he had failed to register the drawings precisely; rather it was a question of whole sequences needing to be reimagined. Max thought he was being overly fussy, and Max was probably right. But just outside his window Nature was being far more fussy, far more finicky and precise. The swirling lines of snow were composed of separate flakes, and each flake was a cluster of separate ice crystals—scientists had counted over a hundred of them in a single flake. Under the microscope each minuscule crystal, colorless and transparent, revealed a secret symmetry: six sides, the outward expression of an inward geometry of frozen molecules of water. But the real wonder was that no two crystals were precisely alike. In one of his father's camera magazines he had seen a stunning display of photomicrographs, and what was most amazing about the enlarged crystals was that each contained in its center a whole world of intricate six-sided designs, caused by microscopic air pockets. For no conceivable reason, Nature in a kind of exuberance created an inexhaustible outpouring of variations on a single form. A snowstorm was a fall of jewels, a delirium of hexagons—clearly the work of a master animator. Max, mocking his endless labor, would have done better to direct his scorn at the falling snow. But Max had made Franklin thoughtful as well as irritable. Why this obsessive fiddling, when after all he was a professional used to working quickly under the pressure of rigorous deadlines? Perhaps the answer was this, that for once in his life he preferred to be an amateur. In this realm, at any rate, he was one whether he liked it or not. But there was also something else, something more elusive that he couldn't quite get at but that had to do with entering a place that made you feel you were somehow at the center—though at the center of what, Franklin wasn't sure.

The snow stopped, leaving great drifts that covered the porch steps and swept up to the parlor windowsills; and again the snow came down, burying the world in billions of glittering but invisible six-sided designs. On the cold kitchen windows Franklin showed Stella elegant frost-drawings: spines and needles of ice, ice ferns and ice feathers, ice filings flung over the field of an unseen magnet. Then the sun came out, and there was a great melting and dripping: artful icicles two feet long hung from the porch eaves, transforming the storm-darkened porch into a sunny cavern of glistening and transparent stalactites, all dripping into the snow, all lengthening stealthily as each falling drop partially froze on the gleaming tips. Suddenly an icicle fell, plunging point-first into the snow and vanishing. A small dark bird, startled, flew into the brilliant blue sky and melted away. And again it snowed, and again the sun came out. In the mornings on the way to the station Franklin counted the new snowmen that had sprung up mysteriously overnight or the old ones that had been stricken with disease and lay cracked apart—a head here, a broken body and three lumps of coal there—and one day he looked up from a piece of snow-colored rice paper and knew he was done. It was as simple as that: you bent over your work night after night, and one day you were done. Snow still lay in dirty streaks on the ground but clusters of yellow-green flowers hung from the sugar maples. Franklin delivered the 4,236 drawings, of which nearly 2,000 were entirely new, to Vivograph himself, then screened the film alone. Only after that did he invite Max to a viewing—and now it was Max's turn to confess that Franklin had been right all along, that the reworked version was superior in every way. "Though I suppose you'll want to take it back and redo it again," he added. Franklin was startled. "Well, no. No. Why? Is there something wrong?"

Dime Museum Days, animated by J. Franklin Payne, produced by the Vivograph Company, and distributed by National Pictures, opened on 1 May in theaters across the country, from Grauman's in Los Angeles to the Rialto in New York, as part of a weekly news-travelogue-cartoon supplement. Franklin and Max watched it in the Strand, where the audience burst into applause, and reports from the Abe Blank theaters in Nebraska, from the Karlton in Philadelphia, from the Finkelstein and Reuben chain in Minneapolis and St. Paul, all confirmed the sense of a heady success. Reviews in the film trade journals did not know which to praise more, the meticulous artistry or the haunting fantasy; and with amusement Franklin showed Max a review that, after summarizing the plot, declared that Payne's scrupulous draftsmanship in the service of a grotesque dream-vision separated his animated cartoon from the ephemeral products of the day and lifted it into the region of art.

Three days after the opening Franklin was asked to report to the office of Alfred Kroll, managing editor and chief editorial writer of the New York *World Citizen*. Kroll's office was located at the end of a darkening corridor on the fourth floor, behind a dingy door whose upper glass pane was covered on the inside by perpetually closed venetian blinds. Franklin, walking along the darkening corridor, wondered whether the darkening effect was accidental or, as he preferred to think, a brilliant strategy meant to summon up deep childhood fears. Kroll, who had signed the letter that had brought Franklin from Cincinnati, was second in command to the invisible owner of the paper, Charles Harlan Hanes, whose office was located at the end of an even darker corridor behind an even dingier door, and who was said by Max to be one hundred ten years old and to be composed entirely of artificial parts. Hanes, according to Max, had hired Kroll to keep a tight grip on the *World Citizen* in all its departments, to express Hanes's views in editorials and their attendant cartoons, and to fire anyone who slacked off, was uncooperative, or seemed lukewarm in the service of *World Citizen* ideals. Exactly what those ideals were, it was difficult to say, since the paper regularly attacked both big business and government while remaining violently patriotic, and advocated an isolationist foreign policy while asserting the moral responsibility of the United States in the wake of the new world order. According to Max, Kroll was Hanes's flunkey pure and simple, but Franklin's sense of the man was more complex: he believed that Kroll had been hired because he had strong views of his own, which happened to be exactly those of Charles Harlan Hanes. He might shade an opinion slightly in deference to his boss, but he was never required to express an opinion in which he did not believe; and it was precisely his belief that gave his editorials a kind of crude passion they would otherwise have lacked, and made him a force to be reckoned with in his own right. Kroll was also known to enjoy certain freedoms in return for his loyal service, among them virtual control over the comic strips of the daily editions and the color comics of the Sunday supplement. Approval by Kroll could mean for a strip a chance it might otherwise not have.

As Franklin continued along the always-darkening corridor, he tried to foresee his meeting with Kroll, which almost certainly had to do with his animated cartoon. He felt both uneasy and cautiously hopeful—uneasy because a summons from Kroll usually, though not invariably, meant trouble, and cautiously hopeful because his cartoon had been a success, and Kroll liked success—and as he pushed open the door, rattling the blinds, he was surprised once again by the perpetual twilight of the reception room, with its one window covered by closed blinds, its tarnished brass floor lamp with a tasseled shade, and its faded secretary with sharp shoulders and thin, reddish nostrils, who looked up at Franklin and then at Kroll's door as if a disturbing connection between the two were slowly dawning on her. Franklin, who had expected to wait, was told to enter immediately.

Kroll sat in his gloomy office behind a cluttered desk with a small neat space in the center, under a yellow bulb that hung from a chain. He was a big broad-shouldered man with a heavy fleshy face and melancholy eyes. His sparse black hair was combed sideways across the top of his head and seemed to match the dark hairs on his fingers, which looked as if they had been combed carefully sideways. Franklin had never seen Kroll except behind his desk, and he wondered, as he sat down on a wheezing leather chair, whether Kroll ended in a straight line where the desk cut him off.

For all Kroll's air of heaviness, of rueful immobility, Franklin knew he was not a man to waste time. Kroll began by saying that he had waited to see the cartoon himself before speaking with Mr. Payne, who might for that matter have informed him of a project that was bound to be of interest to the *World Citizen.* The little film was admirable—he had expected no less from a man of Mr. Payne's undoubted abilities—and well deserved the attention it had been getting. But he hadn't called Mr. Payne to his office in order to discuss the craft of animated drawings, despite the interest such a discussion would hold for him; for as a matter of fact, he had been following the work of the animation studios for some time. No, what he wished to discuss with Mr. Payne was the subject of his little film. He had to confess that he had become—what was the word?—thoughtful, very thoughtful, upon hearing that a member of the art department had chosen to animate a strip no longer published in the *World Citizen* but still published in the Cincinnati *Daily Crier* and imitated in a number of New York papers. He had assumed that the report must have been mistaken; but now that he had seen the cartoon himself there could no longer be room for doubt. During the time of his association with the *World Citizen,* Mr. Payne had shown himself to be a loyal member of the staff. It was therefore difficult to understand his motives for engaging in an enterprise that could serve only to benefit the circulation of rival papers. He did not at this time wish to discuss the issue of motives; he wished simply to inform Mr. Payne that he was to cease at once all professional activities not calculated to advance the interests of the *World Citizen*, that he was to keep the editorial office apprised of all future projects relating to the animation of comic strips, and that, in order to take advantage of the attention aroused by his film, he was immediately to revive his old strip, under the new title "Dime Museum Days." He trusted there would be no misunderstandings in the future, and wished Mr. Payne a good day.

As Franklin coolly reported the interview to Max, he realized that what had most upset him about it had been Kroll's crass assumption that he had animated his old strip. Of course he had drawn on "Dime Museum Dreams," but there had been no attempt to drag his old strip out of the attic, brush off the cobwebs, and present it to the public all over again. Rather he had sunk into a familiar place in his mind and emerged with something entirely new, something mysteriously connected with his father's grave voice in the kitchen darkroom. At the same time Max's savage attack on Kroll, who he said had the look of a debauched Humpty-Dumpty, struck Franklin as wide of the mark, for he recognized with a kind of irritation that he did not entirely disagree with Kroll's position. Kroll was by no means the corrupt buffoon Max made him out to be; his alertness to possible injuries to the *World Citizen* was surely proper. Franklin hadn't given a moment's thought to the possible consequences of his animated cartoon, his kingdom of shadows, and his carelessness seemed to him blameworthy. His next cartoon would give Kroll no grounds for concern, since it would have nothing whatever to do with any of his strips. Meanwhile he intensely disliked the idea of reviving the old strip, which no longer interested him; but he supposed he could stand it for a few months.

Perhaps it was the talk with Kroll, perhaps it was the sense of having completed a long and arduous task, in any case Franklin felt tired—very tired—tired deep in his bones. In the mornings when he heard the rattle of milk bottles in the wire box on the front porch he lay in a heavy stupor of half waking, thinking how nice it would be to lie there a little longer, only a little longer; and the heaviness, the sense of being bound to his bed, made him think of his child's illustrated *Gulliver's Travels*, in which Gulliver was shown lying on his back with disturbingly thick, taut bolts of hair tied to little stakes in the ground. In the graying light of late afternoons, on the commuter train that made its way along the river toward the Victorian station one township south of Mount Hebron, Franklin sat back with half-closed eyes and listened to the soft squeak of the conductor's shoes, the soothing click-click of the ticket punch; and in the lamplit evenings, sitting in the soft armchair in the parlor, he listened to Cora practice her Czerny exercises while Stella bent frowningly over sheets of paper at her round worktable or played on the rug with her little wooden wash set: her washtub, her clothes wringer, her clotheshorse, her washboard. Sometimes he read aloud to Stella while she sat in his lap with her hair tickling his cheek. He read *The Young Folks' Story Book, Shining Hours, Grimm's Household Fairy Tales,* and a boxed set of four small books called *Polly's Jewel Case,* which included *Fireside Fancies, Very Pretty, Dear Little Buttercup,* and *Miss Mugglewump and the Thugglebump* ("Just kidding, Stel"). Later, when Stella had been put to bed, he would sit at the kitchen table with Cora and play one of the board games she sometimes enjoyed, like Innocence Abroad, or Steeplechase, or The Game of Life. Then he would retire to his armchair, where he would sit heavy-lidded and heavy-limbed, weary but not sleepy, while Cora sat reading on the couch. Sometimes he thought of his tower study, which seemed as remote and inaccessible as a tower in a fairy tale: to reach it he would have to climb innumerable flights of stairs, only to find, behind a moldering door, in an old room so thick with cobwebs that he would have to part them like layers of gauze, an old clock with a rusted key, a pile of yellowed pages, a cracked bottle of dried ink.

On a Saturday house visit to Stella, who lay in bed with a sore throat, Dr. Shawcross lingered to examine Franklin. In a grave voice that reminded Franklin of his father in the darkroom, Dr. Shawcross said that he was suffering from nervous exhaustion as a result of overwork. He recommended rest, a curtailed work schedule, and as much time as possible in the fresh country air. Franklin, struck by the kindness in the doctor's voice, thought how odd it was that this kind man, the very opposite of a Kroll, nevertheless reminded him somehow of the harsh editor, and later that night, as he lay in the dark staring up at the black ceiling that was the floor of his forbidden study, he suddenly made the connection: both Kroll and Shawcross had issued warnings, and both had exacted from him promises of obedience—as if they had secretly conspired, though for different reasons, to punish him for straying.

As the weather grew warmer and the leaves of the sugar maples, spreading their elegant designs into sunlight, cast broad patches of shade, Franklin played outside with Stella after supper under the still-light sky. On weekends he liked to explore with her the two acres of woods that were part of his property and rose up behind the deep backyard. He showed her little tight-coiled ferns that hadn't yet unfurled, birch bark and beech bark, hickory nuts that looked like small green pumpkins, the striking shapes of maple leaves: sugar maple and red maple and silver maple. Each leaf looked as if it had been cut from a pattern with a pair of scissors. It struck him that leaves were the snowflakes of summer, each tree a storm of slight variations on a form. Sometimes he walked with Stella down to the village to buy seed packets and balls of twine at the general store. From there he liked to continue down to the river and sit quietly with her on the bank: he leaning back on his elbows with his legs stretched out, she sitting with her arms around her raised knees. He was a little concerned about his daughter, who was very quiet, seemed sullen around Cora, hid when anyone except Max came to the house, and preferred staying indoors with Mrs. Henneman or taking walks with Franklin to playing with children her own age. Across the sunny brown water rose long low hills of pine woods with a scattering of blue spruce, oak, and birch. There were a few houses among the trees, and a patch of bare earth on which sat a brilliant yellow bulldozer. "When I die," Stella said, hugging her knees and staring out across the water, "I'm going to keep my eyes open." "Look," Franklin said. "Over there: do you know what that is? It's a blue jay. It looks a little like the kingfisher in your book, but take it from me, it's a jay. I bet *he's* not thinking about dying. Why would you want to keep your eyes open?" "Because that way it won't be too dark. I hate the dark. When people die, do they come back again?" "Well," Franklin said, and cleared his throat. Stella said vehemently, "They do come back again. They do." She paused. "But not always."

On weekends when Max visited, he and Cora and Franklin and Stella took long walks on country paths, had picnics in the woods, played croquet in the front yard, and drove to a landing ten minutes away, from which they took a small ferry across the river to the wooded hills on the other side.

"Stel's been talking about death," Franklin said one night. "I think she's lonely. I'm away all day, and she doesn't really have any kids her own age to play with." He and Cora and Max were sitting on the open porch, despite a chill in the air.

"Death," Max said. "A woman after my own heart. You know, I've seen two new bulldozers in those hills since my last visit. People are buying land up and down the river. In twenty years you'll be living across from Chicago."

"God, I love it up here sometimes," Cora said, shaking back her hair and drawing her sweater close.

"The only land I've ever owned," Max said mournfully, "is in a flowerpot on a window ledge on East Twenty-third Street."

"Well," Cora said, "we've all got to start somewhere," and Max burst into high, nervous laughter.

The weekend outings, the lazy evenings, the hours in the sun, the self-banishment from the tower study: Franklin had to admit that it was all having an effect, that he had never felt better in his life. In the mornings he rose before the rattle of the milk bottles and, filled with a kind of energetic serenity, went downstairs in the bird-loud dark, showing its first streak of gray, to put up a pot of coffee and prepare fresh orange juice. He sliced the plump Florida oranges in half on the breadboard, pressed the juicy halves firmly against the upthrust knob of the juicer, and carefully checked for pips. Freight cars loaded with slatted boxes of oranges picked from sun-drenched trees in orchards in Florida had rushed through the night at sixty miles an hour, through Georgia, the Carolinas, Virginia, all the way to the state of New York, where husky men with bulging veins in their upper arms had loaded the boxes onto trucks and driven them to country stores in northern villages, solely in order that he, Franklin Payne, could buy one dozen sun-ripened oranges and stand in his kitchen to make fresh orange juice for his wife and daughter. It was all astonishing, as astonishing as the milk that arrived in clear glass bottles every morning, with the cream clinging to the top, or the brightening air that poured through the large windows in their solid oak frames—yes, the whole world was simply pouring in on him. Soon he would make a breakfast of soft-boiled eggs, sputtering bacon, and toast with butter and apple jelly, and later, in his office, he would work hard, but not too hard, so that he would finish by the end of the day; and in the warm evenings he would walk with long strides, taking in the dark green scents of early summer. His body was trim, his step light, the skin of his cheeks and neck radiant with weekend sun and air; and at night he had begun to visit Cora in her room again.

As his health returned, as his energy increased, Franklin sometimes felt a touch of restlessness. In the warm summer evenings, sitting on the front porch as the last light drained from the sky and the green hills turned black beyond the darkening river, he would feel a vague regret, a wistfulness; and somewhere far back in his mind he would have the sense of an inner itching, as if he were on the verge of remembering a word that kept eluding him. Then he would get up from the porch glider and go inside, letting the wooden screen door slam behind him; and in the lamplit parlor he would look at the mantelpiece clock, flanked by a glass-covered oval photograph of Cora's parents and a glass-covered photograph of Stella, in matching pewter frames.

One night Franklin woke beside Cora and sat up in bed. His heart was beating rapidly; the remnant of a dream floated just beyond his inner sight and vanished. The muscles of his legs itched. Through the screen beneath the raised shade the night sky was deep blue. Franklin slipped out of bed, glanced at Cora, and stepped out of the room. He walked down the hall, opened a door, and began climbing the stairs to his tower study. On the dark landing he paused; his heart was beating wildly; his temples felt damp. Somewhere a floorboard creaked. For a long time he stood on the landing before turning back down the stairs.

"No no no," Max said a few days later. It was a hot blue Sunday afternoon. "My lips are sealed. Not a word until we're there." The wheels of the Packard made snapping and crunching sounds as they passed over pinecones on the rutted dirt path. Through overhanging branches, sunlight fell in trembling patterns, rippling over Cora's straw hat, glinting on bits of mica in granite rocks, sliding over foot-high tufts of grass that sprang from the dirt between the ruts. The ferry had carried the car across the river, and Max had guided them onto a hard dirt road that became narrower and bumpier, sprouting ferns, buttercups, clusters of Queen Anne's lace. "This will do," Max said, "this is fine, stop right here. Now follow me, one and all." He led them along the vanishing dirt path, looking back impatiently. Suddenly he stopped and stepped into the woods. "Come on, come on, you lazy city slickers, get a move on, shake a leg. Watch it, we're coming to a stream. Easy now. Easy does it." After a while he stopped and held out his arms. "Well? What's the verdict?"

"A nice spot for a picnic," Franklin said. "We could sit in that oak tree." Through the trees he could see the river below and, half a mile downriver, the village of Mount Hebron.

"Humble," Max said, placing a hand over his heart, "but mine own. Three and a half acres of pinecones and fungus."

Cora clapped her hands. "You're not serious, Max! You're not serious!"

Franklin said, "Do you mean to tell me—"

"It cost me an arm and a leg, let me tell you." Max shrugged. "But I figure I've got two of each. I think of it as an investment. A larger flowerpot. Hey, Stella Bella, look: see this pebble? I own it. That leaf's mine."

"This calls for a celebration," Franklin said, patting his pockets over and over again, as if he expected to find a corkscrew.

Two days later Max sat in Franklin's office, his legs outstretched, his left arm hooked over the back of the chair, his right hand rippling through the air. "I feel like a kid with a new train set, Franklin—only my trains are trees. Is this crazy? It's not even Wednesday and I'm counting the hours till the weekend. This place doesn't help. Monday morning I don't even have my hat off and already there's a note on my desk. From the Troll himself. You know who Alfred the Fat is? I'll tell you who he is. He's the fat little drip-nose kid we all knew in the third grade, the one whose pants were always getting stuck in his behind. Now he's sitting behind a desk and making us pay for knowing what we know about him. I'm telling you, one of these days— one of these godforsaken days—and take a look at this place, will you? Look at it. It's like working in a loony bin designed by

one of the resident loonies. Christ, I'm raving. I've got a dead-
line." He stood up. "You have a good life, Franklin." He turned
abruptly and left, rattling the blinds.

Franklin disliked being told that he had a good life—for some
reason it made him feel that he didn't have a good life at all—
and he disliked Max's abuse of Kroll because it had the effect
of making him rise secretly to Kroll's defense, and he preferred
not to be nudged into Kroll's camp against his will. His own work
for Kroll was going well. For the revived Cincinnati strip, now
called "Dime Museum Days" in honor of the popular animated
cartoon, Franklin changed Danny to a girl and brashly borrowed
incidents he had invented for the film. There was a daily black-
and-white version and a separate Sunday one in color. Moreover,
the daily strip was no longer closed, but continuous: a long adventure, each day's installment ending in a suspenseful sixth
panel, with an occasional small resolution and the introduction
of secondary characters, who replaced the rather passive hero-
ine from time to time in adventures of their own that took them
to new rooms of the museum. Franklin worked swiftly, scarcely revising a line; the strip proved popular, although he knew
that the drawing was inferior to that of the original strip, the sit-
uations less surprising and original, the whole thing hopelessly
uninspired. Kroll had canceled "Figaro's Follies" and rejected
each of the new strips Franklin had invented to replace it; he
was urging Franklin to create a strip in a more realistic vein to
replace the old "Phantom of the City." After several failed at-
tempts, including a humorous domestic strip in which the husband stayed home with the baby while the wife worked as a
newspaper reporter, and a mischievous-kid strip in which the
real culprit was the cute little dog, Franklin returned to an idea
in one of the late Phantom strips, replaced the Phantom with a
likable street urchin with a patch on his pants, and set the strip
entirely underground, in the subway and its tunnels. It was a
continuous strip, in which the boy had a series of menacing ad-

ventures in subway cars and in the system of tunnels under the city; the settings were precise but verged on the fantastic. Kroll was pleased, though he insisted that Franklin name the boy Sammy and the strip itself "Subway Sammy." Franklin had suggested "Adventures in Underland."

But for the most part, Franklin spent his time drawing the editorial cartoons that were Kroll's particular passion. Kroll wrote a daily editorial, seven days a week, in which he thundered at an abuse, attacked a senator or a budget proposal, turned his attention to the Allied war debts or German reparations, raised questions about the advisability of naval limitations, and for each of his editorials he required a striking one-panel cartoon. At first Franklin experienced the daily assignment as a punishment, but he soon became adept at seizing the central point in a Kroll editorial and teasing it out into the skillfully exaggerated lines of a cartoon. Kroll, a severe and fussy critic, was pleased with his work; and on the first of September Franklin opened his pay envelope to discover that he had been given a handsome raise.

Sometimes, poring over a Kroll editorial, Franklin would feel a sudden impatience. Then taking up his pencil he would begin making tiny sketches all over the margins: funny noses, grinning gnomes sitting under toadstools, little people stuck upside down in mustard jars and sugar bowls, pieces of broccoli with arms and legs, snarling creatures with spiked tails and spotted wings.

One December morning about eleven o'clock there was a familiar knock at Franklin's door. "Enter," Franklin called curtly; he had a busy day before him and was irked at being interrupted by Max, who was wearing his hat and an open coat. "I won't stay long," Max said, throwing himself into the faded armchair, stretching out his legs, and setting his hat on his knees. "I have to run down to the corner and pick up a couple of ribbons for Helen and be back in time for what's-his-name, the typewriter repair guy—her ribbon stopped reversing and it's driving her crazy. There's a little wheel in there, but I can't get at it. Incidentally, I quit a few minutes ago. I showed Helen how to take the front off and move the lever with her finger, but she says, and I quote: 'I can't live like that.' "

"I assume you're not serious."

"Dead serious. 'I can't live like that': her very words."

"But what'll you do?" said Franklin, who had stood up and begun to pace. "You can't just quit like that."

"You sound like my wife," Max said, "if I had a wife. Congratulate me, dammit all."

"Congratulations," Franklin said quickly.

Max explained that from time to time he had made discreet inquiries at rival papers, but nothing had turned up. Then, about two months ago, an idea had come to him, a bold and stunning idea that at first he had dismissed as mere daydreaming but that had refused to leave him alone. Despite his impulsive nature, he insisted he was cautious when it came to business, and he hadn't thrown in the towel before making certain he knew what he was doing. And now he was ready: ready to quit the newspaper business entirely and go to work for Vivograph. They liked his art, business was brisk, and there was money to be made. His plan was to start at the bottom, as an inker, though at the same salary as his present one, and work his way up. Then one day, when the time was ripe, he'd strike out on his own.

"What does that mean—strike out on your own?"

Max shrugged. "Start my own studio. Run the whole show." He put on his hat and stood up. "I've got to pick up a couple of ribbons for Helen. Listen, I'll be around till the end of the week. Lunch tomorrow?"

On the weekend Franklin and Cora celebrated Max's new job with a roast leg of lamb, ginger ale, and a bottle of bootleg gin supplied by Max; and as Max spoke of the studio system of animation, with its division of labor among inkers, in-betweeners, and animators, as he spoke of production and promotion and distribution, of press releases, full-page ads, and the European market, Cora listened closely and asked precise questions.

"Do you mean to tell me," she said, "that one of these cartoon films can be made every two weeks?"

"That's right," Max said. "There's a man at Vivograph—"

"So if you had a good distributor," Cora said, "you could make quite a lot of money."

"Exactly. Always assuming, of course, that your product satisfies a demand. And that means understanding your audience."

"I see," Cora said. "And how do you learn to understand this audience of yours?"

Max looked at the ash of his cheroot and raised his eyes. "You give ten years of your life to Alfred Kroll. That refines you. That sharpens the old sense of smell."

Max's absence from the second floor of the *World Citizen* at first confused Franklin: it seemed a kind of trick. In the long hours at his desk, with the drawing board slanted down against his lap, he kept listening for the sound of sudden footsteps outside his door, the impatient rap, the door swinging open with a clatter of blinds. His relations with his colleagues remained amicable and playful but somewhat distant; once he had lunch with Max's office mate, Mort Riegel, who suffered from asthma and, when he breathed, made soggy sounds that reminded Franklin of shoes pressing into waterlogged sod, and who spent the entire lunch hour complaining bitterly of having to share an office after eight years of service. For the most part Franklin stayed alone in his office, sketching in pencil on white bristol board, carefully going over the finished drawings in India ink, and erasing unwanted pencil lines—and as he fell into the soothing rhythms of his work he imagined, not without pleasure, the days of his life moving steadily toward him, passing through him, and coming out the other side.

Sometimes once a week, sometimes once every two weeks, Franklin had lunch with Max, who was frantically busy. As

Franklin had foreseen, Max was soon complaining about his new job. It was boring, it was burdensome, it provided him with paychecks mysteriously lower than he had been led to expect; but to Franklin's surprise, the disgruntlement only fed Max's ambition. Max wouldn't hear of returning to newspaper work, despite an attractive opening at a rival paper; he was determined, as he repeatedly put it, to strike out on his own. Besides, the work wasn't all bad; he was learning something new about the business every day. The Vivograph system of studio production saved time but was also stupidly makeshift and haphazard: to save time they did a little of one thing and a little of another, and failed to see that the consistent application of a single method would be far more efficient. Franklin began to argue that efficiency wasn't everything, that the Ford system as applied to the commercial cartoon had certain drawbacks, since each car was supposed to be identical to the others whereas each cartoon—but he let the argument slide, Max looked irked, it had been a long week for both of them, and besides, Franklin had other things on his mind.

In late March Stella had come down with a low fever that kept her in bed and refused to go away. She had no sore throat, no cough, no cold symptoms of any kind, and only a very slight decrease in appetite, for which her inactivity could be held accountable. What puzzled Dr. Shawcross and disturbed Franklin was her weariness and languor. So long as she continued eating well, the doctor had assured him, there was no cause for alarm; Franklin wasn't so certain. Stella was a quiet and moody sort of girl, but she had her own sense of fun, which anyone could recognize; and it was the absence of this sense of quiet delight, of secret inner glee, that worried Franklin. Cora was impatient with what she called Stella's moodiness and was herself too restless to spend much time at a bedside, especially of someone who refused to speak a word or even look at her. But Stella liked Franklin to sit with her while she lay drowsily in her bed with her dark eyes half-closed. He would read to her and tell her long stories that never really stopped, but only reached suspenseful resting points, and one evening he took up her box of colored pencils and began drawing pictures on a small pink pad. "Now look at this, Stelly Bumbalelly," he said, holding out the pad close to her and flipping it with his thumb: a kangaroo hopped headfirst into a barrel, kicked its legs wildly, and hopped out again. "Again," Stella said, watching earnestly, crawling up onto her elbow. "You see," Franklin explained after the sixth time, "it's really very simple. You draw the pictures in sequence: see? One after the other. Then when you flip them, your eye puts them all together. I can't believe I've never showed you this stuff. Do you have any more of these little pads?" On a plain white pad he drew swiftly, bent over his knee. Then leaning toward Stella, he watched her watching: a turtle dived off a rock and went down, down, passing startled fish until he came to a small house with a smoking chimney; and swimming through the door, he floated onto a bed and went to sleep. Stella was enchanted. Franklin made four more flipbooks for her before she fell asleep, and that night, after Cora had gone to bed, Franklin rose from the armchair in the parlor and climbed the two long flights of stairs to his tower study. Nothing had changed: the bottle of India ink sat on his desk beside two Gillott 290 pens, the little reapers on the faded wallpaper still slept among their faded haystacks. Franklin was calm, but his mind was streaming with images, and when he rose from his desk at four in the morning he had filled an entire sketchpad and had in his brain, in vivid detail, the structure of a new animated cartoon.

As he sat by Stella in the evenings, turning the upper sheet back to form a smooth border over her blanket, or holding his palm against her slightly warm forehead, he felt, beneath his anxiety, an odd tenderness for her illness; and he was grateful to his daughter, for releasing him into a sweet, intoxicating realm of freedom.

A week later the fever vanished as mysteriously as it had come, and as Franklin worked long into the night, he wondered whether he had somehow drawn Stella's fever into himself, where it flared up into images. The new animated cartoon or fever-vision was likely to be ten or even twelve minutes long, which meant ten thousand or twelve thousand separate drawings; and Franklin let himself sink into his night world with deep and secret joy.

The secrecy was crucial, he felt it in his bones: he must never let Kroll know what he was doing, never speak of it even to Max, who would suggest shortcuts, give well-meant advice, surround him with an air of reproach and expectation that would only get in his way. Cora, who knew he was back at work in his study, chose not to speak of it—and Franklin was glad, for he knew that his work irritated and exasperated her, as if it were a form of secret disobedience. Only to Stella did he sometimes speak of the growing piles of rice paper, the slow and loving work of retracing each drawing and inking over the pencil lines, and one evening when Cora had a headache and retired to her room after dinner, he took Stella up to the tower study and showed her his pile of inked drawings and his handmade viewing machine. Stella turned the crank carefully and made the pictures move: a doll with large, wondering eyes was walking through a moonlit department store. Stella watched to the end of the sequence, which broke off abruptly as the doll discovered the top step of an escalator. Then Franklin started at the beginning, with all the dolls waking in the toy department—the fluttering dance of the paper dolls had cost him a week of nights and lasted ten seconds. Stella watched all the way to the top of the escalator and started from the beginning again. Franklin sat down at his desk, and when he raised his head he was startled to find Stella fast asleep on the floor. It was past midnight. He carried her down in his arms and went back up to work.

The cartoon had presented itself to him in part as a series of formal problems to be solved. In *Dime Museum Days* he had introduced his girl into a strange world of scrupulously drawn settings and realistic freaks, both of which gradually assumed the distortion of nightmare. The girl herself had remained a frightened visitor from the sane, outside world. In *Toys at Midnight* the protagonist was a doll who magically came to life and would herself undergo a series of physical transformations that called for continually changing perspectives. Franklin felt the desire to accept a certain challenge posed by the artificial world of animated drawings: the desire to release himself into the free, the fantastic, the deliberately impossible. But this desire stimulated in him an equal and opposite impulse toward the mundane and plausible, toward precise illusionistic effects. As the violations of the real became more marked, the perspective backgrounds became fuller and more detailed; and as he gave way to impulses of wild, sweet freedom, he found himself paying close attention to the look of things in the actual world: the exact unfolding of metal steps at the top of a down escalator, the precise pattern of reflections in the panes of a revolving door seen from inside. One morning before entering the *World Citizen* he went down the steps of a nearby subway entrance and squatted beside a turnstile with sketchpad in hand, recording the turnstile arms viewed from below, while busy people looked at him with amusement or indignation. And one dark afternoon during a sudden storm he left his office and stood under a grocer's awning, recording the distorted reflections of stoplights and store lights in the wet black avenue, the halos of rain-haze about the street lamps, the wavelike sweeps of rain blowing across the street like the bottom of a blown curtain.

The doll went round and round in the revolving door and was flung out onto the sidewalk: he had the complex sequence of motions exactly right. For some reason the simple descent into the subway was more difficult, and the nightmare subway ride, with carefully exaggerated perspectives of looming seats and menacing faces, was causing him a lot of trouble—and as Franklin felt himself falling deeper and deeper under the spell of his cartoon, as he patiently traced backgrounds over and over again on the thin, crackly rice paper, throwing away entire sequences and studying the results in his viewing machine, he had the sense that he was living in the rain-haze of his shadow world, through which objects showed themselves waveringly, with an occasional hard edge peeping through. Somewhere beyond the rain-haze he and Stella and Max and Cora were walking in checkered sunlight on a green, wooded path, but when he arrived home he had to drag his feet through piles of red and yellow leaves; the wind howled as he climbed the stairs to his study; from the high windows he could see the ice skaters on the river, turning round and round, faster and faster, until they were a whirling blur—and emerging from their spin they sat back lazily in sun-flooded rowboats, their straw hats casting blue shadows over their eyes.

"The Coca-Cola bottle," Max was saying as he pulled the oars, "is instantly recognized by a wheat farmer in Iowa, an adman in Manhattan, and a housewife in Wyoming. It's the most powerful image of a civilization since the pyramid. And what is its secret? I'll tell you its secret." Stella sat with one arm over the side of the rowboat, letting her fingertips drag through the water. Cora, leaning back on a cushion with her straw hat pulled low, brushed at a fly on her shoulder.

"What, Max?" Cora said. "What's its secret?"

"The Coca-Cola bottle is shaped like a woman. That's its secret."

"Oh, Max," Cora said, "I can't believe that. Do you really think I look like a Coca-Cola bottle?"

"In a general way, yes. I mean it strictly as a compliment, of course."

"Did you hear that, Franklin? Max says I look like a Coca-Cola bottle."

"I read the other day," Franklin said, "that a woman found a mouse in her bottle of Coca-Cola."

"Really, Franklin," Cora said. "How disgusting."

"When she complained to the company, they apologized and sent her a free case of bottles. You see? It had a happy ending."

"That's what I mean about them," Max said. "They always satisfy the customer."

"What about the mouse?" Franklin said.

"I don't think anyone," Cora said, "has ever compared me to a Coca-Cola bottle. Y'all say the sweetest l'l ol' things."

"The mouse," Stella said, "turned into a giant rat. Then she ate the lady up."

"Stella," Cora said, "please don't interrupt when we're trying to talk."

Under overhanging branches Max brought them to shore. He pulled the boat onto a strip of sandy earth and held out his forearm for Cora, who seized it with one hand while holding onto her hat with the other. Franklin lifted Stella out and followed Max and Cora through the trees. "All this stays the way it is," Max was saying. "The road will be in back of the property. Watch your step. Up there—on the other side of the stream— that's where things will begin to look different." On the other side of the stream they passed through more woods and came to a clearing. Sawed-off branches lay about, and here and there stood a few smooth stumps. On one of the stumps someone had left a tin mug. "You see how private it is," Max said solemnly, narrowing his eyes as he stared down through the trees at the river.

He had established himself quickly at Vivograph, passing through the ranks and revealing a talent for direction and organization that had not gone unnoticed. When the head of the studio, a former animator who had become increasingly preoccupied with matters of business and was spending more and more time away from Vivograph, began to look about for someone to stand in for him and oversee daily operations, Max was the clear choice. His transition to virtual studio head was immediately successful. He hired three new animators and increased the production schedule from a biweekly to a weekly cartoon. But his particular talent was for detecting and eliminating wasteful steps in the animation process itself, while at the same time insisting on a high level of technical accomplishment. To this end he divided his animators into two ranks based on talent, limited the drawing of his chief animators to complex gestures, and introduced among his group of assistant animators a new and unheard of degree of specialization, assigning one man to avalanches, collapsing bridges, and storms at sea, another to mill wheels, stagecoaches, and windblown hats, a third to snowflakes and swarms of bees.

"Even so," Max said as he rowed them back across the river, "my hands are tied. The big decisions are made by the high-muckety-mucks who pay for my meat loaf and mashed potatoes while they serve T-bone steaks to their pet poodles."

"What you need," Cora said, "is a studio of your own."

"Exactly. I've talked to most of the guys about it and they're with me to a man. Frankly, I've been nosing around for low-rent office space. Putting out feelers. Waiting for the right moment to jump ship."

"Not now!" said Franklin, placing a hand on his chest and looking at the water in alarm.

As the excavation got under way, Max took to coming up each weekend in order to keep an eye on things. Franklin, whose weekends were devoted to work, was at first irritated at the prospect of weekend visits, and annoyed at his own irritation— what kind of friend was he, anyway?—but quickly felt a rush of gratitude to Max, who sternly insisted that everyone do what they wanted to do without fussing over him and who spirited Cora away for day-long outings, leaving Franklin free to bend over his animation board in the tower study, while Stella drew pictures of cartoon animals with her box of pastel pencils. Through the tower windows he could see down to the sunny brown river and, if he stood to the left of the right-hand window and looked out to the right, he could see, far up the river, Max's pale new house rising among the dark trees.

Perhaps because he could see the house rising, perhaps because he was moving forward swiftly after several wrong turns, Franklin had the odd sensation that Max's house and his own animated cartoon were springing up together under the rich blue summer sky. As the first-floor joists were laid and long floorboards began to be nailed diagonally over them, Franklin brought the doll up the stairs of the subway station onto the moonlit avenue. Under the oppressive height of skyscrapers, depicted in nightmare perspective, the doll seemed to grow smaller and smaller. A sudden storm burst out, driving the doll to huddle in a doorway as partition studs with door openings were raised and braced in place. Waves of rain blew along the avenue, halos of rain-haze glowed about the street lamps; and as the rain cleared and Franklin began the crucial scene in which the terrified doll slipped through the keyhole of a candy store and in the presence of tiny candy animals felt herself growing larger, the corner posts and outside wall studs began to rise among the dark trees.

"A perfect place for a picnic," Max said, half-sitting on a sawhorse with his legs outstretched and crossed at the ankles as he carefully salted the top of a hard-boiled egg. Franklin and Stella sat on barrels facing a board set across two sawhorses. On the board sat plates of sandwiches, bowls of strawberries and purple grapes, a dish of hard-boiled eggs. Cora sat in a window opening, leaning back against the window stud with half-closed eyes and slowly raising to her lips a single plump grape. Through the second-floor joists shone slices of brilliant blue sky. The floorboards were striped with crisscross patterns of joist shadows and stud shadows. Curled wood shavings lay in a little heap

beside Max's sawhorse, and here and there lay a few shiny nails.
"Tell them to stop work," Franklin said. "The rest is superfluous. Look, Stel, some pigs have lost their tails."
    "And this is the living room," Max said. "Open, free—plen-
ty of light. Exposed timber, everything simple and straightfor-
ward—none of your Queen Anne quaintness for Uncle Max. I've
said it before and I'll say it again: the shut-in family parlor has
had its day. That's the dining room over there, and through
there's the kitchen, big as a barn. I plan to cram it full of every
up-to-date gadget on the market. And that room over there—
it's the American dream. I refer of course to the noble bathroom.
I'm installing a tub the size of Grand Central Station, oak tank,
siphon-jet bowl, brass trim, the works. Tell me a man's house is
his castle and I say hear, hear: but his bathroom is his church."
    "It might be a bit drafty," Franklin said. "You might want to
add walls."
    "How did they lose their tails?" Stella said.
    Cora, stretching her arms slowly into sunlight, said, "What on
earth are you talking about?"
    "Hey," Max said. "Off of there, buster. This is private prop-
erty." A squirrel, scampering along an overhead joist, stopped
abruptly, its head erect, its front paws raised, as if it had been
turned to stone.
    "You haven't lived," Cora said, "till you have squirrels in the
attic."
    "The workmen took off the tails by mistake," Franklin said.
"It happens sometimes. But luckily they left some nails behind."
    Something about the picnic disturbed Franklin, and that night
in his tower study it came to him: he hadn't looked back at the
squirrel, which in his mind remained fixed forever on the joist,
caught in an evil spell. His own work was progressing nicely.
Out on the street the doll continued to grow, higher than the
candy-store awning, higher than the candy store, while far up
the river, horizontal boards rose along the walls and the outline

of the roof took shape: king post and ridgepole and rafters. And still the doll continued to grow: higher than the Flatiron Building, higher than the Woolworth Building, until, placing one foot in the East River and one foot in the Hudson, she loomed above the island of Manhattan. Bending over, she picked up the little Brooklyn Bridge as tiny cars and trains spilled from the edges. She set the bridge down in Central Park, placed the Statue of Liberty on top of Grand Central Station, picked up the Flatiron Building and used it to smooth a wrinkle in her dress. Stella awaited each stage of the cartoon with quiet excitement; she had become quite skilled at detecting slight waverings caused by faulty alignment. Looking up, the gigantic doll saw the moon not far away. She removed it from the sky and began tossing it back and forth between her hands. Then she began to bounce it on rooftops like a white rubber ball, while through the right-hand tower window the house assembled itself as if it were the work of a skillful animator: red shingles spread across the roof-boards, a chimney rose into the blue sky. The final sequence was difficult: as the first light of dawn became visible the doll shrank swiftly down to her proper size and hurried back to the department store, to take her place on the shelf with her head leaning against the side of a puppet theater—lifeless as each of the drawings that composed an animated cartoon but, like them, irradiated by a secret. Max spoke of moving in by the first of September. Franklin, bothered by the subway sequence, began it over again.

One hot night toward the end of August, when heat lightning flickered in the blue-black sky and the chirr of crickets through the adjustable screen sounded like the tense hum of electric wires, Franklin placed a pen in his box of penholders, screwed the cap onto his bottle of drawing ink, and sat back in his leather desk-chair with his arms hanging heavily over the sides. The lacy black hands of the glass-covered clock showed 12:55. He was tired; the front of his neck felt wet; the back of his shiny brown vest stuck against the leather chairback. Everything was still, as still as in his father's darkroom when the enlarger light clicked on and shone down through the negative onto the magic paper. His father had counted slowly, in a grave voice, marking each number by the slow downward motion of his index finger, reddish in the light of the darkroom lamp. The enlarger light clicked off; the cream-colored paper, empty of images but charged now with secret life, slipped into the developer tray; he was allowed to hold it under with the tongs. He watched very closely in the light of the red lamp. Now in the white paper a shadow appeared, and another, a hardening edge, a hazy foot, a face, a tree—and there he was, darkening, smiling up at himself in the developer tray, as clear as life, but motionless, hardening: spellbound. And as he grasped the edge of paper carefully with the tongs in order to lift it from the developer into the stop bath, in his mind he saw the boy in the photograph walking across the picture, one foot after the other, through trembling spots of sun and shade. And he had done it; now he had done it; and scraping back carefully in his desk chair, Franklin began pacing about the room, his heart beating wildly, and in his temples a ripple of headache. He had done it, and he needed to tell his father. But his father was dead. What did it mean? The clock tick-tocked. Hearts ran down and you couldn't wind them up again. Time was passing—even here. Franklin, filled with exhilaration and a kind of wild melancholy, stepped to the door of the tower room. He began to hurry—quietly, quietly—down the stairs.

At Cora's door he stopped and placed his hand on the fluted glass knob. The handle squeaked as it turned; through a sliver of door-opening he saw Cora asleep on her back, her head turned to one side. Heat lightning flickered beyond the screen, showing a glimmer of branches. "Cora," he whispered; he heard the gentle rasp of her breathing, a racket of crickets. Quietly he closed the door. He made his way down the hall and placed his hand on another fluted glass knob. The door opened with a squeak: he would have to remember to oil the bottom hinge. Stella lay on her side in a wildness of bedclothes. Franklin knelt by the bed. "Stella," he whispered, "are you awake? Stella." He shook her shoulder. She opened her eyes and looked at him gravely. "Stella," he whispered, "I just wanted to tell you: I'm done. Now go back to sleep."

Stella sat up and gave a shuddering yawn. A ripple of slept-on hair fell across her cheek and touched the corner of her yawning mouth; she swept it back as if she were brushing at a fly. Then she pulled up a shoulder of her short-sleeved nightshirt, which slipped down again, and held out her thin arms. "Carry me," she said, and reached quickly for her bear.

Franklin carried her up the stairs to his tower study. On the floor he sat with her on his lap and turned the handle of his viewing machine. In the department store at midnight, the toys woke to life. The nightmare flight through a world of giant furniture, the revolving door, the menacing subway ride, the looming buildings, the night storm—all was calculated to make the doll smaller and smaller until, in the candy store, came the turn: then larger and larger she grew, as the scrupulously reduced world grew smaller and smaller, and at last she straddled Manhattan. The coda was swift: the return to her proper size, the flight back to the department store, the stiffening of the toys as the city woke from its dream. It had taken him seventeen months. He had seen it all a hundred times, five hundred times, his back ached and his temples were throbbing, but he knew that nothing like it had ever been done before. He glanced down. Stella, faithful and exhausted, was asleep in his lap. Her one-eyed bear lay on his back on the floor. "Thank you," Franklin whispered. "Sorry," he whispered. "Easy does it," Franklin said, scooping them both up in his arms as joy leaped in him and headache, like heat lightning, flickered across the back of his brain.

FIVE

In the arcade building, cool and shadowy after the hot sunlight of
the avenue, Franklin passed a flower shop, a cigar store, a shoemaker's shop where a sad-eyed man in a leather apron sat staring at an upside-down red high-heeled shoe, a newsstand, and
a barbershop where a man lay with a towel over his face. Franklin
wondered whether it was the same man the barber had murdered almost three years ago. Next came an archway that contained a dim-lit staircase with a rattly handrail. At the top of the
dark stairs he entered the Vivograph studio, where he was told
that Max had gone down for his morning shave. In the barbershop, empty except for the man with the towel over his face and
a barber shaking out an apron, Franklin was surprised that he
hadn't recognized Max, though even now there was something
a little unfamiliar about the look of his legs and the shiny black
leather shoes. He sat down in the barber chair next to Max and
leaned back against the adjustable neck-rest as a second barber
rose heavily from a chair in the corner. To the soothing sound of
the blade slapping against the strop—the swing of the blade and
the steady slap-slap reminded him of the pendulum in the glass-

cased clock—Franklin closed his eyes and settled into the soft
leather seat. "I'm done," he said to Max. "Twelve thousand three
hundred twenty-four drawings—over twelve minutes. I want
Vivograph to shoot it. I wonder whether I can screen it early next
week? Do you do this every day?" The barber began lathering
his cheeks; the warm thick soap, the soft bristles of the brush,
the smell of scented oils, the barber's firm plump stomach pressing against his elbow, all this soothed him deeply. He was very
tired. "Max," he said quietly, "are you asleep?" He opened his
eyes and glanced at Max as the first barber leaned over and slowly removed the towel. He saw flushed red cheeks, bristly gray
eyebrows, and a pencil-line gray mustache. "So there you are,"
called a familiar voice, and Max strode into the barbershop.
"They told me I'd find you here. I had to pick up a few things."
He sat down in the empty chair on the other side of Franklin.
"So what brings you to my neck of the woods? Give him the
spray job, Benny. Make a new man of him. Irwin, I'd like you to
meet Franklin Payne: friend of mine. Irwin Marcus." Still leaning back in the barber chair, the man with brick-red cheeks and
a gray mustache solemnly extended a hand.

In a booth in an arcade coffee shop Max agreed to photograph
the drawings, which sat in twelve cartons in the trunk of
Franklin's Packard; he had driven into the city and parked around
the corner from the arcade building. Two young men from Vivograph, with identical vests and four white shirt-sleeves rolled
up above the elbows, helped Max and Franklin carry up the boxes and set them on the floor of Max's small office. Franklin eyed
the growing pile ruefully. Individual drawings flashed in his
mind, but he could not put them together. They were lifeless—
boxes of corpses. He had wasted a year and a half of his life.
"Don't worry," Max said, "I'll guard them with my life," and as
Franklin stepped past the flower shop into hot sunshine, he was
so startled by the loud car horns, the explosion of jackhammers,
the flash of sun on black and red and green cars, the reflections

of striding people in plate-glass windows, the sharp smell of gasoline and baked cookies, that his visit to Max seemed to have taken place under the ground, in a dark burrow, long ago, in some other life.

A week later he recalled that other life as he sat in his office at the *World Citizen,* his drawing board slanting from the edge of the desk to his stomach. He was sketching another cartoon for one of Kroll's editorials, in which he showed a German house-wife buying a single egg with a wheelbarrow full of money sacks. The idea was hopelessly trite. A trapped fly buzzed between the half-open venetian blinds and the window. Franklin won-dered how long it took to photograph 12,324 drawings, and for some reason he remembered the sad-eyed shoemaker staring at the red high-heeled shoe. He wondered whether flies ever died of boredom. Perhaps he should turn the housewife into a witch trying to purchase a toad for her pot. There was a knock on the door, and Franklin looked up. He was about to say "Come in" when the door opened and Max entered.

"You look as if you haven't moved for two years," Max said.

"I haven't," said Franklin.

Max sat down on the edge of the desk and drummed his fin-gers on a pad of paper.

"You could have saved three hundred to five hundred hours if you'd used cels. Our inkers could have saved you another two-three hundred hours, our in-betweeners ditto. At a conservative estimate I'd say you threw away four to six months of your work-ing life making unnecessary wiggles. The alignment's shaky— there's a flicker—strictly amateur stuff. A kid of seventeen without a scrap of talent can align perfectly using the peg sys-tem. Now listen to me. Here's what I propose. Last month we decided to ditch National Pictures and distribute through Cin-emart, where we can cut a much better deal. This one needs to be handled a little differently because of the length, and Cine-mart is the best in the business when it comes to special angles.

They can get it out there like nobody's business and once it's in the theaters we think it will draw. We'll work with them on publicity and we'll supply the art for the lobby poster. You don't have to worry about a thing. I'll have Milt draw up a contract. Don't forget the housewarming on Saturday. By the way, congratulations. It's a masterpiece. The boys are gaga over it."

"The reason I don't like cels," Franklin began, but Max had already put on his hat. The door shut behind him. Franklin pulled over his drawing board, picked up his pencil, and did not draw. Had he wasted four to six months of his life through sheer stupid stubbornness? He had no dislike of technological progress, of up-to-the-minute systems and methods. He was fascinated by the latest advances in the art of home refrigeration, by recent developments in camera shutters and the steering mechanisms of automobiles. Above all he loved the machinery of newspaper production, from the zinc plates with their dots of blue or red or yellow ink for printing Sunday comics in color to the automatic cutters and folders that transformed the long rolls of paper into thick, perfectly folded newspapers. In the early days in Cincinnati he had taken time to visit the composing room and watch the Linotype operators at work, and observe the splendid machine itself as it dropped the correct brass matrix in place after each key was pressed and, after the slug was cast, distributed the individual matrices back to their original locations in the magazine. His objection to the cel system wasn't that it saved labor, or that it represented a technological advance; his objection was that it encouraged stable backgrounds, whereas his experiments in changing perspective required continual slight shifts in the entire background image. The cel system also encouraged a split between background and animation, expressed in the studio as a division of labor among different kinds of artists, whereas for him the image was a single complex unit of interconnected lines. Moreover, he had seen dozens of Vivograph cartoons, he had followed the cartoons of other studios, and he had passed judgment: the sequences were smooth, the motions fluid, the gags clever, but the drawing—the drawing was mediocre. And there was another thing, something he had no name for but felt in his mind's fingertips: the cartoons lacked something, they left him restless and disenchanted; and this thing that they lacked, that had no name, was the only thing that mattered, and was somehow connected with his father's grave voice in the darkroom and the mystery of the developer tray. And yet—and yet. He had to admit to himself that Max's words had disturbed him. After all, it wasn't true that every one of his backgrounds was different from the others; there was a great deal of repetition, of mechanical and laborious retracing. In the future he would have to consider adopting a partial cel system. And one more thing bothered him: the flickers from faulty alignment. If he ever made another animated film, he would use pegs instead of crosses. And at the thought of making another cartoon, tiredness rippled in his temples like a flutter of headache.

On Saturday afternoon Cora went into town to pick out a present for Max's party and try on hats, while Franklin took Stella rowing on the river. It was a sunny blue day in September. The pines and oaks at the river's edge, the blue sky, the lifted white oars, all showed clearly in the shiny dark water; here and there the green was streaked with red and yellow. Franklin rowed downriver, away from Max's house. Mount Hebron ended and hilly farms came down to the water. Strands of green cornstalks edged with brown lay burning in the September sun. Stella, in her straw hat with the brilliant red wooden cherries, sat trailing her hand in the water. In the shade of a spreading oak, seven cows resting on their stomachs all raised their heads and stared at the passing rowboat. "They've never seen cows like us," Franklin said. Stella looked at him with a faint smile; her grave beauty was a darker version of Cora's. The shadows of branches rippling across the straw hat, the brilliant blue air, the sudden orange and yellow of a turning sugar maple, the distant barns, the lazy amble of cows—all this filled Franklin with delight and a gentle, yellow-orange melancholy. Their first summer in Mount Hebron, he and Cora and Stella had gone picnicking on the riverbank every Sunday. Was it so long ago? Cora had told him about family outings on the banks of the Ohio when she was a child: from the picnic basket had come wineglasses and a bottle of wine and a silver cream pitcher and silver bowls and fresh strawberries. "I wish Mom was here," Franklin said, watching drops of water fall from the oars. He too remembered childhood picnics by a river, not far from Plains Farms: a willow had trailed its branches in the water. "Mom hates going anywhere with us," Stella said sharply. Panic flared in his chest. "Well now," he said, "I wouldn't exactly say that," and kept on rowing.

Back at the house he found a note from Cora on the kitchen table. "Ran into Max all jittery in town. Agreed to help set up for party. Meet us there 5:30—yes? Stella can wear her new patent leathers. Don't let her wear the blue dress—it's a fright. C." It was half-past three. For the next hour Franklin played croquet with Stella and then went inside to change for the party: a dress-up affair, for which he chose his tuxedo jacket. Stella wore her red party dress with the white lace collar and her white straw hat with the black velvet band. Franklin drove to the ferry and missed the five o'clock crossing by two minutes; he stood on the dock and watched three yellow-green leaves bobbing in the ferry's wake. Half an hour later he stood with Stella at the rail and looked down the river toward Mount Hebron as they crossed. The warm air had an underlayer of chill; a tang of autumn filled the late afternoon. On the other side, dusk had fallen; he drove on a dirt road through a gloom of pines. A new road ran behind the house, but Franklin preferred the old one, which grew gradually impassable and stopped in the middle of the woods. Through the trees he could see the house, its lights burning in the green dusk. He and Stella walked through the underbrush and came out of the trees onto a path leading to the long front porch. The porch and sloping lawn were crowded with guests in pale dresses and summer suits; Max and Cora stood with drinks in their hands, talking to a young couple both dressed in white.

"Ah, there they are!" cried Max, breaking away and bounding down the steps. Cora, in a shimmering green sleeveless dress with a long transparent scarf flowing down her side, followed slowly. Max seized Franklin by the elbow. "We thought you'd drowned. Everyone's here. And who's this? Please introduce me to the princess. No—I don't believe it. You don't mean to tell me. It can't be . . . Stella?

> *Stella*
> *You're so bella*
> *You make a guy feeeel*
> *Like one heck of a fella.*

Oh Cora, I'd like you to meet a friend of mine: Franklin Payne. You've met? Over here, Milt, over here. Milt Crane: man who drew up your contract. There's not a thing he doesn't know about the business. We're very hopeful, Franklin, very hopeful. Drinks are on the porch. Lemonade or strawberry punch for the princess, and you can water yours down with a little high-class hooch. Excuse me. A little crisis over there. Cora, would you mind? Excuse us for just a second."

Franklin wandered onto the porch with Stella, where he poured lemonade for her from a big pitcher into a tall glass. An expressionless man in a red dinner jacket and black pants held out a silver tray of little triangular sandwiches with toothpicks in them as a man with wavy gray hair, wearing a white dinner jacket, said, "Franklin Payne, isn't it? Max introduced us." "I'm afraid I," Franklin said, looking for his drink and remembering that he'd forgotten to pour one, and all at once recalling the man under the towel. "Not *the* Franklin Payne?" a woman said; she had bare shoulders and on one shoulder lay a tiny shimmering drop of liquid. "The other one, I think," Franklin said. He looked about for Stella, who seemed to have disappeared. He heard a shriek and turned violently; down on the crowded lawn a woman was brushing furiously at her dress as a man held out a handkerchief. Through the trees he could see glimpses of river and, far downstream, the village of Mount Hebron and his tiny house with its tiny tower. "Excuse me," Franklin said, "I've misplaced someone." She wasn't on the porch; on the lawn he saw a green dress and made his way down to it. "I can't find Stella." Cora said, "I thought she was with you." With a swift glance she took in the lawn and porch. "I'm sure she'll be all right, Franklin. I'll help you look for her in just a minute."

He found her in the depths of the house, in a large leather chair in a dark study. Through the partly open blinds was a darkness of trees and patches of dusky sky. "I've been looking for you," Franklin said. "Well," Stella said, "here I am." "Yes, you are. What're you doing in the dark? Don't you like the party?" "I'm just sitting here. You're not supposed to ask two questions, you know. Can we go home soon?" "Pretty soon," Franklin said, sitting down on the floor and leaning back against the side of the chair. He felt a hand shaking his shoulder and opened his eyes to see Max bending over him in bright electric light. "We've been looking all over for you," Max said. Franklin said, "Is this a dream?" His neck hurt; Stella was asleep in the chair. Then he was handing Cora her shawl and Max was holding a flashlight as he led them to the car. The ferry had stopped running an hour ago, and while Stella slept in the backseat and Cora sat with closed eyes in the front seat, Franklin drove slowly over a bumpy dirt road to the nearest bridge crossing, ten miles away.

Despite Max's assurance that *Toys at Midnight* was perfect—perfect—Franklin insisted on a screening. The flicker was un-

mistakable, but except for one short sequence that needed fix-
ing, oddly satisfactory: the effect of a slight continual tremor, of
a black-and-white shot-silk iridescence, charged the images with
the shimmer of dream. Franklin was pleased with the episode
in the nightmare subway when the enlarging train appeared to
be coming out of the dark directly at the audience, closer and
closer, until it seemed ready to burst from the screen, though
he was now bothered by the transformation in the candy store.
On the whole he was less disappointed than he had expected to
be, and hoped to iron out the rough spots in a few months.

"I can't believe I'm hearing this," Max said. "All right, all
right: now listen to me. You can have one month—thirty days—
and not a billionth of a second more. We've got a tight production schedule and you'll gum up the works with your crazy
fussing. Christ almighty, Franklin. Shakespeare wrote *Hamlet* in
ten minutes on the back of a grocery list and Beethoven wrote
the entire Ninth Symphony while eating a bowl of Post Toasties
Corn Flakes, and you need two years to tinker with a cartoon.
Is this just? Thirty days: I'm warning you."

Franklin, who had been feeling idle and restless since deliv-
ering up his boxes of drawings, took up Max's challenge almost
gratefully. On weekday nights he worked four-hour stretches in
the tower study, coming down only to read Stella a bedtime story at half-past nine; and on the weekends, which Max now spent
at his new house, Franklin was able to work in the mornings and
afternoons, while Stella sat sketching in a corner of the study
and Cora and Max went shopping or rode through the countryside in Max's new Peerless. Sometimes Franklin stopped work
and, turning to Stella, offered to take a walk down to the river
or play croquet; but she, looking at him gravely, said that he
wasn't allowed to play until he finished his work. Then Franklin,
tired and joyful, returned to his task; and at dinner, which took
place sometimes at his house and sometimes at Max's, he had
the sense that he had fallen asleep at his desk and was dream-

ing this moment, with its steaming ears of buttered corn, its big shining pots in the kitchen, its summer sky darkening to dusk outside the windows and the shadows rising on the sun-topped trees.

Franklin finished in twenty-nine days; on the thirtieth, a Sunday, he took Stella to the circus in a nearby town. He had hoped to make it a family outing, but Cora begged off with a headache. The clown with his three tufts of orange hair jumped from the burning building, the tightrope walker in spangled blue tights rode a unicycle across the high wire, the balloon man and the popcorn man and the man selling live chameleons walked up and down the steep aisles between the wooden benches stretching up and up, while Stella watched with tense, held-in excitement and Franklin watched Stella watching and worried about Cora's headache. She had been having a lot of them recently, but she refused to see Dr. Shawcross, and that night after dinner, as he handed three new boxes of drawings over to Max, who agreed to let Franklin view it one more time but refused to allow a single additional change, he saw, in the smooth space between Cora's eyebrows, two shadowy lines of strain.

In the morning Cora laughed her old laugh and said that her headache had lifted. Franklin, despite her laughter, seemed to see the same shadowy lines between her eyebrows, and on a Saturday afternoon two weeks later when he happened to glance at her, seated between him and Max in a darkening movie theater, he thought he saw the same shadowy lines, as if she had a slight perpetual frown. The newsreel and travelogue barely held his attention, though he found *Toys at Midnight* interesting enough. He noted several flaws, was pleased by the night storm and the rings of rain-haze about the lampposts, and in general had the slightly confusing but not unpleasant sense that, thrown up on the big screen before an audience, none of it any longer had anything to do with him. They left after the first film of the double feature, a cloak-and-sword adventure, and as Franklin pushed open the heavy doors he stopped in confusion as he saw not the dark autumn night but the brilliant afternoon sunlight shining through the glass doors, flashing on the glass-covered lobby posters, polishing the silver posts, lying in warm parallelograms on the crimson rug.

The reviews in the film trade journals were lengthy and laudatory, though several critics complained that the deliberate rejection of studio techniques, the elaborate detail, the painstaking finish, set the cartoon so radically apart from its contemporary rivals that it existed in a world by itself and could exert no influence. One critic, attempting to define its baffling quality, said that it was at once daring and old-fashioned, casting one eye boldly toward a realm of animation that had not yet come into being and the other eye back to the comfort and stability of a vanished past. "I wonder what sort of eyeglasses he'd recommend," Franklin remarked, while Max reported that the overall marketing strategy he'd discussed with Cinemart and the jazzy promotional posters in particular had been so successful, so very successful, that other studios were already beginning to copy them and the head of Cinemart had paid him a personal compliment.

On Wednesday morning, four days after he had sat in the darkening movie theater and seen shadowy lines between Cora's eyebrows, Franklin was asked to report to the office of Alfred Kroll. As he walked down the darkening corridor toward the dingy door whose glass pane was covered by perpetually closed venetian blinds, he wondered vaguely what possible cause for complaint Kroll might have against *Toys at Midnight*, if indeed that was the reason for the unusual summons; for although the cartoon bore Franklin's name, it was an entirely original creation that made no use of any comic strip and could in no way injure the *World Citizen*. His relations with Kroll had been coolly cordial since the summons three years ago, for Kroll practiced among all his employees a kind of cryptic amiability, and as

Franklin pushed open the rattling door and stepped into the twilight of the reception room he had the sudden sense that no time ever passed in this realm of gloom, with its tarnished floor lamp and its faded, barely visible secretary.

In his dim-lit office Kroll sat immobile behind his desk, looking out from melancholy and intelligent eyes above their dark pouches. Franklin, as he sat down across from him, had the sensation that Kroll had been deftly sketched by a cunning hand: the large head boldly indicated by three or four strokes, the powerful plump body roughly outlined, here and there a few skillful shadings. His large, soft hands lay folded on the desk before him. Without moving, Kroll spoke.

In no way, he said, did he wish to meddle in the private affairs of his employees, except, to be sure, when those private affairs affected the fortunes of the *World Citizen*. For some time he had sensed a—what should he say?—a slight falling off, a lack of verve, a loss of passion or energy in Mr. Payne's editorial cartoons. He had not known whether to attribute this puzzling deficiency to general fatigue, to overzealousness in the performance of his other newspaper duties, to a failure to engage imaginatively with the crucial issues of the day, or to some other cause. It had now come to his attention that Mr. Payne had been engaging in an activity that in no way concerned the *World Citizen*—an activity that, however admirable it undoubtedly was in itself, was bound to consume considerable time and energy. He had no wish to go into the matter, which he had had the pleasure of discussing with Mr. Payne on another occasion. He did however wish to insist, indeed he was incapable of not insisting, that workers in the employ of the *World Citizen* devote their full energy to the business of the *World Citizen* and refrain from any activities that might detract from or diminish that energy. In a word, he was forced to order Mr. Payne to cease immediately to occupy himself with animated films, on pain of severing his happy association with the *World Citizen*. In addition, he was taking it upon himself to cancel two of Mr. Payne's three comic strips so that he might devote himself with full energy to the editorial cartoons for which in the past he had demonstrated so great an aptitude. If there were no questions, he wished Mr. Payne a good morning.

The cool brashness of it impressed Franklin, even as the gray meaning of it, like an exhalation of Kroll's gloomy cave, came over him in a thickening drizzly fog. The sense of clouds and chill was still with him at lunch the next day in the arcade building, where he told Max that he felt as if his hands had been cut off at the wrists. Max, saying that he'd recently thrown out a rotten eggplant that looked better than Kroll, leaned forward and spoke in a low voice.

"I have news, Franklin: big news. It's not official yet, so your lips are sealed, but listen to me now. I'm leaving Vivograph next week. I've got the office space lined up two blocks away and all the guys are coming with me. I'm calling it Maxograms, Inc.— don't laugh. It's a surefire thing. In a week I'll be a corporation. I'm sick of working for clowns like Kroll, and so are you. Franklin, listen to me. Tell fatso you're kissing the old dump goodbye. Tell him thanks for the buggy ride but it's time you rode your own jalopy. Franklin: listen. Come to work at Maxograms. I'll give you the freedom you need to do the work you want to do and I'll put my staff at your disposal—inkers, in-betweeners, all the little guys who can take care of the dreck while you take care of the art. Franklin: forget Kroll. You need him like a hole in the head. He's nothing but a five-and-dime Buddha. Ask yourself what you'd rather do with your life: have free run of Maxograms and do what you want to do, or spend the rest of your life drawing funny faces for the likes of Alfred Kroll, who sits there drowning in his own butterfat scribbling trash about the fate of the nation and jiggling his wienie under the desk."

Franklin told Max he'd think the offer over, but even as he spoke he knew he would say no. At night he lay awake, trying to

understand what was wrong with him. To work every day on animated drawings, to be paid for his work as he did it, to have at
his disposal the camera, the projection room, the help of skilled
assistants, the practical advice of professional animators, to watch
his work take shape under an expectant and well-wishing com-
munal gaze, above all to have time: all this was not to be refused
lightly. But even as he felt the temptation of it he was aware of
an inner recoil. For the flaw was this: even if Max should remain
true to his word, and an unlikely freedom should in fact be granted to Franklin within the strictly run studio, his work, for better or worse, had always originated and flourished in secrecy.
Whatever Max thought he was offering—perhaps a room of
Franklin's own, with a locked door, at the farthest end of the studio—Franklin knew that Max could never prevent himself from
following each day's work, making suggestions, urging one direction rather than another. For the spirit of a studio was com-
munal, and it was precisely this public and open spirit, which in
one sense was a temptation, that in another was sheer death to
the solitary, secretive, perhaps unhealthy, but utterly necessary
spirit in which he did his work. There was one more thing. Kroll
might be harsh, Kroll might be pompous and cold, Kroll might
enjoy exercising power to the point of tyranny, but he wasn't corrupt, he wasn't self-serving, and he was in no sense a fool. His
passion was not for himself but for the *World Citizen*, and his fa-
natical demand for total devotion to the paper was not in itself
ignoble. And Kroll's instinct, when all was said and done, had
been entirely right: Franklin had in fact been slacking off, even
the comic strips no longer engaged his deepest interest, his passion lay elsewhere. Kroll's decision had been ruthless, but not
unreasonable—or if it had been unreasonable, it had at any rate
been understandable. Kroll's fanaticism ran deeper than Max's;
in some black corner of Franklin's brain, he felt an odd kinship
with Kroll, even as he raged at his punishment.

Max received his refusal wryly, as if he had thrown a drowning man a rope that the poor devil refused to take because it felt a little rough to the touch, and Franklin bent to the task of seeing exactly how things stood with him. Kroll had canceled "Dime Museum Days," which had long ago played itself out and was dragging a shadowy half-life through the dailies for no conceivable reason. He had assigned "Subway Sammy" to another artist, and he had asked Franklin to revive one of his old Cincinnati strips, about a likable hobo whose dreams were continually shattered by reality but who kept on dreaming anyway. But Franklin's real task was to supply Kroll with editorial cartoons— not only for Kroll's daily column but for other news articles as well. Franklin threw himself into the task, intent on making amends for his halfhearted work in the past; and as the days flowed by, and his editorial cartoons grew more accomplished, he found a kind of contentment in his work, marred only by sudden sharp bursts of irritation or restlessness.

Two weeks after his refusal of Max's offer, Franklin received in his office mail a three-color circular announcing the birth of Maxograms, Inc., and including a scribbled line from Max: "Think it over. It's never too late." The next day Max called to say that the whole staff had gone with him, leaving Vivograph on the brink of collapse. Since Vivograph was under contract to supply their popular cartoon series to Cinemart, Max had been forced to abandon the series, which he himself had mostly created. But he had signed a fat two-year contract with Cinemart for a spectacular new series, which would make the rival studio look like a bunch of bush leaguers. Meanwhile Vivograph had refused to go under and had hired a whole new staff to churn out the old stuff. But since the copyrights to all the cartoons were held not by the studio but by the distributor, Cinemart was under no obligation to renew the contract with Vivograph, and had given Max to understand that the old series would revert to Maxograms when the contract with Vivograph expired. Cinemart had insisted on holding onto *Toys at Midnight*, which was still attracting bookings, but Max had worked out a deal that gave Maxograms the option of purchasing the distribution rights twelve months down the road. All this was part of a larger plan to combine production and distribution and leave the other studios choking in his dust. In the meantime Max wanted Franklin to know he had faith in his work. He hoped Franklin would rethink his offer and keep Maxograms in mind when it came time for the next cartoon. Franklin said he was miles away from even thinking about a cartoon. "That's okay," Max said quickly. When Max hung up, Franklin had the sensation that Max had been talking to someone else, whom Franklin had been impersonating for obscure reasons.

Again he avoided his tower study, which seemed the haunt of a mad scientist with a foaming beaker; again he sank into family life as into his soft armchair. The sharp sense he sometimes had of falling into a pattern was blunted by the equally sharp sense of a difference, for if Cora was present at these family occasions she was also somehow absent. Often she complained of headaches and went to bed early, leaving Franklin to put Stella to bed. One evening she sat down at the piano and played a few bars, but suddenly stood up, raising a hand to her temple and shutting her eyes. She refused to see Dr. Shawcross; and once, trying to raise a window in the parlor, she kept banging her palms against the upper rail, over and over again, while a muscle worked in her cheek and the hair on her forehead grew damp.

He was often alone with Stella. In the evenings, after dinner, she seemed content to sprawl in a lamplit corner of the sofa reading *Anne of Avonlea,* or to sit at her old worktable cutting out paper costumes that she designed herself and fitted to her paper dolls. Franklin drew a series of hats for her: a dashing cloche to go with her flapper's dress, a broad-brimmed straw hat with fruit and flowers, a checkered beret, a cowgirl's hat with a picture of a steer on it. Max, obsessed with his new studio, was rarely visible on weekends; and while Cora went on errands or sat practicing scales to the click of a metronome, that eerie clock without a face, Franklin and Stella took long walks on autumn trails or went rowing on the river.

At the office he was spending more and more time on editorial cartoons, fussing over details, making small adjustments, adding minute refinements; and holding out a sketch at arm's length he would examine it carefully, searching for defects of composition.

One darkening autumn day when Franklin drove home from the station he walked up the porch steps and saw through the window Stella reading *Chronicles of Avonlea* on the lamplit sofa. In the front hall he hung his hat on the coatrack and was about to call out to her through the partly open parlor door when he noticed a pale blue envelope on the hall table. It was Cora's stationery. On it she had printed his first name. Franklin opened the envelope, unfolded the pale blue piece of paper, and read: "Dear Franklin, I can no longer live a lie. Max and I"—he crumpled the letter, thrust it into his jacket pocket, hung up his coat, took out the letter and scanned it wildly, then thrust it into his pocket again and walked into the parlor. "Dad's home. Did you have a good day at school? Your mother won't be having dinner with us tonight, something came up—did she say anything about the lamb chops?" In the kitchen he uncrumpled the letter and tried to read it through, but his brain was pounding, something was wrong with his vision, the words kept splitting apart and falling into fragments—"six mon," "unf," "tter for ev," "nbear"—and later that night, after he had put Stella to bed early and, evading her sharp gaze, explained that Mom was visiting friends far away and might not be back for a day or two, he went down to the parlor and unfolded the letter, but the words were crisscrossed by hundreds of little creases and kept falling into cracks, abysses.

He turned off the lamp and sat in the dark, staring through the windows at the night and waiting for Cora. His temples throbbed, his stomach trembled and rippled, his eyelids felt burning hot. At two o'clock in the morning he heard a car approaching on the road below. He felt his mouth open, as if to emit a cry, but the car slowly passed. Toward three he heard footsteps on the stairs, and suddenly he realized it was all a hideous joke, Cora had been punishing him, he would forgive her despite her cruelty, and when the parlor door opened he saw Stella staring at him gravely, her eyes heavy with sleep and her hair wild. Without a word she sat down next to him and fell asleep against his arm. In the morning he made her breakfast and drove her to school. All day he sat in the parlor, closing his eyes from time to time but not sleeping. Stella came up the walk at four, and that night after he had put her to bed he climbed the stairs to his tower study. In the dark room he stood to the left of the right-hand window. It was a clear night, and he could see far up the river. Max's toy house was well lit. Through the dark pines the yellow lights seemed to tremble like candleflames and on the black river they lay in wavering lines.

He became aware of the glass-cased clock on his desk. The pendulum, immobile, hung down heavily over the slumbering key. And an irritation came over him: it was not right; someone should have wound the clock. In a burst of anger he opened the glass door, seized the clumsy key, and wound the clock tightly. Then he took out his pocket watch and set the clock hands to the precise hour. He pushed the pendulum to one side, releasing it into its arc. The clock ticked. His father had once shown him what made a clock tick: it was the sound of a toothed wheel escaping from first one and then another little hook. The sound of time was the sound of a continual effort to escape from something that held you back. He replaced the key on the mirrory floor beneath the pendulum and the exposed gears and closed the glass door. The clock ticked, the pendulum swung back and forth. And he felt soothed, soothed deep in his bones, as the clock ticked and the pendulum swung back and forth. Slowly the pendulum swung back and forth. The clock ticked.

Toward eleven the last light went out in the little house far up the river. Then pictures streamed in his mind: Cora in her lavender nightgown, Max and Cora laughing in the rowboat, Cora frowning and running a hand through her hair, Cora as a girl of ten in the Vaughn family album, wearing a white dress and straw hat and reaching up to pick a rose from the rose trellis. Then he imagined, in careful detail, Max making love to Cora; and when she reached her three short sharp cries, he began again from the beginning, more slowly, as if he had been a little hasty the first time, a little careless and irresponsible.

A sound startled him. When he turned his head sharply toward the door he felt a dizziness seize him, as if he had turned and stopped his head while his brain, unattached, continued to turn slowly. A dark form stood in the doorway.

"It's late," Franklin said. "You should be in bed."

"You should be in bed too. She's not coming back, you know."

Toward dawn he stumbled and lay on the floor with a fiercely beating heart. Pictures streamed through the deep blue of the room: the façade of Klein's Wonder Palace, his father's finger rising and falling slowly as he counted out the numbers, the green leather chair in Judge Vaughn's study, Cora's hip bumping open the wooden screen door, a mouse scampering across the back of his hand in the cellar of his home in Plains Farms, Max's tin mouse moving along the boards of the porch. He remembered his moonlit walk across the roof; and suddenly he longed to be out of this world entirely, up there on the cool white moon, far from his heavy body lying in blue light.

On the second day of his vigil Franklin walked about the house, looking in every room, as if he were searching for something, as if he were trying to solve a mystery.

On the third night of his vigil he returned to the tower and looked at the little yellow windows in the far trees and the wavering lights on the water. His temples pounded, his chest hurt, he felt heavy as a bag of loam but light, very light, as if at any moment he might float away, and when the lights in the house went out there appeared in his mind a journey to the moon: he saw terrifying ice caverns, haunting crevasses and fissures, white cities, melancholy moonfolk—and then the dangerous journey to the dark side of the moon, where the cartoon would burst into images of startling freedom and terror. He did not know exactly how it would end, but he knew already that it would be called *Voyage to the Dark Side of the Moon* and that it would be his longest effort—perhaps thirty minutes, which was to say, some 30,000 drawings.

Before dawn of the third night of his vigil, the details of the new cartoon were clear in his mind. Toward morning Franklin drew the shade over the window that looked toward Max's house, went down to his room, and fell into deep, dreamless sleep.

His new life, once he had settled into it, was surprisingly like the old. It struck him that Cora had withdrawn from him gradually, so that her absence was merely the last step of a series to which he had almost grown accustomed. He hired Mrs. Henneman as a full-time housekeeper, whose primary duty was to look after Stella: to be in the house when Stella came home from school each day, to take care of Stella when she was sick, and to be with her during school holidays. She shopped and did the laundry, had charge of the groundskeeper, and prepared dinner five days a week, Monday through Friday. She combed Stella's hair, tied her ribbons, sewed on her buttons and mended her petticoats; and she was given a special allowance for the purchase of Stella's clothes. Sometimes on the weekends he hired her to be in the house for Stella, while he worked in the tower, but Stella preferred to sit with him in the high room, drawing quietly at a small table—keeping an eye on him, he sometimes thought.

For although she was still his grave and brooding daughter, he was aware of a change in her. Cora, even at her most distant, had a large and dramatic temperament; she filled doorways, swept into rooms, flung her head onto the backs of chairs in utter exhaustion. Stella had grown up warily, a little off to one side, where it was safe; she guarded her gestures, walked quietly as if to escape notice, led a secret, hidden life. Cora's escape across the river had left the house lighter as well as emptier, and Stella, who at first had crept into some dark corner of herself, quickly felt the attractions of lightness and began to move about more freely. She expressed opinions clearly, told pointed anecdotes about school, and asked precise questions about Franklin's work at the *World Citizen*, the management of household expenses, the operation of the furnace, the reason for the little holes at the side of a strip of film. Above all she asked technical questions about animated cartoons. Why did he fasten the sheets of paper with pegs instead of using the old crossmarks? Was it possible to make cartoons in color, like the Sunday comics? What about cartoons that talked? She invented an eight-panel comic strip of her own that she carried through six adventures, coloring the panels carefully with her pastel pencils and printing the words in the speech balloons in small capital letters; she overcame her fear of roller skates; and one day she asked for piano lessons. At first the sound of the piano made Franklin desperately unhappy, but he grew used to her simple tunes, her finger-strengthening exercises, her versions of "Oh, Dem Golden Slippers" and "My Old Kentucky Home." In the mornings she checked to make certain his socks matched, since once he had worn a maroon and a brown, and to see that his vest was buttoned properly; at dinner she asked questions about his work at the office and listened attentively to his answers. Sometimes he detected in her a primness, a slight maternal fussiness, that secretly annoyed him, as if she were growing a little askew. Then he would pretend to be drunk and stagger around the room until she whooped with laughter. And once, stepping into the parlor, he saw her sitting motionless in the armchair, staring out the window; and when she turned to him he saw for a moment, before she leaped up to greet him, her grave eyes, stricken with sorrow.

His work for the *World Citizen* was going well. For some time Kroll had been obsessed by the issue of German reparations; at first he had insisted on immediate and unconditional payment as the one assurance of stability in postwar Europe, but the French occupation of the Ruhr had roused his indignation, and in a sharp reversal he had argued that Germany should pay at a fluctuating rate determined by her degree of economic prosperity. His opposition to the French adventure in the Ruhr led him to thunder against the dangers of French militarism, but at the same time he began to question the strength of the French armed forces and to hint that all was not well. Franklin had become adept at picturing a cruel, powerful, and vindictive France, setting its heel on a prostrate Germany, but he had also begun to reveal a talent for inventing variations on the theme of a weak, boastful, decadent, doddering France, concealing its impotence behind gestures of ridiculous vainglory. In a scribbled note, Kroll himself commended Franklin's recent version of The Emperor's New Clothes: in front of the Arc de Triomphe the gigantic, effeminate Emperor, with rings on his fingers and a long curly wig, marched naked before a stream of soldiers, while crowds along the Champs Élysées looked on doubtfully and a little boy in one corner pointed his finger. In front of the Emperor marched two tiny generals, who held up long poles between which was stretched a banner than concealed the Emperor's genitals and read: CLOTHES PROVIDED BY PÉTAIN.

At home he hurled himself into *Voyage to the Dark Side of the Moon*. On weekday evenings he climbed to his tower study at half-past eight after reading Stella a bedtime story and came down at half-past midnight or one in the morning, and on the weekends he stayed shut up in the tower, coming down only to take an afternoon walk. Stella, who liked to be with him for much of the day, did not sit idly while he worked. It was her job to number the finished drawings, to erase carefully the pencil lines that showed through the India ink, to fasten each drawing to a cardboard backing, to attach the cardboard to the metal drum of the viewing machine, and to check carefully through the window of the machine for flickering due to faulty alignment. Franklin had modified his animation board: directly above the rectangle of glass he had screwed two pegs into the wood for exact registration of the drawings. In addition to his rice paper he had purchased a supply of transparent sheets of celluloid, which he used for moving figures during certain sequences. With a paper cutter he trimmed each piece of paper or celluloid to the proper size; then with a punch he carefully made two holes at the top, to fit over the pegs. He had arrived quickly at the moon, but the early lunar landscapes, with their mixture of enchantment and menace, were coming along slowly. His characters, a boy and his pet monkey, had to be led through three adventures, including a crash through the lunar surface and the discovery of an ancient underground civilization of Selenites, before he could bring them to the shore of the river that separated the white side of the moon from the dark side.

The long hours of work, the four to five hours of restless sleep, the strain of an immense task requiring rigorous concentration, the sense of some menace lying in wait for him if he should relax his will for one second, all this began to tell on Franklin's health, and by midwinter he fell sick. His arms felt heavy, he could barely hold up his head, the thermometer recorded a low, persistent fever; and after ten days of increasing exhaustion he called Dr. Shawcross, who found nothing more than a viral infection that was making the rounds but who warned of nervous exhaustion and ordered two weeks of bed rest. For one week Franklin lay in a stupor of mild fever, burning eyelids, and bone-deep weariness, during which Mrs. Henneman brought him bowls of soup and turkey sandwiches. Stella, as soon as she came home from school, sat on a chair by the side of his bed and from time to time took his temperature, carefully shaking down the mercury in the glass rod, telling him to be sure to keep the thermometer under his tongue, and timing him for three minutes by the second hand of his gold pocket watch. On the eighth day Franklin took the train to work. At his desk, with the drawing board sloped against his lap, he felt as if his brain were wrapped in cotton wool that itself was wrapped in crinkly blue paper; when he stood up he had an attack of dizziness and stood bent over his desk, supported on a trembling arm. He spent three more days at home before returning to work again; the fever had lifted, he was no longer dizzy, but he felt tired, always tired.

One night in the tower study Franklin looked up and saw through the unshaded window that it had begun to snow. The thick white flakes looked like shavings of wax from a candle. The snow lay in white lines on the black branches of the maples, it stood heaped on the wooden swing like the top of a loaf of bread. Only on the black river, gleaming faintly like dark tin, did it leave no trace. Color was coming to the world of animated cartoons, experiments had been made by more than one studio, and someone had already invented a workable sound track that produced synchronized sound effects, but Franklin knew that the truth lay with the winter night: the world was silent and black-and-white.

Night after night in the black-and-white winter, in the silent tower high over the house, Franklin sat bent over his silent black-and-white world, raising his eyes only to rest them before sinking back into his waking dream, and once, raising his eyes after a long and particularly stubborn sequence that left his neck aching and his temples throbbing, he was amazed to see the light of early morning shining in the window and there, outside, clusters of tender green-yellow flowers hanging from the branches of the maples. Butter-yellow and blood-red tulips glowed in the flower beds. Sunlight trembled on the green-brown river.

She had never called, never tried to visit the house, never

asked for her clothes, her piano music, her oval photograph of Judge Vaughn and her mother. Her absence was absolute—she had crossed the river and vanished away. Franklin gradually stopped expecting her. A dull anger glimmered in him, like the shine of old tin. The rigor of her absence struck him as cold and unnatural, the result of a hard will. Once, relaxing his anger, he permitted himself to wonder whether the completeness of her absence, far from being a sign of contempt for her former life, might not be a sign of doubt, of secret shame, of midnight fear— a fear of seeing Stella's eyes, a fear that her romantic flight had been not daring but banal; but a moment later he imagined her throwing back her head to laugh in the sun—happy, flourishing, indifferent.

One summer midnight Franklin looked up from the drawing of a moon waterfall plunging into a chasm to see a piece of moon in the window. The moon, the luminous blue sky, the hot summer night reminded him of his roofwalk ten thousand years ago. He stood up and looked through the window; the world was blue and still, only the dark river shimmered with trembling points of light. He felt no boyish desire to walk through the window into the sky, but he was restless and needed a breath of night air.

On the second floor he stopped to look in at Stella, who lay fast asleep beside a book on her pillow. He moved the book away from her cheek and pushed up the fallen shoulder of her nightshirt. Then swiftly he descended the second stairway, opened the front door, and stepped into the radiant summer night.

Shadows of porch balusters lay sharp against the moon-bright floorboards. He walked down the porch steps. The night sky was flame blue. A memory came to him: as a child he had liked to look at the world through one of the dark blue circles of glass that his father removed from a little leather pouch to screw into the camera in front of the lens. The night sky was like that: a dark, transfigured day. Franklin wanted to walk; and after passing down the front path past the great maples to the hedge dividing the front yard from the road, he glanced back once at the house, dark except for the light in the tower, and continued on his way.

He knew and refused to know where he was going. He turned down several familiar lanes, breathing the smell of mown grass, loam, manure, the sudden sharp scent of some unknown flower. After a while he came to the deserted main street, lit by two street lamps. In the dark window of the general store he saw the reflection of a maple tree and a clapboard storefront and, through the reflection, a shadowy pyramid of soup cans. On the other side of the street he passed between two stores so close together that he could have touched the shingled walls on both sides. At the back of the stores was a weed-grown lot in which a rusty wheel lay aslant against the side of a rotting hay wagon, and a moment later he found himself on the bank of the river.

A few old rowboats and peeling oars lay outside the boat shed. Franklin pushed a boat into the water and began rowing upstream. Moonlight shone on the back steps of the drugstore, on iron-hooped barrels and piles of lumber; in a backyard garden a scarecrow wearing an old straw hat threw a long shadow across a stand of corn. Franklin was soon past the abandoned knitting mill that marked the end of the village. The water near the river's edge was thick with grass and rushes, and he had to swing away from the bank. The woods on both sides were broken by an occasional dark house; here and there he saw a clearing with a bulldozer, and after a time he came to a well-lit house. It was set halfway up the hill, on the other shore. The house was obscured by the thick woods; from the rowboat he could hear the sound of voices, laughter. A party appeared to be in progress; Franklin could hear the chink of glasses. "Oh, absolutely!" a voice said, very sharply and clearly, before dropping back into the murmur. Through the dark crosshatch of woods he could see patches of lamplit leaves and pieces of people moving in light on the front porch. A burst of high laughter seized his attention, aroused his deepest interest, but in fact he didn't know, he couldn't be certain. Something plopped lightly into the water— a frog?—and sent out ripples that began in shadow and, slowly widening, suddenly trembled in the brightness of the moon. After a while Franklin took up his oars and rowed home.

He sank back into his black-and-white world, his immobile world of inanimate drawings that had been granted the secret of motion, his death-world with its hidden gift of life. But that life was a deeply ambiguous life, a conjurer's trick, a crafty illusion based on an accidental property of the retina, which retained an image for a fraction of a second after the image was no longer present. On this frail fact was erected the entire structure of the cinema, that colossal confidence game. The animated cartoon was a far more honest expression of the cinematic illusion than the so-called realistic film, because the cartoon reveled in its own illusory nature, exulted in the impossible—indeed it claimed the impossible as its own, exalted it as its own highest end, found in impossibility, in the negation of the actual, its profoundest reason for being. The animated cartoon was nothing but the poetry of the impossible—therein lay its exhilaration and its secret melancholy. For this willful violation of the actual, while it was an intoxicating release from the constriction of things, was at the same time nothing but a delusion, an attempt to outwit mortality. As such it was doomed to failure. And yet it was desperately important to smash through the constriction of the actual, to unhinge the universe and let the impossible stream in, because otherwise—well, otherwise the world was nothing but an editorial cartoon. In the long nights the thoughts came to him, streamed in on him, though mostly he merely watched them, a little distrustfully, out of the corner of one eye.

He was moving ahead: by midwinter he had completed more than 20,000 drawings. It took him another month to complete the difficult episode of the vanishing palace, the last adventure before the eruption onto the dark side of the moon. The palace, located on an island in the river that separated the white side of the moon from the dark side, had the property of fading away as you advanced through it. It was necessary not simply to invent a detailed dream-palace, a palace with long corridors and arched doorways, soaring halls and mirrored chambers, but also to make drawings that were lighter and lighter until the passageway or chamber seemed to fade away—and turning his head the boy saw, in perfect perspective, another detailed and alluring corridor, which began to fade as he passed along. At the end of the episode the entire palace faded away, like the Cheshire cat, leaving the boy and the monkey alone in blank whiteness. The monkey, removing a piece of charcoal from his pocket, quickly drew a spit of land, a rowboat, some waves; and as the monkey rowed them across the river toward the dark side of the moon, the boy looked over his shoulder and saw, clearly in the distance, the palace on the island, sharp and clear, growing smaller and smaller.

But it was the dark side of the moon that drew on Franklin's deepest energies, for here he rigorously released himself into a realm of absolute cartoon freedom. Although he continued to draw in India ink on rice paper, he imagined the images in reverse, for he planned to instruct the cameraman to make a negative print, in order to create the effect of white drawings on a black background. In this black world the hero was to undergo a series of phantasmagoric metamorphoses, of dream dissolutions and hallucinatory recombinations. A radical shift in drawing style indicated the change: gone was the intricate perspective background with its preference for the unusual angle, and in its place was a flat picture plane with deliberately simplified figures. The instant the boy set foot on the dark side of the moon he began to unravel, until he was a single wavering line that gradually assumed the form of a spinning top. The top became a clown's yawning face; inside the yawn was a fantastic garden, where the boy reappeared and was at once transformed into a tree hung with many apples, each of which gradually assumed the shape of his head. The faces grew bodies, and a crowd of boys ran off in many directions as each turned into a different animal ridden by a monkey; the animals collided and became a boy surrounded by tall, wavering, menacing figures, who pursued him into a black rock that contained a cobwebbed parlor. Slowly the parlor became an amusement park where the carousel horses grew larger and larger and began to eat the roller coaster, the fun house, the Ferris wheel until there was nothing left—at which point the fat horses melted together and became an open umbrella, beneath which the boy and his monkey floated down, down, down—and as the episodes of metamorphosis multiplied, becoming more dangerous, more sinister, incorporating apparently random images like toasters, icebergs, and blast furnaces whose shapes were cunningly drawn from earlier parts of the cartoon, beyond the edges of the paper Franklin noticed an occasional hard image that swiftly melted away: an edge of window, the hand of Mrs. Henneman holding out a glass, the yellowing slats of the partially open venetian blinds, but already he had sunk back into the dark side of the moon. In a narrow valley he was surrounded by mountains with mouths, somewhere a phone was ringing, his temples were about to burst. A moon bird melted into a river of demon birds. "You have to decide," someone was saying, "whether to build or buy," and when he looked up he saw his own face reflected in a dark train window, through which he saw a passing landscape. Slowly the landscape became a sewing machine that stitched the silently screaming boy onto the sleeve of a shirt. The last snow melted under the spirea bushes by the steps of the front porch, green leaves hung from the maples, and one rainy hot day Franklin saw that he was done. Somewhere the notes of a piano sounded: Stella practicing. A drop of sweat trickled along his cheek. Several sequences needed to be reworked, the voyage was riddled with minor flaws, but he could fix things in a month or two. He wanted to hand it over to the cameraman, he wanted to throw it on a white screen in the dark of his study; and a day came when Franklin began carrying boxes up to Vivograph, which still operated in its old offices in the arcade building, but with an entirely new set of faces.

That evening he felt heavy-limbed and light-headed and went to bed early. When he lay down his heart began to beat very quickly, as if he were running; and he lay alert and exhausted as moon drawings streamed in his mind, with their two peg holes at the top, their numbers in the lower right-hand corner, their hundreds of thousands of carefully drawn little black lines.

As he waited for the drawings to be photographed, he began to fear that something had happened to them, something Vivograph was attempting to conceal. He saw his 32,416 drawings fluttering slowly to the floor, a snowstorm of spilled pages, each flake slightly different from the others; he saw a black footprint, like one of the footprints in a dance manual, stamped in the center of each clean white moonscape; and he saw, rising along the sides of high piles of crisp white paper, little red-and-yellow flames darting higher and higher.

The day came when his reels of film were ready. At once a new worry sprang up in him: suppose Kroll were to discover what he had done? The revelation of an immense secret life, of vast energies directed away from the *World Citizen*, could strike Kroll only as a criminal violation of their agreement; punishment would be harsh and swift. Caution was crucial. At Vivograph a man with a sharp chin and thin pink lips kept plying him with questions, but Franklin, slyly avoiding his gaze, said that he knew nothing about it, he was just there to pick up the cans of film and the boxes. At home he decided to make it a surprise for Stella. He had rented a projector earlier in the week and purchased a portable screen attached to a collapsible tripod. Mrs. Henneman served dinner and left at seven-thirty; she would return at seven-thirty in the morning. "A good night to you, Mr. Payne," she said, and he was startled: surely she couldn't know about the trip to Vivograph, the night's screening? "That's all right, Mrs. Henneman," he said, waving. "I'll be just fine. Don't you worry about me." In the kitchen he played a game of Parcheesi with Stella, who liked each of them to take two colors. At eight-thirty she went upstairs to get ready for bed and Franklin crept up to the study to set up the screen and load the first reel in the projector. By the time she had finished brushing her teeth he was back in the parlor, pacing. In Stella's room he read to her a chapter of *Anne of the Island*, then closed the book and said, "I have a surprise for you: upstairs." He placed a finger over his lips. Stella sat up at once, her dark hair falling over one shoulder, her lips parted slightly, her large, dark eyes grave in their excitement.

She followed him up the stairs and entered the tower room quietly, taking in the projector and screen without a word. On one side of the projector Franklin had placed his leather desk-chair, on the other Stella's small wooden chair from her old work-table. She sat down quietly on the childish chair with her hands in her lap, then slid forward until her shoulders pressed against the chair-top. Raising a hand she began to wind her hair round and round a finger. Franklin turned out the light and started the projector. There was a flickering blankness on the screen, then a briefly flashed numeral *3*, a few scratchy lines, and suddenly the title, in carefully drawn black letters. Franklin shifted the projector slightly; the cartoon began. In the darkroom he had stared at the white paper, waiting. From the depths of white-ness black shapes had come. But the pictures had not moved. On the white screen the black pictures moved—the old mystery made new. Dark and light: night and moon: dark theater and bright screen. In the dark he could see the shaft of light thrown by the projector. It looked like a moonbeam in some old painting of a forest. It struck him that the projector beam was the true modern moonbeam, the ray of light from a new realm of mystery and enchantment that outmoded the poor old moon. And it was good: he saw that it was good, that he hadn't lost his touch. Stella sat rigid, spellbound, tense with attention.

It was shortly after the landing on the moon that a deep excitement seized Franklin, for he realized that something extraordinary was going to happen—and yet, was it really so surprising, after all? The footsteps on the stairs were light but not to be mistaken. Stella, screen-enchanted, noticed nothing. The stairs creaked once, then were still; after a while the door opened. She was wearing a spring dress, one that he remembered, and a white flower in her hair. She looked at him questioningly, a little shyly; he was grateful that she said nothing. A flicker of light from the projector played on one sleeve and on her collarbone. She looked about for a moment or two, then stepped to the back of the room, not far from Stella, and silently watched the shimmering screen.

And he was touched that she had come: after all, she had never much cared for his cartoons. That was only proper, for she played Schubert on the piano and had once talked to him on the porch of her father's house in Cincinnati about the difference between Ingres and Delacroix. He hoped she would like this one, for it was the best he was able to do.

And again he heard a footstep on the stair: he was not surprised. It was a firm step, a confident step—the step of someone who had no doubt about where he was going. After a while the door opened, and Max stood there with a hand in his pocket, the other hand gripping a suit jacket flung over his shoulder. His tie was loosely knotted and his top shirt button undone, and he looked at Franklin with affection and a touch of wryness. Then he removed the hand from his pocket and touched the fingertips lightly to his forehead in salute. He looked quietly about, then stepped to the back of the room, near Cora but not directly beside her.

The first reel came to an end; quickly Franklin removed it

and put in the second reel. Max would like this one: he would understand what Franklin had done.

But hardly had the second reel begun when there was another sound on the stair. It was a heavier tread, the tread of someone not accustomed to climbing flights of stairs, and Franklin listened anxiously to the slow, relentless, gradually approaching steps. For although he had not expected anyone else, on this special occasion, still his little group seemed incomplete. Outside the closed door came the sound of labored breaths and a faint asthmatic wheeze. Then slowly the door opened, and in the doorway, wiping his forehead with a large pocket handkerchief, stood Kroll. Yes, it was Kroll—how could it be otherwise?—Kroll with his melancholy, intelligent eyes, Kroll with his chocolate-brown suit jacket stretched to the breaking point across his great shoulders and massive belly, Kroll with a big polka-dot bow tie, evidently purchased for the occasion, for it still had its price tag. It sat a little askew over a triangle of rumpled shirt. Kroll stepped into the room and closed the door softly behind him. And Franklin was grateful that he had come: he wanted Kroll to see what he could do. Kroll had brought with him a metal folding chair with a leather seat, and after a quick glance he set up his chair in the dark between Stella, seated in front of him, and Cora and Max, standing behind him at the back of the room.

Even as Kroll sat down on his chair, allowing his broad hands, with their little black hairs that looked as if they had been combed carefully to one side, to sink gradually into the dark, Franklin became aware of yet another sound on the stairs. It was a pair of footsteps this time, and Franklin felt a sharp tug of curiosity and excitement, for he had thought his little party complete. And although he was not entirely surprised, for nothing surprised him on this special occasion, even so he could not still the violence of his heart as the footsteps reached the top of the stairs. The door opened and the couple entered, first the woman and then the man, their figures a little more stooped than he had imagined, their faces unclear in the dark. But he recognized the bag of knitting with its faded pink flowers that the woman carried over one shoulder, and the old man's darkroom apron was deeply familiar to him. Arm in arm they made their way to the back of the room, where they stood on the other side, apart from Cora and Max, though Cora, just for a moment, stepped over with a child's wooden chair and helped the woman sit down. Once seated, she took out her knitting needles but watched the screen without looking away; and his father, standing bent beside her with the fingertips of his left hand resting on the back of the little chair, his cheeks waxy smooth and reddened with rouge, his father, giving off a sweet, disturbing odor of lilies, raised and lowered the extended index finger of his right hand, counting silently as he watched the screen.

And it was good: Franklin was touched that they had come. For they were all gathered now, those for whom his work mattered at all; and what difference did it make if he had to shut it all up in a box, so long as they were here to see it, on this special occasion. They had all been very quiet—Stella had noticed nothing, but sat transfixed beside the projector, her face tense with delight—and as Franklin put in the third reel he was pleased that they would see it to the end. For the voyage was not a collection of separate adventures but a gradual accumulation, a pressure in a direction, culminating in the rhythmic release of the dark side of the moon. And as the cartoon entered its last phase, he felt it was working, despite a few adjustments that would be necessary here and there. He could feel the silent excitement in the room. The end was coming: after a nightmare pursuit through melting moonscapes, by creatures who kept changing their shapes, the boy seized a moon bird that changed into a chalk eraser, and with it he began to erase. He erased the fluttering white moongirl with long moon hair, the moon fountains, the line of moon hills, the white horizon line—and at last he and the monkey stood alone in a black world. Then he turned to the monkey and began to erase him, in quick strokes that sent up puffs of chalk dust. He paused for only a moment before he began to erase himself: first his legs, then his body, next his head. He erased both arms, and now there was nothing left but the fingers grasping the eraser. And so it was nearly done. He had made the voyage to the dark side of the moon, from which no traveler returned. Quickly the eraser extracted itself from the fingers and erased them. Now the eraser began to spin: faster and faster it spun, growing larger and larger, vanishing in a blur, erasing the blackness itself, until there was only a white, blank world, on which the words THE END swiftly wrote themselves. And it was good: he had done what he set out to do. Perhaps he could rest now, for he was very tired.

The reel of film continued to click through the projector as the applause began. It was light at first, a spatter of appreciative claps. But it did not stop: led by Max the applause grew louder, Franklin could distinguish Cora's swift vigorous claps and Kroll's little persistent ones, muffled as if he were wearing gloves, but tireless for all that. His mother, standing now, clapped slowly, while his father, still raising and lowering his right hand gravely, struck his left palm against the top of the chair in time to the rhythm of his counting. They were all standing, even Kroll had risen to applaud him in the warm and intimate dark. "Please," Franklin said, holding up his hands, "this is really, this is really." Tears of gratitude ran down his cheeks; and as he bowed his head, for he was very tired, the applause grew louder and louder until it was one continuous roar.

The Princess,

the Dwarf,

and the Dungeon

THE DUNGEON. The dungeon is said to be located so far beneath the lowest subterranean chambers of the castle that a question naturally arises: is the dungeon part of the castle itself? Other underground chambers, such as the storage cellars, the torture chamber, and the prison cells used for detention during trial, are merely the lowest in an orderly progression of descending chambers, and maintain a clear and so to speak reasonable relation to the upper levels of the castle. But the dungeon lies so far beneath the others that it seems part of the dark world below, like the place under the mountain where ogres breed from the blood of murdered children.

THE CASTLE. The castle lies on a steep cliff on the far side of the river, three hundred feet above the water. In bright sunlight the castle seems to shine out from the darker rock of the cliff and to thrust its towers gaily into the blue sky, but when the air darkens with clouds the castle draws the darkness into itself and becomes nearly black against the stormy heavens. From our side of the river we can see the Princess's tower, the battlements of the outer wall, including the vertical stone spikes on the merlons, and two arched gates of darker stone. Beneath the Princess's tower lies her walled garden. We cannot see the garden walls or the garden itself, with its paths of checkered stone, its turf-covered benches, and its shady bower of trelliswork sheltering two couches covered in crimson silk. We cannot see the courtiers walking in the Court of the Three Fountains. We cannot see the Prince's oriel overlooking the slate roof of the chapel, we cannot see the row of marble pillars three of which are said to come from the palace of Charlemagne at Ingelheim, we can only imagine the hall, the brewhouse, the bakehouse, the stables, the orchard, the park with its great alleys of shade trees, the dark forest stretching back and back and back.

TALES OF THE PRINCESS. There was once a beautiful Princess, whose skin was whiter than alabaster, whose hair was brighter than beaten gold, and whose virtue was celebrated throughout the land. One day she married a Prince, who was as handsome as she was beautiful; they loved each other entirely; and yet within a year their happiness turned to despair. Some held the Prince to blame, saying he was proud and jealous by nature, but others accused the Princess of a secret weakness. By this they meant nothing less than her virtue itself. For her virtue, which no one questioned, made her secure against the attentions of admirers, and prevented her from imagining even the possibility of unfaithfulness. Because of her deep love for the Prince and her knowledge of her own steadfastness, she failed to fortify herself with haughtiness, reserve, and a sense of formidable propriety. Instead, while acting always within the strict constraints of court etiquette, she was unaffected in manner, generous in spirit, and open to friendship with members of her husband's intimate circle. Moreover, her love for the Prince led her to follow closely all matters at court, in order that she might understand all that concerned him and advise him sagely. It was therefore in no way unusual that she should take an interest in the stranger who arrived one night on a richly caparisoned horse, and who quickly won the friendship of the Prince by virtue of his nobility of bearing, his boldness of spirit, his thirst for knowledge, and his gift of ardent speech, but who nevertheless, saying only that he was a margrave, and that he came from a distant land, bore on his escutcheon the word *Infelix:* the Wretched One.

THE TWO STAIRWAYS. The stairways are circular and are composed of heavy blocks of stone that wind about a stone newel. Both stairways spiral to the right, in order to give the advantage to the defender, who with his right hand can wield his sword easily in the concavity of the round wall, while the attacker on the lower step is cramped by the newel's outward curve. One stairway winds up past slitlike openings that give higher and higher glimpses of the little river, the little town with its double wall, the little mills along the riverbank, until at last it reaches the chamber of the Princess at the top of the tower. The other stairway begins in a subterranean corridor beneath the torture chamber and winds down and immeasurably down, in a darkness so thick that it feels palpable as cloth or stone. After a time the steps begin to crumble, sprouting black vegetation; gradually the outlines of the steps become blurred, as if the reason for steps has been forgotten. This stairway, which some imagine to narrow slowly until there is space only for the rats, descends to the dungeon.

THE WINDOW RECESS. The Prince, who was often closeted for long hours with his councillors in order to discuss a pressing matter of territorial jurisdiction, was grateful to the Princess for attending to his new friend. Accompanied by two ladies-in-waiting, the Princess walked with the margrave in the walled garden beneath her tower, or sat with him in a small receiving chamber attached to her private rooms in the great hall. The small chamber had a pair of tall lancet windows set in a wide recess with stone window seats along the sides. The many-paned windows looked down upon wooded hills and a distant twist of river. One day as the Princess stood at the window, looking out at the far river, while the margrave with his sharp brown beard and amethyst-studded mantle sat back against the angle formed by the stone seat and the windowed wall, the Princess was startled from her revery by the sound of suddenly advancing footsteps. She turned quickly, raising a hand to her throat, and saw the Prince standing in the arched doorway. "You startled me, my lord," she said, as the margrave remained motionless in shadow. The dark stranger in the corner of the window seat, the startled, flushed wife, the stillness of the sky through the clear panes of glass, all this caused a suspicion to cross the Prince's mind. He banished the thought instantly and advanced laughing toward the pair at the window.

THE RIVERSIDE. Directly to the west of the town, on the bank of the river between the copper mill and a grist mill, lies the broadest of our town meadows. To reach it we must first cross the dry moat on a bridge made of oak planks, which is let down every morning by chains from within the gate-opening in the outer wall, and is raised every night so that it fits back into the opening and seals the space shut. The meadow is supplied with shade trees, mostly lime and oak; a path runs along the river, and there are fountains carved with the heads of devils and monkeys. Here on holidays and summer Sundays the townsfolk play bowls, wrestle, dance, eat sausages, stroll along the river, or lie on the bank. Here wealthy merchants and their wives mingle with pork butchers, bricklayers, rope makers, laundresses, apprentice blacksmiths, journeyman carpet weavers, servants, day laborers. Here at any moment, throwing back our heads to laugh, or shifting our eyes slightly, we can see, through the sunshot branches of the shade trees, the shimmering river, the sheer cliff, the high castle shining in the sun.

THOUGHTS IN SUN AND SHADE. As the Prince walked in the shady park, stepping through circles and lozenges of sunlight that made his dark velvet shoes, embroidered with gold quatrefoils, seem to glow, in his thoughts he kept seeing the Princess turn suddenly from the window with her hand on her throat and a flush on her cheek. The persistence of the image disturbed and shamed him. He felt that by seeing the image he was committing a great wrong against his wife, whose virtue he had never doubted, and against himself, who admired forthrightness and disdained all things secretive, sly, and hidden away. The Prince knew that if anyone had so much as hinted at unfaithfulness in the Princess, he would without hesitation have cut out the false accuser's tongue; in the violence of the thought he recognized his inner disorder. He was proud of the frankness between him and the Princess, to whom he revealed his most intimate thoughts; in concealing this thought, of which he was ashamed, he seemed to himself to have fallen from a height. Walking alone along the avenue of the park, through lozenges of sunlight and stretches of shade, the Prince reproached himself bitterly for betraying his high idea of himself. It seemed to him suddenly that his brown-bearded friend with the amethyst-studded mantle was far worthier than he of his wife's affection. Thus it came about that in the very act of self-reproach the Prince nourished his secret jealousy.

• • •

THE TOWER. From dawn to dusk she sits in the tower. We catch glimpses of what appears to be her face in the tower window, but isn't it likely that we are seeing only flashes of sunlight or shadows of passing birds on the high windowpanes? In all other ways she is invisible, for our solemn poets fix her in words of high, formal praise: her hair is more radiant than the sun, her breasts are whiter than swansdown or new-fallen snow. We saw her once, riding through the market square on a festival day, sitting on her white horse with black ostrich plumes, and we were shocked by the gleam of raven-black hair under the azure hood. But in the long days of midsummer, when the rooftops shimmer in the light of the sun as if they are about to dissolve, her raven hair is gradually replaced by the yellow hair of the poets, until the sight of her astride the white horse seems only a midday dream. High in her tower, from dawn to dark she paces in her grief, and who can say whether even her sorrow is her own?

LEGENDS OF THE RIVER. The river breeds its own stories, which we hear as children and never forget: the fisherman and the mermaid, the king in the hill, the maid of the rock. As adults we recall these legends fondly, even wistfully, for we no longer believe in them as we once did, but not every tale of the river passes into the realm of cherished, harmless things. Such is the tale of the escape of the prisoner: the splash, the waiting boat, the voyage, and there, already visible in the distance, the flames consuming the town and the castle, the blackness of the sky, the redness of the river.

INFELIX. The Princess, who had been startled by the Prince as she gazed out the window in the recess of her private chamber, gave the incident no further thought. Instead she continued to think of the margrave's story, which he had revealed to her one day while they were walking in the garden, and about which she had been brooding when the Prince interrupted her revery. The margrave had told how his younger brother, secretly lusting after the margrave's bride, had stolen the girl and locked her in a tower guarded by forty knights. Upon learning that the margrave was raising an army to free his bride, the brother sent him a jeweled casket; when the margrave opened the casket he saw the severed head of his bride. Half-crazed with grief and fury, the margrave led his knights against his brother, at last slaying him with his sword, cutting off his head, and razing the castle. But the margrave could not rest. Haunted by his dead bride, unable to bear his empty life, he fled from that accursed country, seeking adventure and death—death, which disdained him—and coming at last to the castle of the Prince. The Princess, pained by the margrave's tale, did not try to console him; and now each day, when the Princess dismissed her ladies, the margrave spoke to her of his slain bride, whom he had loved ardently; for though he had vowed never to speak of her, yet speaking eased his heart a little.

THE TOWN. Our town lies on the lower slope of a hill that goes down to the river. The town extends from the bank of the river to a point partway up the hill where the slope becomes steeper and the vineyards begin. Above the vineyards is a thick wood, which lies within our territorial domain and harbors in its darkness a scattering of sandstone quarries, charcoal kilns, clearings yellow with rye, and ovens for manufacturing glass. Except for the grist mills, the sawmills, the copper mill, and the bathhouse, which stand on the bank of the river, our town is entirely enclosed by two meandering walls: an outer wall, which is twenty feet high and eight feet thick, with towers that rise ten feet higher than the battlements, and a vast inner wall, which is forty feet high and twelve feet thick, with towers that rise fifteen feet higher than the battlements. Between the two walls lies a broad trench covered with grass, where deer graze and where we hold crossbow matches and running contests. Should an enemy penetrate the defenses of the outer wall, he must face the defenses of the towering inner wall, while standing in the trench as at the bottom of a trap, where we rain upon him arrows and gunshot, rocks large enough to crush a horse, rivers of molten lead. Flush against the outer wall stands a dry moat, broad and very deep, which an enemy must cross in order to reach our outermost defenses. Although we have enjoyed peace for many years, guards patrol both walls ceaselessly. Inside the walls, steepgabled houses with roofs of red tile line the winding stone-paved streets, carts rumble in the market square, fruit sellers cry from their stalls, from the shops of the ironworkers and the coppersmiths comes a continual din of hammers, servants hurry back and forth in the courtyards of the patricians' houses, in the shade of the buttresses of the Church of St. Margaret a beggar watches a pig lie down in the sun.

THE PEAR TREE. The Princess was quick to sense a change in the Prince, who looked at her strangely, often seemed on the verge of saying something, and lay restlessly beside her at night. She waited for him to unburden himself, but when he continued to keep his mind in shadow, she determined to speak. One morning when she and the Prince were walking in the walled garden, where she had lately walked with the margrave, the Prince stopped beside a pear tree to pick a piece of fruit. With a melancholy smile he handed the yellow pear to his wife. The Princess took the pear and thanked him, but said that she would like to share it with her lord, reminding him that she was not only his wife, but his dearest friend, who asked no higher pleasure than to share his joys and sorrows, and to ease the burdens of his heart. The Prince, who wished only to conceal the ignoble secret of his suspicion, felt a motion of irritation toward his wife, who by her words had put him in the position of having to deceive her, and he replied coldly that he had picked the pear not for himself, but for her alone; and turning his face away he added that he had cause to believe that his new friend, who was also her friend, had dishonest intentions toward him. The Princess, though hurt by his cold refusal of the pear, was nonetheless pleased that he had unburdened himself at last. She replied that she knew not who had been trying to divide the Prince from his friend, but for her part, she could assure her lord that the margrave was as trustworthy as he was honest, and as loyal as he was trustworthy, and that he was entirely devoted to the Prince and to all that concerned him. The Prince, ashamed of his suspicion, convinced of his wife's honor, yet hearing in her words a disturbing ardor, repeated sternly that he had cause to doubt the stranger, and wished to request of the Princess a small service. Though stung by his tone, the Princess put herself instantly at his disposal. Plucking a second pear roughly from the tree, the Prince asked the Princess to test the admirable devotion of his friend by offering to him what was most dear to the Prince in all the world. To put matters plainly, he desired the Princess to go to the margrave in his bedchamber that night, to lie down beside him, and to report the outcome to the Prince the next morning. In that way, and in that way alone, he hoped to be able to dispel the doubt that had arisen in his mind. The Princess, who all this while had been holding the first pear in her hand, looked at the Prince as if she had been struck in the face. The Prince watched the yellow pear fall from her long fingers and strike the ground, where it rolled over and revealed its split skin. Her look, like that of someone frightened in the dark, made the prince taste the full horror of his moral fall, even as it sharpened the sting of his suspicion.

• • •

PATRICIANS. The patricians of our town are powerful men with broad shoulders, keen eyes, and a touch of disdain about the lips. In their steep-gabled houses with arcaded ground floors and three upper stories, furnished well but without ostentation, one sees handsome door panels, table centerpieces of chased silver, and heavy paintings of themselves and their wives: the patricians in their broad berets and their dark robes trimmed with fur, the wives in plain bodices with velvet-trimmed sleeves. From their paintings the patricians stare out fearless as princes. Indeed, in times of danger they leave their counting houses and their seats in the Council Chamber, put on sturdy armor forged by our master armorers, mount their proud horses, and lead well-armed citizens in maneuver and battle. The patricians are wealthier and more powerful than the nobles of the castle, against whom they have relentlessly asserted their rights as free citizens, thereby further weakening the always declining power of the Prince. And yet these keen-eyed merchants, in the pauses of their day, will raise their heads for a moment, as if lost in thought; or striding along the slope of an upper street, suddenly they will stare out between the walls of two houses at the river below, the sunny cliff, the high castle. Some of our patricians purchase for their wives cloaks modeled after the cloaks of court ladies, and hang on their walls ceremonial swords with jeweled hilts. We who are neither nobles nor patricians, we who are of the town but watchful, observe these manifestations without surprise.

THE KEEPER OF THE DUNGEON. The keeper of the dungeon, whom no one has ever seen, is said to dwell in a dark cave or cell beside the winding lower stair, twenty-two steps above the dungeon. The keeper is said to have thick, matted hair so stiff that it is brittle as straw, a flat nose, and a single tooth, shaped like the head of a crossbow arrow; he is so stooped that his face is pressed against his knees. In one hand he clutches, even when asleep, the heavy key to the dungeon, which over the years has impressed its shape in the flesh of his palm like a brand burned into the flesh of a criminal. His sole duty is to open the iron door of the dungeon and to push in the iron bowl of gruel and the iron cup of brackish water delivered from above. The keeper, whom some describe as an ogre, a one-eyed giant, or a three-headed beast, is said to have a single weakness: he is fond of small, bright objects, like glass beads, gold buttons, and pieces of colored foil bound between disks of clear glass, all of which he places in an iron box concealed behind a loose stone in the wall beside his bed of straw. It is by manipulating this weakness that the dwarf is able to work his will upon the keeper, who in all other respects is ruthless and inflexible.

THE MARGRAVE'S BEDCHAMBER. The Princess, who not only loved the Prince deeply but had been raised in the habit of unquestioning obedience to a husband's slightest wish, did not for a moment think of disobeying him. Instead she thought only of persuading him to take back a request that had been born of some unpleasant rumor in the court, and could lead only to unhappiness for her, for his friend, and for himself. When the Prince proved adamant, the Princess lowered her eyes, rose naked from the bed, and sorrowfully, in the chill night air, drew on her long chemise ornamented with gold, her close-fitting underrobe, and her high-waisted tunic with wide sleeves, all the while hoping to be commanded to stop; and over her tight-bound hair she drew her thick-jeweled net of gold wire, so that not a single hair was visible. Then with a beseeching look at her lord, who would not meet her eyes, she betook herself to the margrave's bedchamber, where by the trembling light of her candle she crept fearfully to the curtained bed, parted the curtains no more than a finger's breadth, and looked in. The margrave lay fast asleep on his back with his head turned to one side. The Princess extinguished the candle and, offering up a silent prayer, slipped into the bed between the margrave and the curtain. Anxiously she lay awake, with wide-open eyes, starting whenever the margrave stirred in his sleep, yet hoping that he might not wake and find her there. But as she lay thinking of the change in the Prince, and his cold words beside the pear tree, her heart misgave her and she fell to weeping. The margrave, wakened by the noise, was startled to find a woman in his bed; and feeling sharp desire, he asked who it was that so honored him in his bedchamber, meanwhile reaching out his hand to touch her. But when he heard the voice of the Princess, he drew back his hand, which had grazed her shoulder, as if he had felt the blade of a sword. She said in a strained voice that she had come to offer him companionship in the night; she hoped she had not disturbed his sleep by her visit. Now the margrave loved the Prince, and revered the noble Princess above all women; and a sorrow came over him, even as he felt desire in the dark. He replied that he was more honored by her visit than by a gift of gold; and because he honored her above all women, he would remember this night until his dying day. Yet he thought it most fitting that she should return to the Prince, her lord and husband, and not trouble herself about one who longed only to serve the Prince and do her honor. The Princess was well pleased with this speech; but mindful of the Prince's cruel command, that she test the margrave in the night, she said that she hoped he did not find her so foul that he would wish to banish her from his bed. The margrave replied that far from finding her foul, he found her of all women the most fair; and so far was he from wishing to banish her from his bed, that he would abandon the bed to her and lie down on the floor of his chamber, in order to keep watch over her rest. The Princess thanked him for his thoughtfulness, but said she could not dispossess him of his bed, and urged him to remain; whereupon the margrave graciously agreed, saying only that he revered her rest as much as he revered the Princess herself; and drawing forth the sharp sword that he kept always beside him, he placed it between them on the bed, pledging to protect her from all harm in the night. With that he wished her a good night, and drew himself down under the coverlet, and feigned sleep. The Princess, well pleased with his answer, tested him no more, but lay anxiously beside him until the first graying of the dark, when she returned to the Prince, who lay restlessly awaiting her. She reported all that had passed in the night, praising the delicacy of the margrave, who had not wished to injure her feelings even as he revealed his devotion to the Prince, and assuring her lord that his friend had been slandered by evil tongues. The Prince, although soothed by her account, was troubled that his wife had lain all night by the side of the margrave, even at the Prince's own bidding; and whereas before this he had been haunted by the image of his wife in the window recess, now he was tormented by the image of his wife in the bed of the margrave, offering her breasts to his greedy fingers, rubbing her legs against him, and crying out in pleasure. For the Prince so desired his wife that he could not believe any man capable of resisting her, if she offered herself in the night. Wherefore he thought she was deceiving him in either of two ways: for either she had lain with the margrave and pleasured him in the dark, or else she had not gone to him as she had said. Therefore the Prince replied harshly that though the margrave had not betrayed him, yet he could not be certain whether it was from loyalty or sheer surprise, to find the wife of his friend beside him in the dark; and now that the Princess had shown a willingness to deceive her husband, it was necessary for her to pay a second visit to the margrave and test him in his full knowledge. To this the Princess replied coldly that she would do all that her lord demanded; only, she would sooner plunge a dagger into her heart than return to the bed of the margrave.

THE REFLECTION. During three days a year, at the height of summer, the position of the sun and the position of the cliff combine to permit the castle to be reflected in the river. It is said that by staring at the reflection one can see inside the castle, which reveals the precise disposition of its arched doorways, high halls, and secret chambers, the pattern of hidden stairways, the shadows cast by flagons and bunches of grapes on abandoned banquet tables, and there, high in the tower, the Princess pacing wearily, while far below, in the depths of the immaculate reflection, so deep that it is beneath the river itself, a shadow stirs in the corner of the dungeon.

TOWN AND CASTLE. Long ago, in the darkness of an uncertain and perhaps legendary past, a Prince dwelt within our walls, in a fortress where the merchants' hall now stands. One day he decided to build a great castle on the cliff on the far side of the river. The decision of the Prince to move outside our walls has sometimes been interpreted as the desire of an ambitious lord to build an impregnable fortress in an unstable world, but a respected school of historians has argued that the change of residence occurred precisely when the power of the patricians was growing at the expense of the Prince, who after his move was expressly forbidden by the Council to build a fortified home within the town walls, although he continued to receive an increasingly ritual homage as lord of the town. A second school, while accepting the historical explanation, sees in the move a deeper stratagem. The Prince, so the argument goes, sensing the loss of his power, removed himself from the town and placed himself above it in order to exercise over our people the power of imagination and dream: remote but visible, no longer subject to patrician pressure, the Prince and his castle would enter into the deepest recesses of the people's spirit and become ineradicable, immortal. A minor branch of this school accepts the dream explanation but attributes it to a different cause. They argue that our ancestors first settled on the far side of the river, in the shadow of the castle, and only gradually withdrew to our side, in order to be able to look across the river and dream continually of nobler, more passionate lives.

THE PRINCE'S DOUBTS INCREASE. Now nightly the Prince drove his wife to the margrave's chamber, and restlessly awaited her return; and every morning the Princess returned to say that the margrave had remained steadfast. The Prince, tormented by the growing certainty that he was being deceived, and exasperated by the hope born of her daily assurances, longed for proof of her faithlessness, in order to ease his heart of uncertainty. One night, sorrowing alone, he remembered suddenly a time before his life had taken a crooked turn. He and the Princess were walking in the park, in the avenue of acacias, and something he had said made her laugh aloud; and the sound of that laughter, and the sunlight pouring down through the acacia leaves onto the graveled path, and the Princess's throat, half in sun and half in trembling shade, seemed as remote and irrecoverable as his own childhood. At that moment he saw with terrible clarity what he had done. He vowed to beg forgiveness on his knees and not to rise until he was permitted to return to his lost paradise. But even as he imagined the Princess laughing in the sun and shade of the acacia path, he saw her hand rise to her throat as she turned from the window, where a devil with a sharp beard and amethyst jewels on his mantle leaned motionless against the shadowed stone.

SCARBO. Among the many devoted servants of the Prince was a dwarf, whose name was Scarbo. He was a proud little man, with stern features and a small pointed beard; he dressed in the latest fashion, was a master of court etiquette and of all questions concerning precedence, and was noted for his disdainful glance, his penetrating intelligence, and his unswerving devotion to the Prince. Once, after a courtier had humiliated the little man by picking him up and tossing him lightly in the air, while others had watched with smiles and laughter, Scarbo lay on his bed in silent fury for two nights and two days. On the third night he crept into the bedchamber of the offending courtier and plunged his little sharp sword into the sleeper's throat. After that he cut off both of the dead man's hands and laid them with interlocked fingers on the coverlet. The Prince forgave his dwarf, but sentenced him to a month in prison; some say he was confined in the dungeon itself, and absorbed its darkness into his soul. But if his proud and disdainful nature was immediately apparent, earning him an uneasy respect never far from ridicule, Scarbo's most remarkable feature was his delicacy of feeling—for he possessed a highly developed and almost feminine sensitivity to the faintest motions of another person's mood. This unusual development in the realm of feeling, born perhaps of an outsider's habit of extreme watchfulness, increased his danger as an enemy and his value as a trusted servant and councillor. Combing his beard in his private chamber, handing the Prince a goblet of ruby wine, listening at night to the footsteps of the Princess moving past his door toward the margrave's chamber, the dwarf knew that it was only a matter of time before the Prince would summon him.

STORIES. Our town takes pride in the practical and useful arts. We are well known for our door panels and brass hinges, our stove tiles and weather vanes, our tomb effigies and stone crucifixes, whereas our literature rarely rises above the level of doggerel verses, carnival plays, and dull philosophical poems in monotonous meters and rigid rhymes. Our imagination is far bet-

ter expressed in the famous work of our metal masters, above
all in the brilliant productions of our church-bell casters, our
bladesmiths, our makers of spice mills, astrolabes, and articu-
lated figures for clocks. And yet it would be a mistake to think
of us as entirely deficient in the art of the word. Although we
are practical citizens, who keep our accounts strictly and go to
bed early, we have all listened to tales in the nursery, tales that
are never written down but may appear suddenly in distorted or
fragmentary form in a song heard in a tavern or at a carnival play;
and foremost among these stories of our childhood are tales of
the castle. The same tales are told by minstrels in the courtyards
of inns, and sung by peasants in the fields and villages of our
territorial domain. In another form the tales show themselves in
the early parts of our chronicles, where legend and fact are interwoven, and many episodes have been joined together by unknown hands and written down on sheets of parchment, which
are bound in ivory and metal on wood, purchased by wealthy
merchants, and read by their wives. Such stories, reaching far
down into the deepest past of our town, attach themselves like-
wise to the castle of the present day, so that the actual dwellers
in the castle come to seem nothing but passing actors asked to
perform the changeless gestures of an eternal play. Thus it comes
about that, although we are practical and commercial by nature,
we too have our stories.

THE SUMMONS. One morning after a night of shattering
dreams the Prince summoned his dwarf to a private chamber
and informed the little man that he desired a service of him.
Scarbo bowed, noting once again the signs of change in his master and saying that he desired only to be of service to his Prince.
With a show of impatience the Prince said that of late he had
been preoccupied with pressing affairs, that he feared the
Princess was too much alone, and that he desired his dwarf to

spend more time in her company, attending to her needs, listening to her thoughts, and serving her in every way; and he further desired that he should report to the Prince each morning, concerning the state of her happiness. The dwarf understood instantly that he was being asked to spy on the Princess. His pride thrilled at the gravity of the mission, for the Prince was in effect conspiring with his dwarf against his own wife, but Scarbo recognized a danger: the Prince, while desiring evidence against the Princess, would not necessarily welcome the proof he sought, nor be grateful to his spy for easing his way into his wife's confidence and ferreting out her secrets. It would not do to be overzealous in the performance of his duty. Wariness was all.

ON VAGUENESS AND PRECISION. It is precisely because of our ignorance that we see across the river with such precision. We know the precise carvings on the capital of each stone pillar and the precise history of each soul: they are transparent to our understanding. On our side of the river, even the most familiar lanes bear surprises around well-known bends; we see only a certain distance into the hearts of our wives and friends, before darkness and uncertainty begin. Perhaps, after all, this is the lure of legend: not the dreamy twilight of the luxuriating fancy, in love with all that is misty and half-glimpsed, but the sharp clarity forbidden by our elusive lives.

A WALK IN THE GARDEN. One sunny afternoon the Princess, who had been walking in the courtyard, dismissed her ladies-in-waiting at the garden gate and entered her garden alone. The walls were higher than her head; paths of checkered stone ran between beds of white, red, and yellow flowers; at one end stood a small orchard of pear, apple, quince, and plum trees.

In the center of the garden, surrounded by a tall hedge with a wicker gate, stood the Princess's bower, shaped like a pavilion and composed of trelliswork covered with vines. The Princess, in her azure tunic and her heart-shaped headdress, walked with bowed head among the fruit trees of the orchard, raising her eyes at the slightest noise and looking swiftly about. After a time she began to walk along the paths of checkered stone between the flower beds, passing two turf-covered benches, an octagon of white and red roses, and a white jasper three-tiered fountain with a column surmounted by a unicorn. At the central hedge she hesitated and seemed to listen; then she pushed open the gate and entered, bending low under a trellised arch. In the green shade of her bower sat two couches covered in crimson silk. Scarbo, seated in the corner of a couch, at once stood up and bowed. The Princess sat down stiffly on the couch opposite and stared as if harshly at the dwarf, who met her gaze and did not turn his eyes aside. "I cannot do what you propose," she began, in a toneless voice. The dwarf, rigid with attention, listened patiently. He was well pleased with his progress.

A LACK OF SOMETHING. Although ours is a flourishing town—and we flourish, according to some, precisely to the extent that the inhabitants of the castle have declined in power and serve a largely symbolic or representative function—we nevertheless feel a lack of something. Our metal artisans are admired far and wide, our sturdy houses with their steep gables and oak window frames fill the eye with delight, beyond the walls our fields and vineyards overflow with ripeness. Our church steeples rise proudly into the sky, and toll out the hours on great bells cast by masters. In fact, it is not too much to say that our lives pass in a harmony and tranquility that are the envy and admiration of the region. Nor is ours a dull tranquility, stifling all that is joyful or dark; for not only are we engaged in vigorous lives, but we are human beings like all human beings, we know the joys and sorrows that come to human hearts. And yet it remains true that, now and then, we feel a lack of something. We do not know what it is, this thing that we lack. We know only that on certain summer afternoons, when the too-blue sky stretches on and on, or in warm twilights when the blackbird cries from the hill, a restlessness comes over us, an inner dissatisfaction. Like children we grow suddenly angry for no reason, we want something. Then we turn to the castle, high on the other shore, and all at once we feel a savage quickening. With a kind of violence our hearts exult. For across the sun-sparkling river, there on the far shore, we feel a heightened sense of things, and we dare for a moment to cry out our forbidden desire: for exaltation, for devastation, for revelation.

THE FOUR REASONS. Because of his high gifts in the realm of feeling, the dwarf understood something about the Prince that the Prince himself did not fully understand. The dwarf understood that the Prince, despite great wealth, a beautiful and virtuous wife, devoted friends, and a life that inspired the praise of all who knew him, bore within him a secret weakness: a desire for immense suffering. It was as if the experience of so much good fortune had created in the Prince a craving in the opposite direction. He had at last contrived to satisfy this desire by means of his wife, as though wishing to strike at the deepest source of his own happiness; and it was Scarbo's role to confirm the Prince's darkest suspicion and present him with the suffering he craved. The danger lay in the uncertainty of the Prince's gratitude for such a service. Scarbo, radically set apart from the court and indeed from humankind by the accident of his diminutive stature, was a sharp observer of human nature; he understood that the Prince was furious at himself for being suspicious of his wife, and above all for inviting his dwarf to spy on her. The

Prince's sense that he had done something unclean might at any moment cause him to strike out violently at the instrument of his uncleanliness, namely, the dwarf. It was therefore essential that Scarbo not bear witness directly against the Princess, even though he crept nightly into the margrave's chamber and listened through the closed bedcurtains in order to learn all he could about their lascivious trysts. To Scarbo's surprise—to his bewilderment and anger—the margrave appeared to be innocent. This the dwarf attributed to a deep and still unfathomable design on the part of the margrave, whom he detested as the Prince's former favorite. The Prince would surely have believed a report of lecherous foul play in the margrave's tangled sheets, but Scarbo feared the force of the Princess's denial, as well as the Prince's rage at a witness of his wife's degradation. There was also something else. Although the Prince desired to suffer, and although the means he had chosen was his wife's infidelity, he also desired to be released from suffering, to return to the time of sunlight before the darkness of suspicion had entered his soul. The abandonment of this second desire, even though that abandonment alone could usher in the fulfillment of the first desire, was sure to be so painful that its agent would appear an enemy. The solution to all these problems and uncertainties had come to Scarbo one night after a week of relentless thought. It was brilliantly simple: the Princess herself must denounce the margrave. The Prince could then have the margrave tortured and killed in good conscience and enter into the life of suffering he craved, without having cause to turn against his dwarf. Now, Scarbo knew that the Princess was steadfast in virtue, and would die rather than yield her body to the margrave; his plan therefore was to persuade her to denounce the margrave untruthfully. For this he urged four reasons. The first was this, that such a denunciation would put an end to the torment of her nightly humiliation, which the Princess had confessed to the dwarf during the first of their bower meetings. The second was this, that the Prince longed for her to denounce the margrave, and that by so doing she would be satisfying the Prince's wish. The third was this, that the margrave in fact desired the Princess, and refused to take advantage of her solely because he feared the Prince; the margrave was therefore a traitor, and deserved to be exposed. And the fourth was this, that to confess the margrave's fall would be to reawaken the Prince's desire for her, and put an end to her nightly banishment from his bed. The Princess had listened to the dwarf's reasons in silence and had promised to give her answer in the bower. Her refusal, on that occasion, had been firm, but it could remain only as firm as her inner strength; and the dwarf knew that under the ravagement of her suffering, her inner strength was weakening.

OF STORY AND HISTORY. For the most part we can only imagine the lives of those who live in the castle, lives that may in certain respects depart sharply from the particular shapes we invent as we brood across the river on midsummer afternoons. And yet it has been argued that these imaginary lives are true expressions of the world of the castle, that they constitute not legend, but history. They do so, it is said, not simply because here and there an invented episode set in the dim past may accidentally imitate an actual event, on the far side of the river; nor because our stories, however remote from literal truth, are images of eternal truths that lie buried beneath the shifting and ephemeral forms of the visible. No, our argument has a different origin. The argument goes that our tales are not unknown among the inhabitants of the castle, and in fact circulate freely among the courtiers, who admire the simplicity of our art or take up our stories and weave them into more refined forms, which we ourselves may sometimes hear recited by traveling minstrels in the courtyards of inns or in our market squares. But if our tales are known among the inhabitants of the castle, may it not come about that they begin to imitate the gestures that give them such pleasure, so that their lives gradually come to resemble the legendary lives we have imagined? To the extent that this is so, our dreams may be said to be our history.

THE FACE IN THE POOL. Day after day the Princess suffered the Prince's displeasure, night after night she lay stony cold beside the margrave; and in her sorrowing and distracted mind the voice of the dwarf grew louder, urging her to put an end to her unhappiness, and restore the pleasure of vanished days. One afternoon when the Princess was out walking in the park with two ladies-in-waiting, she came to a pool, shadowed by overhanging branches. Stooping over, she was startled to see, beneath the water, a wrinkled old woman who stared at her with grief-stricken eyes. Even as she drew in her breath sharply she knew that it was her own face, changed by sorrow. For a long time the Princess gazed at the face in the water before rising and returning to her chamber, where she dismissed her women and sat down at a table. There she took up her Venetian mirror, with its frame of carved ivory, and looked into eyes that seemed to be asking her a frightening question. After a time she reached for her jars of cosmetic powders and, mixing a small amount of saliva with several compounds, began to apply skin whiteners and rouge to her cheeks. Faster and faster she rubbed the unguents into her skin with her fingertips, before stopping abruptly to stare at her pink-and-white face. With a sudden motion she reached over to a small silver bell that sat on the table beside an openwork pomander containing a ball of musk, and shook it swiftly twice. A moment later Scarbo appeared, with a low bow. Holding up the mirror, the Princess gestured disdainfully toward her pink-and-white image in the glass. At once the dwarf stepped over, climbed onto a stool covered in green velvet, and picked up a cloth. With a headshake and a sigh of disapproval he began wiping the ointments from her face, while he held forth on the art of cosmetics. Had the Princess never been told that a base of white lead was to be avoided, since it was known to produce harmful effects on the skin? Surely she had seen the telltale red spots on the faces of women of the court— spots that had to be treated with ground black mustard or snake- root. In place of white lead, might he suggest a mixture of wheat flour, egg white, powdered cuttlefish bone, sheep fat, and cam- phor? When Scarbo had finished cleaning the Princess's face, he carefully selected half a dozen jars of powder from the table, holding each one up and studying it with a frown. In a copper bowl he prepared a whitish paste. Then, still standing on his stool, he leaned forward and began to apply the paste skillfully to the Princess's cheeks with his small, jeweled fingers.

THE MARGRAVE. What of the margrave? The tales say little of the Prince's friend, save that each night he lay faithfully on his side of the sword. It is true that in one version he becomes the Princess's lover, and they are caught there, in the bed; but this is a version that few of us heed, for we recognize it to be less daring than the versions in which the Princess remains un- sullied in the margrave's bed. Let us say, then, that the margrave remains nightly on his side of the sword. What is he thinking? We may imagine that he is troubled by the visits of the Princess, who nightly creeps into his bed and lies beside him without a word. We do not disgrace him if we imagine that he desires the Princess, for he is a man like other men and the Princess is the fairest of all women; but even if we fail to take into account his own sense of honor, the margrave is bound to the Prince by the high law of friendship, and by the debt that every guest owes to his host: he would no more think of possessing the Prince's wife than he would think of stealing a silver spoon. Or, to be more precise: he is forced, by the Princess's offer of herself, to think continually of possessing her, and the thought so inflames and shames him that he must exercise all his vigilance to resist the nightly test, while at the same time he must make certain not to offend the Princess by an unseemly coldness. It is also possible that the margrave senses that the Princess has been sent by the Prince against her will, to test him; if so, the knowledge can only strengthen his resistance, while making him question why he has incurred the Prince's suspicion. The margrave is troubled by the displeasure he senses in the Prince, and by the cooling of their warm friendship; he longs to return to the early days of his visit. It is time for him to return to his distant land, but he cannot make up his mind to leave the castle. Is he perhaps drawn to the nightly test, the nightly overcoming of his desire, by which act alone he can assert the power of his high nature? Or is he perhaps secretly drawn to the possibility of a great fall? Thus do we weave tales within tales, within our minds, when the tales themselves do not speak.

RATS. The rats in our town scuttle along the narrow lanes, crawl from the compost heaps before our houses, scamper freely in the grassy ditch between the double ring of walls. They feed on slops surreptitiously spilled in the streets despite our strict ordinances, on scraps from the dinner table, on carcasses brought for burial to the field beyond the gates. The ratcatcher drowns the rats in the river, and it is from the seed of these drowning rats that a darker breed of rat is said to grow. The dark rats swim across the river and burrow in the cliff hollows. Slowly they make their way up to the castle. They penetrate the towers of the outer and inner walls, scamper across the courtyards, invade the larder and the pantry, and gradually make their way down to the underground cells and tunnels. From there they begin their long descent, pushing their sleek bodies through hidden fissures, seeping into the stone like black water, until at last they come to the dungeon. The dungeon rats are long haired, half-blind, and smell of the river. They crouch in the black corners, rub against the damp walls, stumble against an outstretched foot. The prisoner can hear them cracking bits of stale bread, feeding on pools of urine. When he falls asleep the rats approach slowly, scurrying away only when he stirs. If the prisoner sleeps for more than a few minutes, he will feel the rats nibbling at his legs.

THE PRINCESS DECLINES. Scorned and distrusted by the Prince, eluded by the margrave, who no longer sought her company by day, thrown always into closer communion with the dwarf, the Princess began to mistrust herself, and to question her own mind. Always she lay awake at night, on her side of the margrave's sword; and she spent her sunlight hours in a melancholy daze. Weary with sorrow, weak with night-wakefulness, she was yet ravaged with restlessness, and could scarcely sit still. Alone she walked in the green shadows of her garden, or wandered alone in the shady paths of the park; and though her gaze was fixed in an unseeing stare, often she would start, as if she had heard a voice at her ear. She ate little and grew thin, so that her chin looked bony and sharp; and in her wasting face her melancholy eyes grew large, and glowed with the dark light of sorrow. One morning she stumbled in her garden, and would have fallen had the dwarf not sprung from behind a privet hedge and helped to steady her; she felt a warmth on her neck and cheeks, and that afternoon she took to bed with a fever. In her fever-bed she had a vision or dream: she saw a girl at a well, holding a golden ball. The girl dropped the ball, which cracked in two, and from the ball a black raven flew forth and circled round her head, trying to peck out her eyes. And though the girl cried out, the bird put out her eyes; and from the drops of blood that fell to the ground, a thornbush grew. And when the wings of the raven brushed the thorns, instantly the bird died, and the girl's sight was restored. Then the Princess woke from her fever-dream and asked the dwarf what it portended. The dwarf replied that the golden ball was her past happiness, and the margrave the raven, that had ended her happiness; and the thornbush was her sorrow, from whence would come her cure. For there was a cure, but it must come from her own despair. Thus did the dwarf tend the Princess in her sickbed, bringing her goblets of cool water, and telling her dwarf tales, as though she were a child; and always he watched her closely with his brown, melancholy, slightly moist, very intelligent eyes.

OTHER TALES. The tales of the Princess are part of a larger cycle of castle tales; other tales speak of the Prince's daughter, the contest of archers, the Prince and the Red Knight. These are tales of the castle, but we have other tales as well: the tale of the Black Ship, the tale of the three skeletons under the alder tree, the tale of the raven, the dog, and the piece of gold. As children our heads are full of these tales, which we confuse with real things; as we grow older our minds turn to affairs of this world, and to the promise of the world hereafter. But the old tales of our childhood never leave us entirely; in later years we pass them on to our own children, without knowing why. Sometimes when we grow old the tales return to us so vividly that we become caught in their wonder, like little children, and forget the cares of the moment in a kind of drowsiness of dreaming; then we look up guiltily, as if we have done something of which we are ashamed.

OUTBURST. Day after day the Princess lay feverish in her sickbed, attended by the dwarf, who sat beside her on a high stool, held cool water to her lips, and fed her syrups prescribed by the court physician; and bending close to her ear, he urged her to confess to the Prince that the margrave had wronged him. Could she be certain, could she be absolutely certain, that the margrave, who after all possessed a fiery nature, had approached her only in friendship? Had she seen no sign of a more ardent feeling? Could she say, in all truthfulness, that relations between her and the margrave had been entirely innocent? When she looked deep into her heart—and he urged her to look deep, deep into her heart, deeper than ever into that unfathomable darkness where perhaps only a dwarf's eyes could see clearly—when she thus looked into her innermost heart, could she say, in all conscience, that she did not desire the attentions of the margrave? Certainly he was a handsome man, well knit and hard muscled, and in all ways deserving of love, so that it must be difficult, for a woman, not to dream of being kissed by those lips, embraced by those graceful, powerful arms. Could she say, in all honesty, that she had not in some small way, if only by a smile or a look, encouraged in the Prince's friend, who was also, as all the court knew, her intimate friend, some slight bending of his mind toward her, some barely perceptible swerve from the straight line of innocent friendship? And was not friendship itself, truly understood, a passion? Could she, when she looked into the darkness of her heart, deny that she had seen her friendship-passion take on a new and unexpected shape, there in the all-transforming and all-revealing dark? Far be it from him to suggest the slightest degree of deviation from the path of wifely duty—although, in such matters, precise lines were difficult, nay, impossible, to draw. And could she say, in all earnestness, that never once, in the margrave's bedchamber, had the tip of his finger grazed her loosened hair, never once, in all those nights, had he looked on her otherwise than in the purity of an unlikely child-friendship? For surely the ardent margrave had been tempted—to deny it would be to insult him, and indeed to insult the Princess herself, whom all women envied. But where there is temptation, there is the first motion toward a fall. Therefore to say that the margrave desired her was but to speak the truth; and for her to say to the Prince that the margrave had acted on his desire was no more than an extension of the truth, as heavy gold is beaten into airy foil. Thus did the dwarf whisper, as the Princess lay on her fever-bed, thus did he teach her to see in the dark; till looking into the darkness of her heart, the Princess saw disturbing shapes, and cried out in anguish. Then she bade the dwarf bring the Prince to her sickbed. And when the Prince appeared before her, the Princess cried out that the margrave had treacherously desired her, and whispered lewdly to her, and lain with her, and touched her lasciviously by day and by night; and for the sake of her lord, she confessed it. Then the Princess fell back, shuddering, and cried out that she was being stung by devils, so that she had to be restrained. Then the Prince summoned his guards, who seized the margrave in his chamber; and when he demanded to know what was charged against him, they would not answer him.

CRIMINALS. Our torture chamber and prison cells lie in the cellars beneath the town hall. Some say that a passageway leads down to a dungeon, which lies at the same depth as the dungeon of the castle on the other side of the river, but there is no evidence whatever for such a dungeon, which moreover would be entirely superfluous, since our prisons are used solely for detention during trial. It is impossible to know whether our legendary dungeon gave rise to the tale of the castle dungeon or whether the castle dungeon, in which we both do and do not believe, gave rise to ours. Our torturers are skilled craftsmen, and our laws are severe. Murderers, traitors, rapists, thieves, adulterers, sodomites, and wizards are taken in a cart to the executioner's meadow beyond the walls and there hanged, beheaded, burned at the stake, drowned, or broken on the wheel by the public executioner in full view of citizens and nearby villagers who gather to witness the event and to eat sausages sold at butchers' stalls. The peasants say that the seed of criminals buried in the graveyard gives birth to the race of dwarfs. The rigor of our laws, the skill of our torturers, and the threats of our preachers, who paint the torments of hell in lifelike detail worthy of our artists and engravers, are intended to frighten our townsfolk from committing criminal deeds and even from having criminal thoughts, and in this they are largely but not entirely successful. The depravity of human nature is a common explanation for this partial failure, but it is possible to wonder whether our criminals, who are tortured underground and executed outside our walls, are not secretly attracted to all that is beneath and outside the world enclosed by our walls—whether they do not, in some measure, represent a restlessness in the town, a desire for the unknown, a longing to exceed all that hems in and binds down, like the thick walls, the heavy gates, the well-made locks and door panels. It is perhaps for this reason that our laws are severe and our instruments of torture ingenious and well crafted: we fear our criminals because they reveal to us our desire for something we dare not imagine and cannot name.

A CHANGE OF HEART. The margrave was tortured on two separate occasions, on the second of which the bones of both arms and legs were broken, but he did not confess his crime, and at length he was carried unconscious down to the dungeon and flung onto a bed of straw. Some members of the court were surprised by the leniency of the punishment, for committing adultery with the wife of a prince was considered an act of treachery and was punishable by emasculation, followed by drawing and quartering, but others saw in the margrave's fate a far worse punishment than death: a lingering lifetime of lying in darkness, sustained only by sufficient nourishment to keep one sensible

of one's misery, while disease and madness gradually destroyed
the body and the soul. The dwarf, who had advised death by be-
heading, a punishment reserved for rapists and sodomites, saw
in the sentence a secret indecisiveness: the Prince did not entirely believe the confession of the Princess. Or, to put it more
precisely, the Prince believed the confession of the Princess,
but his belief had at its center a germ of doubt, which spread
outward through his belief and infected it in every part with a
suspicion of itself. The Princess, for her part, soon recovered
from her fever, and resumed her former habits; only, there was
a marked reserve about her, and sometimes she would break off
in the middle of a sentence and grow silent, and seem to gaze
inward. She no longer summoned the dwarf, and indeed appeared to avoid his company; but Scarbo well understood the
necessity for his banishment, for had he not caused her to fall
beneath her high estimate of herself? The Prince, uneasily rec-
onciled with his wife, sensed in her an inner distance that he
could not overcome; to his surprise, he discovered that he did
not always wish to overcome it. To the extent that he believed
her confession, he felt a cold revulsion that she had lain with the
margrave, even at his own urging; to the extent that he disbe-
lieved her confession, he blamed her for condemning the margrave to a dungeon death. Meanwhile the Princess withdrew
deeper and deeper into her inner castle, where she brooded over
the events that had estranged her from the Prince, and made her
a stranger even to herself. And as the days passed, a change came
over her. For she saw, with ever-increasing clearness, in the long
nights when she no longer slept, that the Prince had wronged
her, by sending her to the bed of the margrave; and she saw, with
equal clearness, that she had horribly wronged the margrave, by
her foul lies. Then in the dark the Princess vowed to set right
the wrong she had done him. And she who had lain coldly in the
bed of the margrave, brooding over the displeasure of the Prince,
now looked at the Prince strangely, as at someone she had known

long ago; and lying coldly in the bed of the Prince, or lying alone in her private bedchamber high in her tower, she thought of the margrave, in the bowels of the earth, deep down.

WIVES. No burgher or artisan can manage the complex affairs of his household without the aid of his capable wife. The wives of our town are practical and industrious; on the way to market in the morning they walk purposefully, with powerful strides. It is true that our husbands, while admiring their wives, expect them to be obedient. A wife who disobeys her husband will be promptly chastised; if she provokes him by continued disobedience, he has the right to strike her with his fist. Once, when a young bride of high beauty and strong temperament argued with her patrician husband in the presence of dinner guests, he rose from the table and in full view of the company struck her in the face, breaking her nose and disfiguring her for life. A wife's conduct is carefully regulated by law; it is illegal for a wife to permit a servant to place a brooch on her bosom, for no one may touch her on the breast except her husband. The wives of our town are strong, efficient, and never idle. They are fully able to manage a husband's affairs if he should depart from town on business, or his trade if he should die. The wives make up the morning fires, shake out rugs and clothes, tend their gardens, direct their servants to prepare dinner. Only sometimes, resting by a window or pausing beside a well, a change comes over them. Then their eyes half close, a heaviness as of sleep seems to fall on their shoulders, and for a moment they are lost in dream, like children listening to stories by the chimney fire, before they return to their skins with a start.

A MEETING. One morning Scarbo received by messenger a summons from the Princess. He had not exchanged a single word with her since her illness, and he appeared promptly at the bower, shutting the wicker gate behind him and entering the shady enclosure with a low bow. The Princess sat on one of the crimson silk couches and motioned for him to sit opposite. Scarbo was struck by something in her manner: she had about her a self-command, as if she were a tensely drawn bow, and she looked at him frankly, without hostility but without friendliness. As soon as he was seated she said that she wished to ask a difficult service of him. The request itself would put her at his mercy, and she had no illusions concerning his good will toward her; but since she no longer valued her life, save as a means to one end, she did not care whether he betrayed her. The dwarf, instantly alert to the danger of the interview, as well as to the possibility of increasing his power in the court, chose not to defend his good will, but remained warily silent, only lowering his eyes for a moment in order to display to the Princess his distress at the harshness and unfairness of her remark. The Princess spoke firmly and without hesitation. She said that because of her weak and evil nature, a nature abetted by dubious councillors in the service of one who no longer wished her well, she had wronged the margrave, who now lay suffering a horrible and unjust fate; and that she was determined to right her wrong, or die. In this quest she had decided, after long thought, to ask the help of the dwarf, knowing full well that by doing so she was placing herself in his power. And yet there was no one else she could turn to. He was intimate with the Prince, adept at hiding and spying, and, as she well knew, at insinuating himself into the confidence of those he served; moreover, it was he alone whom the Prince entrusted with the task of descending the legendary stairway with the prisoner's daily ration of wretched food, which he placed in the hands of the keeper of the dungeon. The service she requested of the dwarf was this: to arrange for the margrave's escape. In making her request, she understood perfectly that she was asking him to put his life at risk by betraying the Prince; and yet she was bold enough to hope that the risk would be outweighed by the gratitude of the Princess, and the advantage of having her in his power. Here she paused and awaited his answer.

NIGHTMARES. Because of the stories we tell, our children believe that if they listen very carefully, in the dead of night, they will hear a faint scraping sound, coming from the bowels of the earth. It is the sound made by the prisoner as he secretly cuts his way with a pickax through the rock. For the most part our children listen for the sound of the prisoner with shining eyes and swiftly beating hearts. But sometimes they wake screaming in the night, weeping with fear, as the sounds get closer and closer. Then we rock them gently to sleep, telling them that our walls are thick, our moat deep, our towers high and equipped with powerful engines of war, our drop gates fitted with bronze spikes sharp as needles that, once fallen upon an enemy, will pierce his body through. Slowly our children close their eyes, while we, who have comforted them, lie wakeful in the night.

THE ANSWER. To his surprise—and he did not like to be surprised—Scarbo realized at once that he would serve the Princess. The reason was not entirely clear to him, and would require close examination in the privacy of his chamber, but he saw that it was a complex reason consisting of three parts, which under different circumstances might have annulled one another, or at the very least led him to hesitate. The Princess, he clearly saw, considered him morally contemptible, and was appealing to what she assumed to be his cynical lust for power. In this she was quite correct, as far as she went; for indeed he was in part attracted by the vague but thrilling promise of having the Princess in his power, although what precisely she intended to imply by those words was probably unclear to her. She was therefore correct, as far as she went; but she did not go far enough. For her very contempt prevented her from seeing the second part of his complex reason for agreeing to risk his life by serving her. Although Scarbo was ruthless, unscrupulous, and entirely cynical in moral matters, his cynicism did not prevent him from distinguishing modes of behavior one from the other; indeed he would argue that precisely his freedom from moral scruple made him acutely sensitive to the moral scruples of others. Because the Princess was moral by nature, the dwarf trusted her not to betray him; he could therefore count on her in a way he could no longer count on the Prince, whose moral nature had been corroded by jealousy. The third part of the reason was murkier than the other two, but could not be ignored. For the first time since her decline into weakness and confusion, Scarbo admired the Princess. He was helplessly drawn to power; and the Princess, in her proud bearing, in the intensity of her determination, in the absolute and, yes, ruthless quality of her conviction, was the very image of radiant power that he adored, in comparison to which the Prince, gnawed by secret doubt, seemed a weak and diminished being. Yes, Scarbo was drawn to the Princess, looked up to her, felt the full force of her power, in a sense yielded to her, and could deny her nothing, even as he felt the thrill of having her in his power. Such, then, were the three parts of the reason that led to his immediate inward assent. Aloud, the dwarf said to the Princess that there was much to be thought about, in a request that only honored him, and that he would deliver his answer the following day.

A RTISTS. Our tombstone effigies, the carved figures on our altarpieces, the faces of our patricians on medallions, the decorative reliefs and commemorative images in our churches, the stone figures on our fountains, the oil or tempera paintings that show an artisan in a leather cap, or the suffering face of Our Lord on the cross, or St. Jerome bent over a book between a skull and a sleeping lion: all these receive high praise for their remarkably lifelike quality. So skillful are the painters in our workshops that they vie with one another to achieve unprecedented effects of minutely accurate detail, such as the individual hairs in the fur trim of a cloak, the weathered stone blocks of an archway, the shine on the wood of a lute or citole. The story is told how the dog of one of our painters, seeing a self-portrait of his master drying in the sun, ran up to it to lick his master's face, and was startled by the taste of paint. But equally astonishing effects are regularly created by our master artisans. We have all watched our master wood-carvers cut from a small piece of pear wood or linden wood a little perfect cherry, on top of which sits a tiny fly; and our master goldsmiths, coppersmiths, silversmiths, and brass workers all delight us by creating tiny fruits and animals that amaze less by virtue of their smallness than by their precision of lifelike detail. Such mastery of the forms of life may suggest a disdain for the fanciful and fantastic, but this is by no means the case, for our painters and sculptors and master artisans also make dragons, devils, and fantastic creatures never seen before. Indeed it is precisely here, in the realm of the invisible and incredible, that our artists show their deepest devotion to the visible, for they render their monsters in such sharp detail that they come to seem no more fantastic than rats or horses. So strikingly lifelike is our art, so thoroughly has it replaced the older and stiffer forms, that it may seem as if ours is the final and imperishable end toward which the art of former ages has been striving. And yet, in the heart of the thoughtful admirer, a question may sometimes arise. For in such an art, where hardness and clarity are virtues, where the impossible itself is rendered with precision, is there not a risk that something has been lost? Is there not a risk that our art lacks mystery? With their clear eyes, so skilled at catching the look of a piece of velvet rubbed against the grain, with their clear eyes that cannot

not see, how can our artists portray fleeting sensations, intu-
itions, all things that are dim and shadowy and shifting? How
can the grasping hand seize the ungraspable? And may it not
sometimes seem that our art, in its bold conquest of the visible,
is really a form of evasion, even of failure? On restless afternoons, when rain is about to fall but does not fall, when the heart
thirsts, and is not satisfied, such are the thoughts that rise unbidden in those who stand apart and are watchful.

DWARF IN THE TOWER. Scarbo delivered his answer at the
appointed time, and now daily he climbed the turning stairway
that led to the private chamber at the top of the tower, where
the Princess increasingly secluded herself from the cares of the
castle to work her loom, brood over her fate, and await the news
of the margrave in the dungeon. As the dwarf ascended the sun-
streaked dark stairway he would rest from time to time at a
wedge-shaped recess with an arrow loop, pulling himself up on
the ledge and clasping his arms around his raised knees as he
stared out at the river winding into the distance or the little city
behind its meandering walls. In the long spaces between recesses the air darkened to blackness; sometimes in the dark he
heard the rustle of tiny scurrying feet, or felt against his hair the
sudden body of a bat. At the top of the stairway he came to a
door, illuminated by an oil lamp resting on a corbel set into the
wall. He knocked three times, with longish pauses between
knocks—the agreed-on signal—and was admitted to a round
room filled with sunlight and sky. The light entered through two
pairs of tall lancet windows, with trefoil tracery at the top; each
pair was set in a wide recess with stone window seats along the
sides. On one stretch of wall between the two recesses was a
wall painting that showed Tristan and Isolde lying side by side
under a tree; from the branches peered the frowning face of King
Mark, circled by leaves. The Princess led Scarbo to the pair of

window seats overlooking the walled town across the river, and there, sitting across from her and tucking one leg under him, the little man reported the progress of his plan. The crusty old keeper of the dungeon had at first seemed a stumbling block, but had soon revealed his weakness: a lust for glittering things. In return for a single one of the red and yellow and green jewels with which the Princess had filled the dwarf's pockets—for she had insisted on supplying him with gems instead of buttons or glass—Scarbo had been able to secure the prisoner's release from the heavy chains that had bound his arms and legs to the wall. In return for a second jewel, the dwarf had earned the privilege of visiting the prisoner alone. It was on the first of these occasions that he had provided the margrave with a long-handled iron shovel, which had proved easy to conceal in the pallet of straw, and which was used by the margrave to dig into the hard earthen floor. And here the tales do not say whether much time had passed, during which the margrave's bones had healed, or whether the report of his crushed bones had been exaggerated. Impossible for the dwarf to say how long the prisoner would have to dig away at his tunnel, for the route of escape had to pass beneath the entire castle before beginning its immense, unthinkable ascent. The ground was hard, and filled with stones of many sizes. A straight tunnel was out of the question, since the presence of rocks required continual swerves; already the margrave had been forced to a complete stop in one direction and had had to strike out in another. The plan, such as it was, called for the margrave to proceed in the direction of the cliff, where a number of fissures in the rockface were known to lead to small cavelike passages; from the face of the cliff he could make his way undetected down to the river, where a skiff would be waiting—not to take him directly across, which would be far too dangerous, but to move him secretly along the rocky shore until he could cross over safely at a bend in the river concealed from the highest of the castle towers. Once in safety, he would raise two mighty armies. One he would lead against the castle, for he had vowed to annihilate it from the face of the earth; the other, across the river, would march up to the walls of the town and demand entry. If refused, the second army would capture the town and use it to control the river, thereby both preventing supplies from reaching the castle by water, and threatening a second line of attack along the low riverbank upstream from the rocky cliff. For the margrave, in his fury, would let nothing stand in the way of his vengeance. Moreover, the town still paid homage to the Prince as supreme lord; and although the homage was well-nigh meaningless, since the Council had wrested from the Prince every conceivable power and was entirely autonomous, nevertheless the margrave, in his blind rage, viewed the town as an extension of the Prince and thereby worthy of destruction. The flaw in this grand plan was not simply the daily danger of discovery by the keeper, whose ferocious love of glitter would never permit him to ignore an attempted escape by a prisoner in his charge, but also the immense and uncertain depth of the dungeon, which was believed to lie far below the bed of the river. Scarbo had repeatedly tried to count the steps, but always he had broken off long before the end, when the number had passed into the thousands, for a strange hopelessness overcame him as he made the black descent, an utter erosion of belief in possibility; and in addition the steps themselves became blurred and broken after a while, so that it was impossible to distinguish one from another. If the idea of tunneling in a straight line had had to be abandoned in the short view, though not necessarily in the broad and general view, how much more tricky, indeed fantastic, seemed the idea of tunneling gradually upward to a point below the foundation of the castle but above the surface of the river. It would be far easier to thread a needle in the dark. At some point, moreover, the tunnel would come up against the solid rock of the cliff, at which moment a stone-cutter's pickax would have to replace the shovel. But the prisoner was strong, and driven by a fierce thirst for vengeance; it was possible that in five years, in ten years, in twenty years, the plan might reach fruition. Then woe betide the margrave's enemies, and anyone who tried to stand in his way; for, truth to tell, the margrave was much changed from the elegant, melancholy courtier he had been, and all his force was now concentrated into a fierce and single aim, culminating in a fiery vision of justice. Thus the dwarf, recounting the underground progress of the margrave to the Princess high in her sunny tower, while across from him she sat in silence, now staring at him intently, now turning her head slightly to gaze out the tall windows at a black raven in the blue sky, at the greenish blue riverbank far below, at the little stone town at the bottom of the wooded hillside.

INVASION. Should an enemy decide to attack us, he must first make his way across the dry moat, one hundred feet deep, that surrounds our outer wall. To do this he must begin by filling with earth, rubble, or bundles of logs that portion or portions of the moat he wishes to pass over. Next he must attempt the crossing itself, under cover of one or more wheeled wooden siege towers supplied with scaling ladders and containing archers, assault soldiers, and perhaps a copper-headed battering ram hung from leather thongs. But while the enemy is still engaged in the laborious task of filling up our moat, we ourselves are by no means idle. From behind our battlements we rain down a storm of flaming arrows and gunshot, while from our towers with their stores of catapult artillery we direct upon the enemy a ceaseless fire of deadly missiles. Should an enemy, against all odds, manage to advance to the outer wall, we are prepared to pour down on him, through openings between the corbels of our projecting parapets, rivers of molten lead and boiling oil, while we continue to shoot at men who are climbing highly exposed ladders that rise against our twenty-foot wall; and since, by design, our towers project from the wall, we are able to direct a murderous fire at the enemy's flank. Should he in all unlikelihood succeed in knocking down or scaling a portion of our outermost wall, he will find himself in a broad trench before a still higher wall, with its higher battlements and towers; and in this trench he will be subject to attack not only from the forty-foot wall looming before him, but from the uncaptured portions of the wall that is now behind him. So inconceivable is it that an enemy in the trench, however numerous, can survive slaughter, that our concern is directed rather at the sappers who, even as we triumph on the battlements, may be digging beneath our walls and towers in an effort to collapse them in one dramatic blow. Therefore we assign soldiers to listen carefully for the sound of underground digging, and we are prepared at any moment to countermine and take possession of an enemy tunnel. Should sappers succeed in toppling a tower or a portion of wall, we are prepared to erect behind it, swiftly, a second wall or palisade, from behind which we can fire upon the invaders as before. Although it is less conceivable that an enemy should penetrate our formidable defenses than that the nine crystalline spheres of the universe should cease to turn, sometimes we dream at night of enemy soldiers scaling our walls. In our dreams they are running through our streets, setting fire to our houses, raping our women and murdering our children, until we can smell the blood flowing among the paving stones, taste the smoke on our tongues, hear the shrieks of the mutilated and dying in a roar of falling and flaming walls and the mad laughter of the margrave as he strides like a giant through the ruins.

A DISTURBING EPISODE. It was about this time that the dwarf began to lust secretly after the Princess, who lived apart from the rest of the castle, and with whom he spent many hours alone in her tower. Perhaps it would be more exact to say that a desire which had always lurked in the dark corners of his soul now first revealed itself to the dwarf, who had not dared to lust after the wife of his Prince when the Prince was his true master. Nightly in his chamber Scarbo imagined scenes of such melting and devouring bliss that he would sit up in bed with pounding temples and press his hands over his chest to still the violent beating of his heart. But when he climbed the stairs to the Princess's tower, and saw her seated proudly and scornfully by the tall windows, he could not recognize in her a single trace of that wild and yielding Princess of the Night, and in his skin he felt an odd confusion, as if he had opened the wrong door and entered a room never seen before. Now, the dwarf was above all a courtier, and had drawn deep into his own nature the court's conventions of love, which managed to combine delicacy of feeling, refinement of speech, longing for self-abasement, and relentless lust, all directed toward another man's wife. Therefore his feelings for the Princess, although new to him, were at the same time quite familiar. But in addition to being a courtier, Scarbo was also a dwarf, and herein lay an important difference. As a dwarf he was threatened at every turn with ridicule, with secret laughter; although no one had dared to touch him since he had committed murder in defense of his honor, he was always aware of hostile and secretly mocking eyes. Once, in his early days at court, a lady-in-waiting had sat him on her lap and fondled him laughingly, placing his small hand on her half-bared breast and touching him on the thigh, calling him her little puppy, whispering that he should visit her at night. When he entered her bedchamber that night and groped his way to the curtained bed, she looked at him in surprise and suddenly burst out laughing, so that her naked breasts shook and tears of hilarity streamed along her cheeks. Scarbo drew his sword in order to cut off her breasts, hesitated, sheathed his sword, and left without a word. After that he never permitted

himself to be touched by anyone. His sudden desire for the
Princess, which grew stronger each night, was therefore frustrated not only by the courtly convention of hopeless love-long-
ing, but by fear—not simply the fear of ridicule, which in itself
was intolerable, but the fear that the Princess would look at him
in bewilderment, without understanding that she might exist
as an object of desire for such a one as he. Secretive and cautious by temperament, Scarbo had trained himself over many
years to murder any feeling that might interfere with his ad-
vancement at court. Should he not do so now? But the Princess
had placed herself in his power. What could that mean except
that she was his to do with as he liked? She was entirely dependent on him for the life of the margrave; she could not possibly refuse him the trivial favor of her body, which he longed
for so violently that sometimes, as he walked along a corridor,
tears of desire sprang into his eyes. But even though he held her
in his power, as she herself had repeated more than once, so that
he need only exercise that power by a simple act of will in order to take possession of her incomparable body, his pride demanded more—demanded, indeed, that she invite him to take
his pleasure with her, that in no vague or uncertain terms she
welcome him to her bed. And because he was tormented by
ever-increasing desire, and because at the same time he was extremely cautious, Scarbo began to reveal his desire to the
Princess, in her tower chamber: at first obliquely, through sly
hints that might be taken up or ignored, and then more open-
ly, though not directly. He spoke to her of love affairs at court,
describing budding passions, unhappy marriages, and secret
trysts, and soliciting her opinion concerning specific questions
debated at court, such as whether a wife neglected by her husband had the right to take a lover, or whether a woman should
prefer an ugly lover with a noble soul to a handsome lover with
an ignoble soul. He contrived whenever possible to pay the
Princess intimate compliments, praising the way a sleeve set off

the whiteness of her skin, alluding to her fingers and neck, and deploring the threadbare phrases of court poets, who settled for the same old expressions and therefore could not see the precise color, for example, of the Princess's hair, which was not the color of beaten gold but rather of the field of wheat by the bend of the river in the light of early morning, or of a wall of pale stone darkened and made bright by the late afternoon sun. The Princess's failure to acknowledge these compliments, which in one sense might have seemed discouraging, in another sense was almost heartening, for it could at least be said that his words had not awakened her active displeasure; and thus encouraged, the dwarf proceeded, as if by cunning, and yet quite helplessly, to more daring and intimate expressions. One day he spoke disparagingly of the fashion lately taken up by court ladies of binding their breasts with bandeaux, instead of leaving them free to assume their natural shape, as was still, he was pleased to observe, the custom of the Princess herself, who unlike certain of the ladies did not need to wrench into false and misleading forms those gifts of Nature which, as anyone with eyes could see, were of a beauty, indeed a perfection, that made one impatient with the shams of artifice and filled one with a longing to experience the naked truth of things—and as the little man continued to speak, shocked by his boldness, sickened by the sense of having gone too far, but unable to stop, he had the dreamlike sensation that he had entered a forbidden realm of freedom and transgression, for which at any moment he would be severely punished. Often he longed to reach out and touch the Princess. She sat across from him on her sunny stone bench, thoughtful, a little tired, with signs of a slight dishevelment; she had grown a trifle slack of late. The subtle laxity in her rigorous deportment, the startling wisp of hair escaping from beneath her headdress, the hint of indifference toward her own body, all this gave her a kind of softness or languor that caused his mouth to become dry, his stomach to tighten, his hands to tremble visibly—

but always at the last moment he held back, fearful of waking
from his sensual dream. At last, sick with desire, he told the
Princess that he often found himself awake at night, thinking
of their conversations. He would, at such times, have been
pleased to visit her, had he not feared to disturb her rest; and
the Princess remaining silent, he added in a low voice, as if not
wishing to hear himself speak, that he would like to visit her that
very night, in order to discuss certain matters best left to the
hours of darkness, unless of course she did not wish to be disturbed. At this the Princess turned her head and looked at him,
with a gaze of immense weariness and disdain, and said that he
was of course at liberty to visit her when and as he wished. Un-
settled by the look of disdain, which he quickly thrust to the
back of his mind, but thrilled by the words of assent, the dwarf
could not sit still a moment more and abruptly took his leave.
In his chamber he lay down on his small bed, made for him by
the court carpenter in obedience to precise specifications he
himself had furnished, and pressed both small hands against his
thudding heart. A moment later he sprang up. He combed his
beard in the glass, paced about, lay down on his bed, sprang up.
He hadn't expected her to agree so quickly, indeed the details
of the scene were unclear in his mind, except for the troubling
look that ought to have been accompanied by a refusal, but
which perhaps could be explained as a last vestige of loyalty to
the husband who had wronged her. She had accepted him, had
she not? She hadn't accepted him in the spirit he would have
wished, but she had not refused him outright: far from it. In such
thoughts he passed the afternoon and evening; and long after it
had grown dark he waited in his chamber. At last he looked at
himself in the glass, combed his beard with his fingers, slipped
a dagger under his mantle, and closed his door softly behind him.
The Princess's bedchamber lay in the tower, directly beneath
her high room, and as the dwarf climbed the familiar stairs he
tried to recall the long history of his relation to the Princess, but

his mind produced only disconnected images: sunlight and leaf-shade trembling on the red silk of a couch, the face of King Mark peering out of the leaves, the body of a bat brushing against his hair. At the door of her bedchamber he paused, listening, then stood on his toes to place his hand on the iron ring that served as a doorknob. The heavy door, unbolted, gave way to his push. In the dark chamber, shuttered against the moon but lit with a single taper, the Princess lay propped on two pillows in her canopied bed, with the curtain open and the coverlet thrown back across her waist. She had removed her headdress, her wide-sleeved tunic, and her underrobe, but not her snow-white chemise threaded with gold. In the dim light of the taper she seemed a shimmer of snow and gold; and the tops of her breasts and her wheat-colored hair were white and gold. She looked at him coldly and said not a word. Scarbo closed the door behind him and began walking toward the bed, which soared above him; when he reached the side his head barely came up to the coverlet. At the bedfoot stood three steps leading up. Scarbo climbed the steps and began to walk along the coverlet toward the Princess. He was keenly aware of the ludicrous figure he cut as he marched along the trembling bed, and he felt almost grateful to her for not ridiculing him, for not requiring him to cut her throat. As he drew close he saw in her eyes a weariness so deep that it was deeper than disdain. When he reached the place where the coverlet had been turned back, he stopped beside the Princess and stood looking down at her. He saw with utter clarity that she did not and could not desire him, but that she would permit herself to endure his pleasure. He saw further that this permission was in part a desire to punish herself for the wrong she had done to the margrave, and in part a sign of her growing indifference to herself. He felt constrained, formal, and immensely melancholy. He understood that he was not going to tear the chemise from those longed-for breasts and plunge into a night of bliss that would change his life forever. No, he would spare her the need to endure his undesired desire. For this she would be grateful, and her gratitude would increase his power over her. He understood suddenly that renouncing his dream of bliss would not be difficult for him, for he was skilled at renunciation—had he not spent a lifetime perfecting self-denial? Exhausted by his inrush of understanding, almost forgetful of the actual Princess lying at his feet, he understood one final thing: the Princess, who believed that she was acting solely to right a wrong, had not yet realized that she had fallen in love with the doomed and inaccessible margrave, who alone occupied her thoughts, and for whom she was willing to endure any indignity. Tired now, Scarbo sat down on the bed and crossed his little legs. He reached under his mantle and removed the dagger. "A gift for you, Milady," he said, handing it to her hilt-first. "To protect yourself against unwelcome guests." She took the dagger hesitantly; and as he began to speak of the margrave's progress, he saw, in her weary and mistrustful eyes, a first faint shine of gratefulness.

CELLAR TALES. Each of us has heard innumerable versions of the tales of the Princess. From this multiplicity of versions, varying from single details of wording to entire adventures composed of many episodes, each of us selects particular versions that eclipse or obscure the other versions, without eliminating them entirely. The versions selected by any one of us rarely replicate the versions chosen by others, but gradually, in the course of our town's history, certain versions come to take precedence over other ones, which are relegated to a secondary status. It is here that an interesting development takes place. For these secondary versions, which have not been able to survive in the full light of day, continue to carry on a hidden life, and give rise to growths of a dubious and fantastic kind. Such offspring of rejected, inferior, but never-forgotten versions are

known as cellar tales, for they grow in the dark, unseen by anyone, mysterious as elves or potatoes. In one cycle of cellar tales,
the Princess and the dwarf have a child, whose face is of a beauty unsurpassed, but whose body is hideously deformed. In another series of tales the margrave in his dungeon begins to
change: a pair of black wings grows on his back, and one day he
appears in the sky above the river as a black angel of death. Although the cellar tales are never admitted to the main cycle of
castle tales, they nevertheless do not wither away, but multiply
inexhaustibly, staining the other tales with their hidden colors,
exerting a secret influence. Some say that a day will come when
the daylight tales will weaken from lack of nourishment; then
the cellar tales will rise from their dark places and take over the
earth.

THE PRINCE. As the Princess withdrew to the solitude of her
tower, the Prince retired to the privacy of his oriel chamber, with
its great hearth, its hunting tapestries in which the yellows were
woven with gold thread, and its many-paned window that over-
looked the chapel roof. Here he kept his favorite falcon in a cage,
his library of rhymed romances inked on parchment and bound
in ivory covers mounted on wood, and a locked chest containing the horn of a unicorn. Alone on his window seat, the Prince
brooded over the Princess, the margrave, and his own unhappy
fate. Had his suspicions perhaps been ill founded? Had he acted unwisely in sending the Princess to the margrave's bedchamber? Should he perhaps pardon the margrave and release
himself from the worm of doubt that gnawed at his entrails? But
such a step was impossible, for at the heart of his doubt was a
still deeper doubt, a doubt that questioned his doubt. The Prince
remembered reading of a cunning Moorish labyrinth in which a
Christian knight had wandered for so many years that when he
caught sight of himself in a puddle he saw the face of an old man,

and it seemed to the Prince that he was that knight. Sometimes the castle, the margrave, the Princess, his own hand, seemed images in an evil dream. He no longer called for his dwarf, who alone might have been able to soothe him, for he sensed that the little man detected in him a secret weakness, an indecisiveness, a softening of the will to rule. Should he perhaps have the dwarf killed? In the late-afternoon shadows of his oriel chamber, the Prince half-closed his eyes and dreamed of another life: surely he would have been happier as a shepherd, tending his flock, playing his oaten pipes, leaning on an elbow beside a babbling brook.

DWARF DESCENDING. The tales say only that the dwarf passed back and forth between the Princess and the prisoner, but in the hillside vineyards beyond the upper gates, or along the well-laid paving stones of a winding lane, we imagine the details: the walls of damp stone, the crumbling edges of the steps, the sudden softness of a scuttling rat. Always, as he descended, Scarbo had the sensation that he knew the moment when the stairway passed beneath the surface of the river: the air became cooler, water trickled along the walls, the stone steps grew slick with moisture and erupted with soft black growths. Later, much later, the darkness changed, became blacker and more palpable: he had the sensation that he could feel it brushing against his face, as if he were passing through the wing of an enormous raven. It was at this point that the castle far above him began to waver in his mind, like vapor over a pool; somewhere a dream-Princess sat in a dream-tower; but for him there was only the long going down in darkness, as if he were a stone plunging into a well. Later still, he heard or thought he heard a faint tapping sound. This was the sound of the margrave's pick, slowly cutting its way through rock. No longer did Scarbo expect to find the prisoner in the dungeon, but rather in one or another branch of a complex tunnel that veered off in many directions as the margrave evaded obstacles, gave way to discouragement, or followed sudden inspirations. So elaborate had the tunnel become, so crisscrossed with intersecting passageways, that it seemed less a tunnel than an ever-widening labyrinth; the dwarf no longer thought of it as a route of escape, but as a fantastic extension of the dungeon, a dungeon caught in the throes of delirium. Scarbo encouraged the margrave, brought him additional tools and measuring devices (a mason's level, a measuring cord), helped estimate his progress, and discussed with him the most promising direction along which to proceed, but his secret plan was the precise opposite of the margrave's: it was to confuse the path of escape, to delay it indefinitely, to prevent the prisoner from breaking free and throwing the world into chaos. But to confuse the path of escape was a difficult task, for Scarbo himself was unsure of the way out, and it was always possible that he would unwittingly direct the margrave toward the correct route. Therefore he contrived plans, made careful measurements, and brooded over sketches as passionately as the margrave himself, but solely with the intention of misleading him and thwarting his escape. For although Scarbo's allegiance to the Princess was profound, it ceased at the point at which he could imagine a change of any kind in the world of the castle; and as he descended through the always darkening dark, it seemed to him that what he most desired was for the Princess to remain forever in her airy tower and for the margrave to dig forever toward an always elusive freedom, while he himself passed ceaselessly between them, in a darkness that never ended.

THE UNIVERSE. The universe, created out of nothing in an instant by a single act of God's will, is finite and is composed of ten parts: the central globe of Earth and, surrounding it, nine concentric crystalline spheres, which increase in circumference as they increase in distance from the Earth. Each of the seven planets lies embedded in its own sphere; if we move outward from Earth, the first sphere is the sphere of the Moon, followed by the sphere of Mercury, the sphere of Venus, the sphere of the Sun, the sphere of Mars, the sphere of Jupiter, and the sphere of Saturn. The eighth sphere is the sphere of the fixed stars, which remain unchanging in relation to one another. The ninth or outermost sphere is the *primum mobile*, turning all the rest. Beyond the ninth sphere, which marks the boundary of the created universe, lies the *coelum empyraeum*, or empyrean heaven, which is the infinite abode of God. Some churchmen say that on the Last Day, when Christ, robed in glory, comes to judge the living and the risen dead, the entire universe will be consumed in fire; others argue that only that part of the universe will perish which lies beneath the sphere of the Moon; but all agree that a great fire will come, and Time will end, and generations will cease forever. Although we admire the architecture of the universe, which seems to have been created by one of our own master artisans, and although we fear its fiery destruction, we are rarely moved by its immense and intricate structure to the condition of wonder. Rather, our wonder is aroused by the tiny silver insects of our silversmiths, by the minuscule steel wheels of our watchmakers, by the maze of fine lines cut by the burin on a soft copper plate to represent the folds in a cloak, the petals of a dandelion, the eyes and nostrils of a hare or roebuck.

ENDINGS. Just as we are familiar with many versions of the tales of the Princess, so are we familiar with a profusion of endings. Sometimes we no longer know whether we have heard an ending long ago, remembering it carelessly, with changes of our own, or whether we have dreamed it ourselves from hints in earlier episodes. Thus it is told how the margrave, suspicious of the dwarf, binds him in irons and climbs to the tower, where he lies down with the Princess and is tended by her for thirty nights and thirty days; on the thirty-first night they are discovered by a servant, and a great battle takes place, in which the Prince is slain. It is told how the Prince, longing for expiation, one day goes down to the margrave in the dungeon and insists on changing places with him, so that the margrave reigns in the castle while the Prince languishes in darkness. It is told how the margrave escapes from the dungeon after twenty-four years, and returns to defeat the Prince and marry the Princess, who in other versions dies in her tower after hearing a false report of the margrave's death. Far from deploring the multiplicity of endings, we admire each for the virtues it possesses, and even imagine other endings that have never been told. For a story with a single ending seems to us a bare and diminished thing, like a tree with a single branch; and each ending seems to us an expression of something that is buried deep within the tale and can be brought to light in that way and no other. Nor does one ending prevent the existence of another, contradictory, ending, but rather encourages other endings, which aspire to be drawn out of the tale and take their place in our memory. Sometimes, to be sure, it happens that endings arise that do not seize us like dreams, and so they pass lightly by and are quickly forgotten. And it is true that among those that remain, however numerous and diverse, we recognize a secret kinship. For we understand that the endings are all differing instances of a single ending, in which injustice resolves in justice, and discord in concord. This is true even of the popular prophetic version, which changes suddenly to the future tense while the prisoner is digging through the rock. A day will come, says the tale, when the margrave will break free. A day will come when he will exact a terrible vengeance on all who have wronged him. A day will come . . . Thus we are able to imagine that long ago, in a past so distant that it blurs into legend, a great battle took place, in which the castle and the town were destroyed, while at the same time we imagine that now, at this very moment, the Princess is waiting in her tower, the dwarf is descending the lower stairway, the margrave is digging his way through the rock, the day is steadily approaching when he will burst forth to visit the world with fire and ruin.

A DAY WILL COME. A day will come when the margrave's pick will suddenly break through the rock. Through cracks of stone he will see a burst of blue sky, brighter than fire. For a day and a night he will cover his eyes with his hands. On the morning of the second day he will widen the hole and peer down at the sun-bright river far below. Unseen by the castle watch he will lower himself on a rope to the river and swim to a waiting skiff. He will row downstream, hugging the cliff wall, for eighteen miles and disembark at the edge of a forest. In a hermit's hut he will sleep for seven days and seven nights. After a long journey he will reach his domain and raise a mighty host, which will exact a terrible vengeance on all those who have wronged him or who attempt to stand in his way. One army will advance against the castle and one army will cross the river and advance against the town; and as both banks of the river burst into towers of fire, the margrave, grown gigantic with avenging fury, will stand astride the river with his face in the heavens and his arms raining destruction.

AN AFTERNOON STROLL. Far from the river, beyond the upper wall on the slope of the hill, lies the executioner's meadow, where criminals are put to death and buried. Beyond the field, higher up the hillside, the vineyards begin. At the top of the vineyards runs a long path of beaten earth, which divides the vineyards from the forest above. Here one can walk undisturbed

in the sun-broken shade of overhanging branches, passing an
occasional vintner in a cart, or another wanderer from the town
below. We recognize each other at once, we solitary ones who
seek the heights above the town, and pass each other with a
sense of fraternal sympathy not unmixed with irritation, for it
is not society we seek on the upper path where the wood begins. From the path we can see a pleasing view of the town below, with its red tiled roofs, its church steeples, the twin towers
of the guild hall, the merchants' fountain in the market square,
the garden of the Carthusian monastery, the courtyards of the
patrician houses with their wooden galleries, the draw wells in
the stone-paved streets. From the town rises a rich interweav-
ing of sounds: the ringing of hammers in the blacksmiths' street,
the honking of geese hanging by their feet from the poulterers'
stalls, the clatter of cart wheels, the shouts of children, the bang
of bells. They are the sounds of an industrious, prosperous, and
peaceful town, prepared to defend itself against disturbance
from within or without, honoring work and order above all, proud
of its wealth, stern in its punishments, suspicious of extremes.
The divisions of its day are well accounted for, with no room for
idling or dreaming. But now and then, unbidden, a shadow passes across the mind of an artisan in his shop or a merchant in his
counting house, and turning his head he looks up to see, across
the river, the high castle shining in the sun. Then an image returns, perhaps from a tale heard in childhood, of a dark stairway,
a princess with golden hair, a dungeon buried deep in the earth.
Long ago these tales unfolded, long ago the prisoner escaped,
the dwarf faded into darkness, the Princess closed her eyes. And
yet even now we can sometimes see, in the high tower, a flash
of yellow hair, we can sometimes hear, in the clear air, the sound
of the prisoner cutting through rock. Ships pass on the river,
bearing away copper bowls, armor plate, and toothed wheels for
sawmills, bringing us spices, velvet, and silk, but under the river live trolls and mermaids. For these are the images that linger,

of the river, of the castle, these are the town in dream. Then we smile to ourselves, we solitary ones, we who are of the town but bear toward it a certain reserve, for we see that the town reaches toward higher and lower places than those it honors. But the sun is halfway along the arc of the western sky, it's time to go down to the town, which after all is our home, even ours. Grapes swell on our slopes, deer graze in the grassy trench between our walls, and in the winding streets, bordered by houses of whitewashed wood and clean stone, sunlight and shadow fall equally.

Catalogue of the Exhibition:

The Art of

Edmund Moorash

(1810–1846)

[1]

THE BELLE AFTER THE BALL
Circa 1828
Ink and brown wash on paper, 9 1/2 x 11 5/8 in.

As an undergraduate (Harvard College, 1826–1830), Moorash composed a series of six satirical drawings in the lively vein of Hogarth, only one of which has survived. Despite a certain crudity of execution, it possesses the boldness of his more mature work, as well as a savage and almost disturbing air of mockery. The Belle is shown among her partially cast-off clothes, with her wig at her feet and her teeth on the table, but Moorash carries the well-worn theme much further: one glass eye lies beside her mask, one naked breast lies under the table, her left arm, still gloved, lies on the floor beside a bouquet of withered roses, and in her lap she holds her bald, toothless, and half-blind head, which stares at the viewer with an expression of malignant hatred. The details of the grotesque scene are scrupulously observed; each minuscule link in the graceful gold chain that hangs from the headless neck is drawn with a miniaturist's precision.

[2]

WILLIAM PINNEY
1829
Black chalk, heightened with white, on buff paper, 10 x 8 1/4 in.

William Osgood Pinney (1808–1846) was born in Philadelphia, the son of Thomas Pinney (a lawyer and publisher of legal papers) and Ann Osgood. Although two years older than Moorash when they met at Harvard College in the fall of 1828, he befriended the younger man and introduced him to others of his set. Moorash's moody nature and fierce independence of spirit made him a difficult friend, but he warmed to Pinney as to no other man. Chester Calcott, an undergraduate friend of Pinney's who later became a fashionable portrait painter and a harsh critic of Moorash's work, noted in his diary a difference between the two men: "In any gathering, Pinney will cross the room to greet you with his hand held out and a smile of welcome on his lips, but Moorash will always hang back, looking at you as if you intended harm." Moorash once said of Chester Calcott that he had the looks of a god, the mind of a devil, and the esthetic sense of a brewer's assistant.

Pinney intended to study law but appears to have been deflected from that purpose by his association with Moorash. Upon graduation he sold his share of the family property to finance his study of art in London, where he was joined by Moorash in the following year. Pinney returned to Cambridge in 1832 and spent two unhappy years as an apprentice in the studio of Henry Van Ness, a leading portraitist who was noted for his brilliant rendition of transparent silk sleeves, ermined capes, velvet armchairs, and ostrich plumes, and who permitted William to paint backgrounds and draperies under close supervision. After a year of indecision Pinney became an architect's apprentice in Boston, where Moorash, who refused to paint portraits, was working in cramped quarters and eking out what he called an "unliving" by a series of obscure jobs, including the painting of panels for the backs of fire engines.

Pinney is shown in the fashionable dress of the day: the black coat with its glimpse of lining, the white linen shirt and high collar, the rippling neckcloth. The coat is unbuttoned below to reveal the vest, to which is attached a delicate chain and a small key; a dark jewel set in pearls is visible on the shirt front. Pinney wears his hair curling, long, and a little wild. Moorash has captured a peculiar expression: Pinney seems to have been caught unawares, and he is shown half-rising, looking at the viewer with a kind of irritated surprise.

[3]

RAT KRESPEL
1835
Oil on canvas, 30 x 25 1/8 in.

E. T. A. Hoffmann's "Rat Krespel" appeared in 1819 in Volume One of *Die Serapionsbrüder*. Although it is not known whether Moorash was able to read German, his sister Elizabeth was well read in both German and French; she may have translated the story for him directly from the German, or from the French translation by Loève-Veimars of the *Oeuvres complètes* (1829–33). Moorash has depicted the scene of Councillor Krespel's wild grief after learning of the death of his daughter:

> Deeply shaken, I sank into a chair. But the Councillor, in
> a harsh voice, began singing a merry song, and it was tru-
> ly horrible to see how he hopped about on one foot, the

crepe (he still had his hat on) fluttering about the room and brushing against the violins hanging on the walls. In fact, I couldn't help giving a loud shriek when the crepe struck me during one of his sudden turns; it seemed to me that he wanted to enfold me and drag me down into the horrible black pit of madness.

The details of the scene are faithfully recorded in the painting: the violins on the wall are draped in black, in place of one violin there hangs a wreath of cypress, and Krespel wears a black sword-belt beneath which is tucked a violin bow instead of a sword. What is striking, however, is not the careful rendering of detail but precisely the opposite: the furious distortion of details as they are swept up into lines of force, the deliberate and expressive blurring of form. Thus the streaming of Krespel's hair and coat is seen in the violins, which in the dark radiance of the candlelight seem to writhe like snakes, and the ripple of the fluttering band of crepe is echoed in the curve of the piano's music rack, while the piano itself appears to be dissolving into reddish darkness. The effect is of a center of violent energy diffusing itself throughout the entire painting. Krespel himself, partially plunged in blackness and partially illuminated by the red candleflames, has the distorted features of a grimacing dwarf. Despite such distortions, the painting retains a number of illusionist features, such as definite though at times ambiguous perspectival lines and a stable, centralized vantage point.

If the scene attracted Moorash for its painterly possibilities, the story itself has significant implications in light of what is known of Moorash's theory of the demonic properties of art. It will be recalled that Krespel's daughter is blessed with a supernaturally beautiful singing voice, which derives in part from a defect of the lung; if she continues to sing, she will die. The dubious origin and fatal effect of art—twin themes that haunted the romantic imagination (see Hawthorne's "Rappaccini's

Daughter" for a later variation)—is here given one of the earliest and most memorable expressions by the German fabulist.

The painting, believed lost until 1951, when it was discovered in the attic of a descendant of William Pinney's maternal uncle, shows some damage: the paint surface is abraded in the top right corner and in a small area to the right of the cypress wreath. There is also some loss of paint along the upper and lower edges of the picture, where the canvas has deteriorated.

Note. Because *Rat Krespel* is frequently connected with the Phantasmacist movement of the early 1830s, it may be worthwhile to distinguish Moorash's work from the paintings of that minor and short-lived school. In works such as *The Headless Horseman* (1832) by John Pine and *Lenore* (1833) by Erastus Washington we see the typical Phantasmacist interest in macabre scenes drawn from literature, the use of violent contrasts of light and dark, and the attraction to shrill discords of color, but in essence the technique of this school is diametrically opposed to that of Moorash. The Phantasmacists attempt to capture the macabre, the eerie, the fantastic by the method of scrupulous precision; even their fondness for unusual effects of light (flickering lantern-light, cloudy moonlight, stormy daylight, the flames of hell) is expressed in an almost scientific method of distortion. Their concern for detail, for exact representation, for high finish and smooth facture, connects them with the academic art against which they appear to be rebelling. But Moorash, even in this early painting, has begun to dissolve the outlines of objects, to blur linear identity, to infect all parts of a painting with an energy that appears to erupt from within the canvas.

It would nevertheless be interesting to know whether Moorash ever visited the Boston studio of Erastus Washington, whom he once ambiguously praised in a letter to William Pinney (5 December 1843): "All the same, I'd rather have painted one devil

by old Erastus Washington than all the landscapes by Hudson."
(Moorash liked to speak of an imaginary artist called Hudson
who was supposed to have painted all the pictures of the land-
scapists working in the Hudson River valley and not yet known
as the Hudson River School.) Erastus Washington (1783–1857),
one of the more eccentric artists of the 1830s, spent ten years
completing a cycle of over five hundred paintings in red, burnt
sienna, and black called *The Underworld,* which he intended as
Part I of a three-part cycle and which he burned along with his
entire library after a mystical revelation at the age of sixty. He
spent the last fourteen years of his life writing religious tracts in
which he inveighed against the idolatry of art and asserted that
Nature itself is a great painting composed of images that obliquely reveal an unseen Master. If Moorash ever admired him, it was
for his wildness and sincerity rather than for his art.

[4]

LANDSCAPE WITH FOG. STONE HILL,
EARLY MORNING
1836
Oil on canvas, 26 x 32 in.

In the early spring of 1836, at the urging of fellow painter Edward Ingham Vail, Moorash left Boston, where he had been
struggling for two years, for the village of Strawson in northern
New York. Here he rented a cottage "dirt cheap" on the out-
skirts of town. The country appeared to agree with him, and in
June he moved to the nearby village of Saccanaw Falls, where
he rented a rural cottage about half a mile from the village center on sixteen acres of fields, woods, and streams. He was soon
joined by his sister Elizabeth, who had been living restlessly
with her parents in Hartford, Connecticut. She had recently
been left a small annuity upon the death of a favorite aunt, and

saw in the move a chance both to free herself from unhappy domestic circumstances and to watch over her beloved and careless brother. The property contained a decaying barn that Moorash used as a studio.

His new life delighted him, in part because he was happy to put distance between himself and Vail, whose dreamy landscapes and sentimental portraits grated on his nerves. The cottage was situated on a small rise known as Stone Hill, a name that in Elizabeth's Journal refers sometimes to the hill itself, sometimes to the entire property, and sometimes to the cottage. Moorash's life at Stone Hill was by no means as isolated as has been claimed (see Havemeyer, pp. 56–58, for the classic statement of Moorash's "romantic solitude"); Elizabeth records frequent visitors, such as William Pinney and his sister Sophia, Edward Ingham Vail, the miniaturist Thomas Swanwick, the itinerant folk artist Obadiah Shaw, who specialized in perspective views painted on cigar-box lids and Biblical scenes painted on glass, and the poet and portraitist Lyman Phelps (later a successful attorney-at-law). In addition, the Journal mentions numerous excursions to Strawson and the surrounding countryside, as well as twice-weekly walks into Saccanaw Falls, a small but bustling village of two churches, four taverns, a dry goods store, two bakeries, three butcher shops, a cooper's shop, three smithies, a tannery, a mason's shop, a furrier's, a brewery, a hatter's, two druggist shops, and even a musical instrument establishment.

The painting, completed in late summer, should be seen as an attack on the popular topographical views of the day, on the early contemplative landscapes of the Hudson River painters, and perhaps on the entire genre of landscape painting, which by mid-century would supplant portraiture in popular esteem. Indeed there is a distinct element of satire here, despite the absolute seriousness of the work. As one early critic put it: where is the landscape? Moorash has chosen to depict a thick, obliterating fog, in shades of gray, white, and black, with brown and green tints seeping through and, in the right-hand portion, a luminous yellow-ocherish burst where an invisible sun is glowing. Nothing whatever is visible in the picture, aside from the brilliantly rendered fog itself and a single, sharply emergent leafless branch in the lower left-hand corner; here and there dark, wavering forms appear indistinctly. Moorash has completely abolished perspective. There is no vantage point, no center; there is no image, except for the disturbing branch in the lower left hand corner, which serves the ambiguous function of anchoring the viewer in place, of providing stability, and also of radically confusing or destabilizing the point of view, for it is impossible to determine the relation of the branch to anything else. We tend to read it as a sign of height, but its position in the lower left-hand corner either contradicts that reading or forces us to imagine that we are looking down on the sceneless scene from an elevated point. The painting makes no attempt to induce in the viewer a state of revery, or to suggest deep religious meanings infused in a natural setting; rather, its effect is to disturb, to confound, to render uncertain.

[5]

ELIZABETH IN DREAM
1836
Oil on canvas, 26 1/2 x 36 in.

Moorash's early masterpiece was refused by the National Academy of Design in New York and the Boston Athenaeum but accepted for exhibition by the Pennsylvania Academy of Fine Arts in Philadelphia, where it attracted the attention of several critics who subjected it to ridicule mixed with moral indignation. The picture was begun in the spring, set aside for *Landscape with Fog*, and taken up again by the end of August, after which

Moorash worked at it steadily until its completion in mid-November. As the weather grew colder he was forced to move from the barn to the house, where with Elizabeth's help he converted the upstairs parlor to a studio and moved most of the parlor furniture down to the kitchen. The ground floor of the cottage was divided into two rooms—the large kitchen and Elizabeth's bedroom—as well as a small room in back that served as a washhouse; the upper floor consisted of a large front room (Moorash's studio, formerly the parlor) and two back rooms, one of which was Moorash's bedroom and one of which served as a storage or guest room. William Pinney, a frequent visitor in 1836, has left a vivid description (in a letter to his sister of 8 September 1836) of the transformed cottage, where guests were entertained in a kitchen containing an armchair, a writing desk, and a sagging sofa, as well as a pile of canvases leaning against an old churn in one corner.

Elizabeth Moorash (1814–1846) was twenty-two at the time of the painting. We are fortunate to have a likeness of her dating from 1836: a miniature watercolor on ivory painted by Edward Ingham Vail. The glossy brown-black hair parted in the middle and bursting into side curls, and the dramatic blackness of the dress, which blends into the dark background, serve to throw into relief her striking face, which Vail rendered meticulously in delicate clear color: the large, heavy-lidded eyes look out with an expression of frankness and passionate intelligence, softened by a kind of dreamy, inward stare, as if her deepest attention lay elsewhere.

Elizabeth in Dream carries to fulfillment the technique first seen in *Rat Krespel*, in which a central image or character infects the entire world of the painting. Here the barely perceptible face, transparent and dissolving, of the dreaming Elizabeth is dispersed throughout the picture: her transparent hair streams into the night sky, her eyes are streaks of purple-black, her bare arms melt into the brilliance of the moon; and the night itself, under the influence of the dream-dispersed young woman, seems to melt into streams of bright darkness or dark brightness. The world and the dreamer intermingle and dissolve. And yet there is nothing soft, gentle, or revery-like about this dream world, which on the contrary is charged with an extraordinary energy, as if the night were composed of black fire.

[6]

THE INFERNAL PICTURE GALLERY
1837
Oil on canvas, 34 1/8 x 46 3/4 in.

Elizabeth's Journal for 15 December 1836 records a visit by John Pope Coddington, a New York art collector and amateur painter, whom she describes as "most bewildered by our kitchen-parlor." Coddington appears to have been even more bewildered by the canvases he was shown, but three days later he wrote to commission a cycle of eight paintings on "The Power of Art." Moorash labored over his unlikely commission for nearly a year before abandoning it after a third painting. He liked to refer to the cycle as his "punishment," which it quickly became despite the attraction of the theme and the lure of income; certainly the first two paintings are disappointing performances and represent a step backward in the development of his art.

As an undergraduate Moorash had frequented the Boston Athenaeum, and in his two years abroad with William Pinney he had spent many days in the art galleries, auction rooms, and temporary exhibition halls of London and Paris, as well as in a number of private collections to which Pinney had entry, but Moorash was at best a restless, impatient visitor of picture galleries, "those most fashionable of graveyards with their numbered headstones" (letter to Elizabeth, 14 May 1833). His refusal to accompany Pinney to Italy is well known; he argued that the entire country was "an interminable picture gallery decorated with olive trees" (letter of William Pinney to Sophia Pinney, 6 June 1833). The only pictures he is known to have viewed with pleasure were not paintings at all, but satirical mezzotints hung in the windows of printsellers' shops. A row of paintings in a gallery, he once remarked to Edward Vail, reminded him of a line of prisoners waiting to be shot. This irritable response to what he called the "necessary evil" of art museums no doubt partly accounts for the infernal theme, but it would be a mistake to see in the painting no more than revenge for the "months of smothering boredom" he claimed to have suffered among the numbered headstones. Moorash believed profoundly in the power of painting to affect the beholder. In a letter to Pinney (undated, c. 1835) he speaks of the *"impressive* nature of art, that is, its power of impressing itself onto the mind and soul, as a knife impresses itself in flesh," and behind the playfulness and mockery of *The Infernal Picture Gallery* we hear the unmistakable note of this deep theme.

The Infernal Picture Gallery is based on no known art museum or private collection. It shows two soaring walls crowded with pictures in carved and gilded frames (in all, thirty-eight paintings are visible), as well as the statue of a naked nymph emerging from her bath on a marble pedestal in one corner. A doorway opens onto a vista of arched galleries. Two copyists are seated at their easels in opposite corners of the room. The gallery holds some half dozen well-dressed visitors, all of whom look up aghast or press their gloved hands to their frock coats and frilled bosoms. From the thick frames, figures are emerging. A fat naked woman who appears to have descended from an allegorical banquet stands smiling before a stiff, startled gentleman in a frock coat, while a red-faced colonel ogles her through his monocle. A naked Jove, covering his genitals with a bunch of green grapes, appears to be abducting a terrified woman in a fashionable cloak; an Indian in war paint brandishes a tomahawk. But it is not always possible to tell which figures are visitors to the gallery and which have escaped from the frames—a confusion that is surely part of Moorash's intention. Indeed this satirical questioning of the boundaries between the illusory and the real is given further complexity by a striking comic detail: one of the copyists is shown leaning uneasily away from his canvas, from which a leg in a shiny black boot is emerging. Since the canvas is a precise copy of a painting on the wall, Moorash has introduced a figure who is twice removed from life. But his artistic playfulness does not end here: the emerging boot casts a clearly delineated shadow on the picture frame, while the boot remaining in the picture casts its own painted shadow. Thus two orders of shadow are established, one "real" and one "painted," although the viewer is meant to be aware that the "real" shadow is itself painted; and to complicate matters a little, the picture being copied contains a statue that casts a shadow, and the copyist himself casts a shadow on the gallery floor. But despite such elements of epistemological playfulness and outright satire, *The Infernal Picture Gallery* has a darker impulse, for a number of the images are disturbing: a lion holds in its jaws the bitten-off leg of a man-about-town, who lies staring in horror at his blood-gushing stump from which hang shreds of veins and sinews; a bandit with a red scar on his cheek is plunging a dagger into the neck of a kneeling woman; and in a dark corner a lady with a torn bodice and disheveled hair is struggling to free herself from a leering satyr, who is pulling her head back by the hair and squeezing the nipple of one bared breast. The painting, with its clearly drawn figures and its reddish light, hovers uneasily between humor and horror.

The grotesque and at times sadistic elements of *The Infernal Picture Gallery* have raised questions about its connection with the Diabolist movement (fl. 1835–36), especially in light of Moorash's defense of their work against the bloodless academicism of the day, but aside from a few features so general as to be

meaningless there is little to connect Moorash's satirical painting with the dubious productions of that school. Typical Diabolist works treat subjects that are intended to be shocking and
titillating: torture, slaughter (especially of half-naked women
by Turkish soldiers in colorful uniforms), orgiastic Roman ban-
quets full of overturned flagons and bared breasts, and studies
of bleeding women mangled by wild animals. John Pine
(1805–1849), who after his defection from the Phantasmacists
became the acknowledged leader of the Diabolist school, was
noted for his meticulous studies of partially dissected female
corpses, his chained women gnawed by rats, and his forest scenes
in which satyrs with very hairy haunches sodomize pale prepu-
bescent girls with dreamy blue eyes, rosy lips, and ivory but-
tocks. Pine was arrested in 1836 and after his release became a
fashionable still-life artist specializing in moist bunches of
grapes, bloody slabs of meat, and sunstruck wineglasses half-
filled with ruby wine. Moorash's alleged praise of Pine (in a conversation with Edward Ingham Vail) should not be misconstrued
as praise for pornography and the eroticism of death, but rather
must be understood as an attack on the fashionable correctness
and tameness of Vail and his set.

[7]

GALATEA
1837
Oil on canvas, 44 x 35 1/4 in.

The second painting of the "Power of Art" cycle was begun in
the last week of March and completed on 21 April, a compara-
tively rapid rate of composition for Moorash. The broad, free
brushstrokes of *Elizabeth in Dream* have here been replaced by
the tight, controlled brushwork of a neoclassical academician
striving for the scrupulous rendition of minute detail and a high

degree of linear definition. So extreme is Moorash's retreat from his earlier experiments in the loosening of contour that one cannot but suspect the artist's deliberate and almost parodic effort to satisfy a taste not his own.

The source of the Galatea legend is Ovid's *Metamorphoses* (X, 243–97), in which, it should be noted, Pygmalion's statue is unnamed; but Moorash treats the incident freely, in a manner without precedent. Galatea is shown in a state of transition, half marble and half flesh: the living half is struggling to free itself from the cold stone. It is a disturbing conception, in which the living creature appears to be trapped in marble. The living half is nearly as white as the marble half, but very faintly suffused with a ghostly flesh tone. Nothing is shown of the sculptor except his tense hand, from whose veins and sinews we infer a response of terror.

[8]

THE UNVEILING
1837
Oil on canvas, 38 1/2 x 29 1/2 in.

The dark sinister light that obscures sharpness of outline, the deliberate sketchiness of the uplifted faces, the flattening of the picture plane, the emphasis on atmosphere, all separate this painting from the first two of the "Power of Art" cycle and show Moorash returning to the true direction of his art after forcing himself to submit to the imagined taste of his improbable patron. The artist, half-concealed in darkness, is here presented as a demonic figure deliberately exercising a spell on the audience, who gaze up fearfully. The uncertain vantage point appears to be above the audience, on a level with the stage, a strategy that permits Moorash to carry through his plan of not showing the masterwork. We see nothing but a piece of velvet drapery trailing on the stage; it is impossible to tell whether a painting, a statue, or something else entirely has been unveiled.

In her Journal (8 November 1837) Elizabeth noted that "Edmund's devil picture has given me a fright." This entry must refer to *The Unveiling*, which was begun in early October, and not to a lost painting, as Havemeyer supposes. On 9 November Elizabeth had a night of "bad dreams" and recorded that she woke "to hear Edmund's footsteps overhead, pacing, pacing. I longed to run to him, and take his beloved head upon my shoulder, but knowing that the suspicion of having waked me would distress him, I could not tell him of my fearful dream, whereupon I held my bitter peace." The painting apparently continued to make a strong impression, for nearly a year later (4 August 1838) we find: "William and Edmund at a quarter past midnight. Merits of painting and literature. William argued for the cumulative force of arts that move in time. Edmund violently opposed: a painting strikes you *all at once*, with its full force, instead of dispersing its effects. A painting *strikes a blow*. William (smiling): Is art then so dangerous? E: Painting is devil's work—let the beholder beware! I instanced the devil picture. Edmund laughed, and said it had given him a month of headaches, but now he thought it a pretty piece of work to frighten a child withal."

[9]

FIGURES IN SNOW
1838
Oil on canvas, 28 x 36 1/8 in.

Moorash appears to have begun work on this picture on 10 November 1837, that is to say, the very day following his night of furious pacing. Elizabeth's terse entry for 10 November reads: "Edmund working like mad." On 22 November she notes that he has been taking long walks in the snow "for his snow picture"; considering his slow habits of composition, it is reasonable to assume that he was still at work on the picture begun on 10 November. In mid-December he put it aside for a *Stormy Night* (letter to William Pinney, 3 December 1837) that he apparently abandoned or destroyed. He was back at work on his "snow picture" by the first week of January and appears to have completed work on it by the middle of February. It remains uncertain to what extent *Figures in Snow* was composed in accordance with the new method he is known to have adopted by the summer of 1840. Instead of discarding canvas after canvas until he achieved the effect he wanted, he began in the summer of 1840 to work obsessively on a single canvas, painting out unwanted portions repeatedly, or else scraping them out with a piece of pumice, so that he gradually built up thick, uneven layers of paint, often with distinct ridges. *Figures in Snow* appears to be transitional; several portions are painted over, but the overall accumulation is notably less than it was to become.

A letter from William Pinney (7 June 1838) to his sister Sophia reports that Moorash was "exhilarated" while working on the painting, and it is reasonable to suppose that part of his exhilaration lay in his triumphant return to the technique of *Elizabeth in Dream*. The heavy, swirling snowfall blurs and distorts the two figures barely glimpsed through the raging whiteness, with its eerie tints of brown and violet. A streak of red in one figure, perhaps indicating a scarf, is carried over in paler and paler tones, as if the redness is staining the storm, or as if the snow is dissolving the figure into liquid.

A pencil study that appears to be connected with the finished picture shows the two figures clearly as William Pinney and Elizabeth, coming up the front path of Stone Hill Cottage; the Journal entry for 6 January 1838 speaks of a visit by William "in wild snow." Evidently Moorash made a quick sketch, which he referred to in completing the painting. If the sketch was in fact made on 6 January, then the two figures were a late addition to the snow picture, but abundant evidence for the composition of other paintings attests that Moorash's conception of a picture often underwent a significant shift during the course of composition, after which he pursued his new vision relentlessly. William Pinney, by now an architect of growing reputation, was a frequent visitor at Stone Hill Cottage; in the spring of the following year he built a cottage of his own on the far shore of Black Lake, about two miles from Stone Hill. It is not certain when he fell in love with Elizabeth Moorash, although his letters to his sister in 1837 and 1838 make it clear that he found Elizabeth enchanting. In the light of later events *Figures in Snow* may seem to have an ominous suggestiveness, as if Moorash foresaw the whole dark history, but nothing in the surviving correspondence or in Elizabeth's Journal lends support to such interpretations. Moorash cannot have been unaware of his friend's growing interest in his sister, but in January of 1838 William was the eagerly awaited friend of the family, who was welcome to stay for a day or a month and who had not yet disturbed the harmony of things by his declaration of love for Elizabeth. *Figures in Snow* is best seen as a study in white, by a young master sure of his way.

[10]

ELIZABETH AT DUSK: BLACK LAKE
1838
Oil on canvas, 30 1/2 x 37 5/8 in.

Elizabeth often walked down to the shore of Black Lake, the large, gloomy lake bordered by cattails that lay some two miles from Stone Hill in a bleak setting of stony fields, clusters of conifers, and a dead ash split by lightning. On the far shore lay the low pine-covered hills where in the spring of 1839 William Pinney was to build his cottage. Edmund sometimes accompanied Elizabeth to Black Lake, where brother and sister would walk along the lakeshore in animated conversation broken by long, peaceful silences. Sometimes they would pull out of the reeds an old rowboat that Edmund had named *Sacagawea* and row about the dark, quiet lake, Elizabeth at the oars and Edmund lying back against the pillow with a novel by Scott or Bulwer that he held open but did not read.

Of the thirty-one surviving Elizabeth paintings—that is, the nineteen paintings in which Elizabeth appears alone, and the twelve paintings in which she appears with another figure or figures—twenty-three show her as a blurred, distorted, or unrecognizable figure, while the remaining eight do not contain any face or figure at all, and are classified as Elizabeth paintings solely on the basis of titles. In a sense, Moorash never painted his sister. And yet there can be no question of her presence in the paintings to which she lends her name. Moorash's use of his sister in the Elizabeth paintings was inspirational, and at times erratic, but it was not only that: even in the earliest paintings he was working out a method. It is significant that he continually asked her to pose for him, as if he were painting a meticulous, highly finished portrait of the popular academic kind. Elizabeth's Journal is filled with accounts of long posing sessions, after which she might discover that a portion of canvas had been covered with a rich shade of brownish black. Moorash's method was not, as Havemeyer supposes, "expressionistic," except in the most general and unhistorical sense. On 12 April 1838 Elizabeth wrote: "In the afternoon I posed for three hours before the window. E very pleased with me, commends my fortitude. Scornful of imitating nature—that old saw. Spoke of his attempt to dissolve the natural world onto its components and reassemble them in order to reveal true nature." On 3 September 1841: "Edmund wants to dissolve forms and reconstitute them so as to release their energy. Art as alchemy." These hints suggest an esthetic that is neither expressive nor imitative, but transformative: Moorash appears to be seeking a way to reveal or release another order of being, a deeper structure than the accidental and physical one that presents itself to the innocent eye.

In the painting Elizabeth is alone, a small, shadowy figure almost swallowed up by the immensity of dark lake and dark sky, which flow into each other indistinguishably. The swirling array of many-hued browns all stream from the dark Elizabeth figure at the center. A mood of deep melancholy pervades the picture, as if a stain of brown sadness has seeped through a crack in the universe. Elizabeth's brief Journal entry for 6 June 1838 reads: "Upon seeing the picture I was seized with a terrible agitation. Edmund has seen into my very soul." Three days later, on 9 June, she writes: "My spirits have lifted on this glorious morning. How deeply I feel the presence of a benevolent Spirit in the hills and valleys. I must pray for guidance." Elizabeth's tantalizing comments have been taken to refer to the coming crisis in her relation with her brother, but it is possible that she had already begun to show signs of the nervous disorder that was to reveal itself more decisively in the years to come.

[11]

DORNRÖSCHEN
1839
Oil on canvas, 19 1/4 x 27 7/16 in.

On 23 December 1838 Elizabeth recorded a single quotation in her journal: " 'The fairy tales of my childhood have a meaning deeper than the truths taught by life.'—Schiller, *Wallenstein.*" There is no further mention of Schiller in the Journal, but among Elizabeth's favorite books must be counted Grimm's *Kinder- und Hausmärchen*, to which she refers frequently in 1839–40 and of which she possessed two different editions: the revised edition of 1819 and the abridged edition, or *Kleine Ausgabe*, of 1825, with illustrations by a third Grimm brother, Ludwig Emil Grimm. It is possible that she read and translated directly to Moorash, although in the case of so well known a tale the memory of a childhood telling cannot be discounted. *Dornröschen*, usually translated "Briar Rose," is the Grimm version of Perrault's *La belle au bois dormant* ("The Sleeping Beauty"); it is one of the shortest and most powerful of the Grimm tales, far more evocative than Perrault's lengthy version.

A surviving sketch (on the back of a bill for canvas and stretcher) reveals that Moorash at one point attempted to depict the great hedge of thorns bursting into blossom, but there is no trace of this vision in the final painting, in which the spell remains unbroken. In this study of darkness we are in Dornröschen's tower room; only as the eye adjusts to the predominantly black tones do we distinguish the thick thorn branches that have pushed through the open casement window and fill the small chamber entirely. Dornröschen remains invisible except for her hauntingly long and vinelike hair, which winds about the thorny branches and hangs in thick, disturbing clusters, although she may also be present as a kind of faint glimmer that appears to come from somewhere in the depths of the dark thorns and permits us to make out the sharp thornpoints, the hair, the tones of blackness. The general effect is uncomfortable, suggesting on the one hand a dark peacefulness, a brooding tranquility, a yearning for annihilation, and on the other hand the oppressiveness of living entombment.

Why did Moorash turn to this tale and this image in the early months of 1839? Unfortunately there can be no clear or certain answer. Was he, as Havemeyer suggests, thinking of his beloved Elizabeth, entombed at Stone Hill Cottage, enwrapped in the thorns of his art and waiting for the unthinkable prince to come? Havemeyer does not mention a brief but crucial entry in Elizabeth's Journal on 2 January: "Visit by Vail and his new bride,

Charlotte. Vail doting, Edmund charming, Charlotte pretty in a girlish way; shy; big clear eyes, pewter gray." It is the first recorded visit of the forty-year-old Vail and his girlish wife, Charlotte (1823–1846), who was sixteen years old but looked two years younger. Moorash might have been thinking of the young bride, spellbound in marriage to the graying Vail—but in that case, whose footsteps would be heard on the tower stair when the thorns burst into blossom? Or should we rather think of Moorash himself as Dornröschen, asleep in the deep spell of his art?

[12]

FACES IN THE STREAM
1839
Oil on canvas, 25 x 32 1/2 in.

Moorash appears to have made a number of preliminary sketches, which have not survived, in April or May of 1839; the painting was completed in late summer, probably during the last week of July. The stream is almost certainly the picturesque rocky brook that flowed, and flows still, from the Saccanaw Hills across a wooded stretch of Moorash's property to empty into Black Lake. A small, railed bridge, no trace of which remains, crossed the stream at the place where an old Indian trail led to the water. The bridge rail can be seen in the painting as a broken and scattered series of brown and yellow brushstrokes in the rushing water. The faces, though recorded as little more than energetic dashes of paint, are unquestionably those of Elizabeth, William Pinney, and Sophia Pinney, as an entry in Elizabeth's Journal makes clear, although even without that entry the student of Moorash's work can recognize the distinguishing marks of all three faces, however dissolved and scattered by the turbulent brook.

Sophia Pinney (1816–1846), William Pinney's sister, had visited at Stone Hill Cottage on three occasions in the mid-1830s but began to accompany her brother regularly in the spring of 1837. In that year alone William and Sophia stayed at Stone Hill Cottage for a week in April, two weeks in May, ten days in June, three weeks in August, a week in October, and four days in November. The frequent visits continued in 1838, and in the spring of 1839 William, now an architect in Boston, built a summer cottage on the far shore of Black Lake at the foot of a wooded hill. The cottage, which was twice the size of the cottage at Stone Hill, included a music room, a library, and a housekeeper's chamber; in a stable behind the cottage Pinney installed a pair of bays equipped with English saddles in the latest style. Sophia had become close friends with Elizabeth, and in the spring and summer of 1839 the two couples visited back and forth almost daily, often rowing across the lake at dusk to one or the other cottage and separating long after midnight. At the Pinney cottage, Sophia, at Elizabeth's bidding, would play selections from Schumann's recently published *Fantasiestücke*, op. 12 (1838), or *Carnaval*, op. 9 (1837), sometimes adding a Chopin étude or nocturne, while Edmund sat with tense fingers and half-closed eyes in a "paradoxical state of dreamy alertness" (Journal, 18 July 1839). Elizabeth was not simply liked by her younger friend (Sophia at this time was twenty-three, Elizabeth twenty-five); rather, she seemed to have inspired in Sophia an outpouring of ardent admiration. At the same time she woke in Sophia a kind of maternal protectiveness that made Elizabeth restless and a little impatient. Sophia would insist that Elizabeth wear a shawl on cool summer nights; she tried to change Elizabeth's careless eating and sleeping habits; she became acutely sensitive to Elizabeth's moods and began to share her headaches. Elizabeth was fond of her passionately devoted friend but refused to permit herself to be reformed. Once, when Sophia reproached her for staying up all night and paying for it with a savage headache, Elizabeth spoke sharply to her, whereupon Sophia burst into tears. The sharp exchange was an exception; the friendship was warm and ran deep, though one senses that Sophia was the more tightly bound of the two, perhaps because the deepest current of Elizabeth's feelings ran toward her brother.

[13]

CLAIR DE LUNE
1839
Oil on canvas, 36 x 32 in.

This picture, which seems to breathe the air of a tranquil summer night, was in fact painted in the fall: begun in mid-September, it was completed during a week of snow flurries in early November. A curious stillness reigns (compare Moorash's two other surviving night studies, the *Nachtstück* and *August Night*): the world seems to be caught in a spell of moonlight. The sense of spell, of enchantment, connects the painting to *Dornröschen*, but the feeling here is quite different: it is a study of calm, of harmony, of an almost weary peacefulness. As if to emphasize the harmony of earth and heaven, Moorash locates the horizon line at the center of the picture: a black line of hills, barely visible and dissolving at top and bottom into blue, divides the brilliant deep blue of the night sky and the slightly darker blues of the lake. The sky is in the lake, and the lake is in the sky, and all is mysteriously irradiated by the light of an unseen moon. Moorash here abandons his thick impastos for an uncharacteristically flat, even surface, though he gives his blues depth by the use of glazes. The dark, glowing blues, the mysterious stillness, the doubleness of earth and sky, all provoke in the viewer a sense of hidden meaning, as if the painting were on the verge of a revelation it refuses to make.

The lake is Black Lake, as a preliminary sketch, which includes identifiable foreground objects, clearly shows; among the black line of hills is the hill where William Pinney had built his cottage. A letter from Sophia to her friend Fanny Cornwall on 3 September 1839 reveals that on the night of 31 August William proposed to Elizabeth, whose Journal remains strangely silent about the entire episode. The proposal shocked Moorash, who was deeply bound to his sister, and who, in a sense that must not be misunderstood, was virtually married to her, but who believed profoundly in her right to lead whatever life she chose. Elizabeth's feelings are more difficult to grasp, in part because of her refusal or inability to write a single syllable about Pinney's proposal. It is clear that she liked William immensely; she may even have loved him; his proposal threw her into a profound state of uncertainty, amounting at times to despair, which lasted three days. On the fourth day, the day William was to return to Boston, she refused him. What she had to overcome in renouncing William, and therefore a "normal" life, cannot be known; certainly her love for Edmund played its part, but her ardent and complex love for her brother should not be twisted into a banal perversion. Among other things, she feared that her absence might harm him, for he was careless about himself in every way, and once quipped that if it weren't for Elizabeth he would starve to death out of sheer absentmindedness. If she sacrificed anything—and it is far from certain that she ever was in love with William Pinney—it was for the sake of Edmund's art.

Moorash was at work on *Clair de lune* by mid-September, less than two weeks after Elizabeth's refusal. It is possible to see in the painting a retreat from the violence of his sensations to an extreme calm, as he returned in thought to the early days of that summer, when the two brother-sister couples visited back and forth night after night across the enchanted lake. Many entries in Elizabeth's Journal suggest his happiness that July and August, painting all day in the barn and wandering the warm and sweet-smelling summer nights in the company of his sister, his friend, and his friend's sister, who was also his sister's friend. It is difficult not to see the doubleness of *Clair de lune* as in some sense a reflection of the two harmonious couples, each itself a double. The friendship among the four was to last for seven more years, but it never recaptured the ease and innocence of that summer.

[14]

NACHTSTÜCK
1840
Oil on canvas, 38 1/2 x 30 5/16 in.

A more deliberate contrast to *Clair de lune* can scarcely be imagined: here all is oppressive, shut in, brooding, menacing, suffocating. A shadowy, unnameable creature hangs in the night like black smoke, looming over the dark landscape, which seems to shrivel beneath it. The placement of the black line of hills near the base of the picture creates a paradox that increases the sense of suffocation and menace: an eye accustomed to the expansive effects of immense skyscapes, which seem to lead the mind upward to a higher world far from the petty cares of earth, here confronts a dark, oppressive force that crushes it back to the frail line of hills that appear to be cowering under a blow. The sky-filling creature or monster is rendered with supreme skill, for the slightest touch of exaggeration would have pushed it into caricature; the creature is disturbingly elusive, at once present and absent, now a mere illusion produced by thundery cloud-shapes with swirls of black instead of eyeholes, now a shadowy form brooding over the world.

The title of the painting may seem to derive from Schumann's *Nachtstücke*, op. 23, but Schumann's "night pieces," or nocturnes, were not published until 1840 and are never mentioned in Elizabeth's Journal. It is more likely that the choice of title was influenced by Schumann's *Fantasiestücke*, op. 12, the collection of eight piano pieces (including the stormy *In der Nacht*) that Elizabeth liked to have Sophia play for her when the four friends were gathered late at night in the music room of the cottage on the far shore of Black Lake. It nevertheless remains possible that the painting does not derive its title from Schumann at all, but rather from E. T. A. Hoffmann's collection of stories *Nachtstücke* (2 vols, 1816–17). The effect of the title, whatever its origin, is to darken the painting with Germanic consonant clusters and so to oppose it in yet another way to *Clair de lune*.

It is not clear when Moorash began the *Nachtstück*, which appears to have been preceded by two or possibly three paintings that remained unfinished and presumably were destroyed. The first mention of a *Nachtstück* occurs in Elizabeth's Journal on 30 March 1840, but on 18 June she records that "Edmund has begun his Night Piece again," which opens the possibility that the *Nachtstück* of 30 March was one of the destroyed paintings, about which nothing whatever is known. What is certain is that Moorash took unusual pains with this canvas, which was not completed until the end of September.

It was during the long composition of this painting that an event occurred which must take its place among the more bizarre episodes in the annals of American romanticism. In late June, at Strawson, Edward Vail's beloved wife, Charlotte, fell ill with a mysterious wasting disease. She could not rise from her bed; she ran a continual low temperature; she could scarcely eat. A local doctor diagnosed pleurisy and recommended mountain air, but a specialist in respiratory diseases summoned from Philadelphia declared her lungs to be sound and urged that the patient be moved to a warm, dry climate. A third physician, from Boston, noted for his work in nervous diseases, prescribed bed rest and absolute quiet and warned that under no circumstances should the patient be moved. In despair, Vail sat by the bedside of his bride from dawn to midnight, holding her limp hand and gazing at her with tender, moist eyes. As the days passed he watched her cheeks grow hollow, her dark eyes grow large, her face fill with weariness and suffering. One night when the end seemed near, Charlotte was seized with a sudden, desperate animation, and struggling up in bed she confessed in a torrent of tears that she had fallen in love with Edmund Moorash. Edward Vail was a mediocre artist, but he prided himself on being a good-hearted man, and he was capable of imagining a noble, perhaps too noble, gesture. Shattered by the news, he at once sat down and wrote a remarkable letter, which has not survived but is summarized in the diary of Elizabeth Moorash's friend Ann Hudley. In it Vail revealed his wife's terrible secret and earnestly entreated Moorash to come to Strawson and save her by any means in his power. Did he understand that he was asking Moorash to become his wife's lover? After reading the letter Moorash stayed shut up in his studio for two days; on the night of the second day he walked the six and a half miles to Rose Cottage and did not return until morning. Precisely what happened during that visit will never be known, but Moorash began visiting Strawson three times a week, and Charlotte's health swiftly improved. All of Charlotte's letters to Moorash were later destroyed, but a fragment was discovered in a trunk in Boston in 1957. It reads as follows:

My dearest Edmund,

Today I looked through the window toward Stone Hill and saw you in the Heavens all fiery bright. Come to me come to me in a shower of fire—O my bright angel—my King— you are a stag of the forest—a lion of the mountains. How my soul aches for you. May God forgive

Vail's journal was also destroyed, but the incidents at Strawson did not pass unnoticed and found their way into several diaries, in particular that of Vail's brother Thatcher, from which we may reconstruct the apparent course of events. It appears that Vail absented himself every other day from Rose Cottage, leaving before dawn and returning late at night. For at least one month and probably two, until the end of August, Moorash visited Charlotte Vail regularly. They never left the house. Where could they go? Thatcher Vail's diary speaks of "disgusting licentiousness" and the "shrill laughter of devils behind muslin curtains"; in assessing such statements it must be remembered that he speaks not only as the outraged older brother but also as a man who, two years earlier, unsuccessfully courted the fifteen-year-old Charlotte Singleton and was rejected in favor of his own brother. The love of Moorash and Charlotte Vail was certainly physical, and desperately unhappy. Charlotte, who had always admired and even loved her husband, was anguished by guilt; Moorash, always scrupulous to a fault, was conscious of injuring his friend in the very act of fulfilling his request; and despite his fierce attachment to Charlotte, he kept waiting for her to ask him to go, please go, and was always conscious of holding himself back. Vail himself could no longer bear the sight of his former friend; he was simply waiting for the hellish summer to end. In early September he wrote a second letter to Moorash, in which he offered to release his wife to him, on the condition that he marry her. This letter appears to have brought about a crisis: Charlotte declared hysterically that she could never abandon her husband, and she and Moorash vowed to "die" to each other forever. The vow was broken in a week, when Charlotte in a state bordering on madness arrived unannounced at Stone Hill Cottage shortly before midnight. Moorash would not see her; she spent the night in Elizabeth's arms, weeping uncontrollably. In the morning Elizabeth returned with her to Rose Cottage, where Vail declared that he was leaving for Boston the next day, and that Charlotte was welcome to accompany him as his lawful wife or to leave him forever. Elizabeth spent the night at Rose Cottage and saw

Charlotte into the coach the next morning. Vail settled in Boston and began his swift rise to fame as a portraitist, noted for the clarity of his flesh tones; he never returned to Strawson. A portrait of him in 1846 by Chester Calcott shows a man with melancholy eyes and a stern mouth. Charlotte remained his devoted wife; only, she was often tired, and liked to keep to herself, out of the social whirl. Moorash shut himself up in his studio and finished the *Nachtstück* before the end of September.

[15]

THE HOUSE OF USHER
1840
Oil on canvas, 39 1/8 x 37 3/8 in.

Edgar Allan Poe's "The Fall of the House of Usher" was collected in *Tales of the Grotesque and Arabesque* (1840). Although Moorash might well have read a copy of the book, there is no reference to it in Elizabeth's Journal, which does, however, mention "The Fall of the House of Usher" in passing (8 December 1840) and never refers to any other tale by Poe. It is therefore possible that Moorash read the story in *Burton's Gentleman's Magazine* (September 1839), a copy of which might have been brought to him or Elizabeth by William Pinney or any one of several other visitors during 1839 and 1840. The painting was begun some time in October and completed before Christmas.

The picture has been taken to represent the collapse of the House of Usher in the famous last paragraph (see Havemeyer, p. 79), but such a reading presents two difficulties: the word "fall" is conspicuously absent from the title of the painting, and the painting does not actually show the dreamlike house falling into the tarn. The second objection is perhaps the less decisive, for Moorash might well have intended to represent the fall in a non-literal fashion, but the title cannot so easily be explained away. The striking presence of red tints, like flakes of fire, that flash up among the browns and blacks are supposed by Have-meyer to represent the murky light of the blood-red moon, but the red tints may with equal justice be seen to allude to other reds in the tale, such as the "feeble gleams of encrimsoned light" that make their way through the trellised panes of Usher's stu-dio, or the drops of blood on Madeline's white robes. It is more to the point that the dissolving, vanishing, visionary house, paint-ed in nervous small strokes separated by intervals of brown or black, is mirrored in the dark tarn. The whole effect is less that of a fall than of the dissipation of a fever-vision: a dream-house over its dream-reflection vanishing into black depths. It is as if Moorash had imagined the House of Usher to be insubstantial by nature, to be perpetually on the verge of dissolving or disap-pearing.

The motif of doubling, so reminiscent of *Clair de lune*, and the allusion to a brother and sister, suggest that the painting, and the tale itself, must have had a strong personal meaning for Moorash. If Moorash saw himself as Roderick Usher, and Eliz-abeth as Usher's sister, then the painting may express his sense of guilt over burying Elizabeth alive at Stone Hill Cottage, and over their mutual, fatal interdependence; but in the last analy-sis, the picture remains enigmatic.

[16]

ELIZABETH AND SOPHIA
1841
Oil on canvas, 28 1/4 x 34 5/8 in.

After Pinney's marriage proposal to Elizabeth on the last day of August 1839 he returned with Sophia to Boston, but we read in

Elizabeth's Journal of a Thanksgiving visit at Stone Hill Cottage, and during the following spring, when Pinney returned to Black Lake, the four friends were once again often in one another's company, though not quite as often as during the first summer. Moorash's summer affair with Charlotte Vail was apparently kept secret from William and Sophia, who nevertheless must have heard rumors and noted his frequent and uncharacteristic absences. The precise state of knowledge among the four remains uncertain, but it appears to have been as follows: Edmund and Elizabeth never spoke of Charlotte Vail to William or Sophia, who half-knew about it and chose not to investigate. William's relation to Elizabeth had by now taken its new shape: he resigned himself gracefully to the role of rejected suitor and resumed, with a touch of wistfulness, his enjoyment of her company. His friendship for Edmund underwent no discernible change, though there is evidence in Sophia's letters to her friends Fanny Cornwall and Eunice Hamilton that he must at times have felt he had lost Elizabeth to her own brother. The one striking change was in Sophia: she grew markedly cool to Edmund, criticized him to her brother, and grew still more devoted to Elizabeth.

A preliminary sketch of *Elizabeth and Sophia* was made during a walking tour with the two women on a day in April 1841 when William was unable to be with them, having had to return to Boston on business and having left Sophia with Elizabeth and Edmund at Stone Hill. The freely drawn pencil sketch shows both women distinctly—Sophia is wearing her straw hat, Elizabeth is bareheaded—but the painting shows only their shadows stretching across a field in the too-yellow light of late afternoon. The long shadows have a slightly sinister air as they ripple distortedly across the darkening grass. The heads are bent close, as though sharing a confidence; below the shoulders the two shadows flow into each other.

[17]

SOPHIA DAYDREAMING
1841
Oil on canvas, 27 1/2 x 34 in.

We know from Elizabeth's Journal that Sophia disliked being painted and agreed to pose for this picture only at Elizabeth's "urgent entreaty" (3 July 1841). It is not clear whether she disliked posing in general, or posing for Moorash in particular; she appears to have felt uneasy at being stared at and "studied to death" (Journal, 6 July). It is difficult to avoid the inference that she was disturbed by the intimacy of a prolonged sitting, in which she had to endure passively Moorash's sustained gaze. Sophia had always had to fight a secret disapproval of her brother's eccentric friend; after the failed marriage proposal she held Moorash responsible for Elizabeth's refusal. Nor did she share her brother's enthusiasm for Moorash's painting: Sophia viewed the pictures with bewilderment and growing distaste, always preferring the meticulously detailed and elegantly precise portraits of Chester Calcott and Edward Ingham Vail.

The sittings began on 3 July and continued for more than a week before they were terminated by Sophia. She appears to have relented, for on 23 July Elizabeth notes another sitting; the last recorded session took place on 8 August. Moorash worked on the painting all summer but did not complete it until October, long after Sophia and William had returned to Boston. Sophia's opinion of the painting is not known, but from what we know of her taste she cannot have cared for it. The painting is reminiscent of Moorash's earlier masterpiece, *Elizabeth in Dream*, although here he makes use of the device of the landscape seen from a window. Part of a window frame divides the painting into two realms, an inner realm indicated by a portion of wall on which part of a picture (unidentified) is visible, and an outer realm of darkening garden and dusky sky. But the contrasts are deliberately undermined and thrown into question, for it is impossible to make a neat distinction between the world of art and the world of nature, or the world of imagination and the world of experience: the room flows into landscape, which in turn echoes the room, and Sophia herself flows wraithlike through the window into the garden, thereby binding the inner and outer worlds. Both worlds of the painting appear to be Sophia's daydream, but she herself is no less dreamlike. It is as if Moorash had attempted to paint the experience of daydream itself, in which the boundaries between inner and outer grow uncertain. Elizabeth was "deeply affected" by the painting, which she considered "masterful" (16 October). Moorash promptly gave it to her, and she hung it in her bedroom between two windows looking out over the garden.

[18]

PHAEDRIA'S ISLE
1842
Oil on canvas, 32 1/16 x 42 in.

In the long winter evenings of 1841–42 Elizabeth read aloud to Edmund, night after night, Sir Walter Scott's *Guy Mannering*, *Quentin Durward*, and *The Black Dwarf*, Hawthorne's *Twice-Told Tales* (the edition of 1837), Byron's *Manfred*, and Spenser's *Faerie Queene*. She appears to have read the latter at the rate of one canto a night, over a period of seventy-four consecutive nights (six complete Books of twelve cantos each, and the two Mutabilitie cantos). During the readings Edmund liked to lie on the sofa in the kitchen with his ankles crossed and his head on a pillow, warming his hands on the bowl of his pipe and staring off into bluish smoke-clouds.

The subject is taken from Book II, canto vi of *The Faerie Queene*, in which Spenser introduces the temptress Phaedria: her aim is to draw knights across the Idle Lake to her pleasant isle and lull them into a life of drowsy sensual pleasure. Like Spenser's more sinister temptress in the Bower of Bliss, Phaedria derives from a rich tradition of Renaissance sorceresses in enchanted gardens, in particular Ariosto's Alcina and Tasso's Armida, both of whom are modeled after Homer's Circe. Phaedria is presented as "loose" and "light," but she represents a powerful temptation: to swerve away from a difficult task, to rest awhile, to relax the will. She is the secret voice whispering in the ear of all those whose lives are bent toward difficult achievement: she is the song the sirens sang, the same song heard by Ulysses lashed to the mast and by Gustav von Aschenbach relaxing on the beach. Moorash, who lived to work, must often have entertained the dream of some other life, in some other world: a life of peace, sweetness, and sensual ease.

Moorash wisely makes no attempt to imitate Spenser's description, but instead seeks to render the island's power of enchantment: the dark island looms before us in an unearthly light, parting here and there to reveal dim, green-shadowy recesses that wind back into velvet darkness. The island, a gloomy mass of overlapping blues, greens, and violets painted in free, flowing brushstrokes, appears to beckon us inward, to soothe us with the scents of green summer dusks, to drug our senses with a dreamlike melting sweetness: it invites us to yield, to bow our weary heads. But even as it does so we are aware of a counterpressure. That dark is too dark, those mossy recesses close too quickly. The unseen bristles everywhere. There are hints that we will never return from the inviting darkness, and that what presents itself as sensual surrender is nothing but Death. Moorash's vision, in fact, reaches to the deep place where love becomes death: the desire to surrender, the longing to lose oneself in another, becomes the final surrender, the longing for annihilation.

The question of the influence of Spenser-derived paintings on Moorash's *Phaedria* remains unanswered. Since the 1770s *The*

Faerie Queene had inspired a host of paintings in England and America; Moorash may have known West's three Spenser paintings of the 1770s (*Una in the Woods, The Cave of Despair,* and *Fidelia and Speranza*), Copley's *Red Cross Knight* (1793), and Allston's *The Flight of Florimell* (1819), although there is no evidence that he ever gave a moment's thought to a single one of these solemn academic studies, and in any case his approach to Spenser is entirely his own. Influence, however oblique, is far more likely to have come from the mysterious Spenser cult that raged in Cambridge during Moorash's first two undergraduate years (1826–28) before ceasing abruptly under suspicious circumstances, and that took its most distinctive expression in the form of a secret society who called themselves the Sons and Daughters of the Faerie Queene. This group of men and women from Cambridge's highest social circle adopted names of characters in *The Faerie Queene* (Busirane, False Florimell, Scudamore, Queen Malecasta, Belphoebe, Sansjoy), met weekly at midnight in the homes of various members, and enacted elaborately costumed *tableaux vivants* based on scenes from their beloved poem, in which women of impeccable moral standards and unquestioned virtue were said to dress like nymphs, shepherdesses, temptresses, and fleeing maidens, in scant and semitransparent costumes, while pillars of male society assumed the garb of satyrs, wicked enchanters, and lustful hermits. The tableaux were enhanced by elaborate stage scenery designed and painted by Richard Henry Daw, later a minor member of the Phantasmacists but at this time known to be an acquaintance of Chester Calcott and William Pinney. Can Moorash have been present at one of the midnight meetings of the Sons and Daughters of the Faerie Queene, who occasionally issued highly coveted invitations to friends outside the charmed circle? Daw's backdrops were destroyed by fire in 1832 but are said to have produced remarkably suggestive atmospheric effects, especially in the dark forest scenes favored by the group, in which he was adept at conveying sensations of lurking evil and hidden menace by means of mossy rocks, shadowy grottoes, gnarled branches, and twisting paths, murkily illumined by red-paned lanterns and obscured by the smoke of concealed braziers.

Moorash had unusual difficulty with *Phaedria's Isle,* taking it up and abandoning it all through the spring and summer, beginning work on several paintings that he never finished and evidently destroyed, and completing it only in November, with the remark that it was "botched work." It is not hard to understand his struggle if we recall that the painting expresses in part a desire to be released from painting. But Phaedria is also a temptress who has a "loose lap" (II. vi. 14); the delights she offers, like those of Acrasia in the Bower of Bliss, are sexual. The precise state of Moorash's feelings toward Sophia at the time of the painting are difficult to determine. His relation to her had become more problematic after the completion of *Sophia Daydreaming;* she refused to sit for him again and did not accompany William on his ten-day visit in January 1842, at the very time Elizabeth had begun to read *The Faerie Queene* aloud. She returned to Black Lake with William in the spring, and the mutual visits across the lake resumed, but an incident of the summer is perhaps indicative of what was to come. On a warm night in July the four friends decided to walk all around Black Lake. They proceeded in continually shifting pairs: Edmund-William and Sophia-Elizabeth, Edmund-Elizabeth and Sophia-William, Edmund-Sophia and William-Elizabeth. At one point when Edmund was walking with Sophia, she lost her footing on a loose stone and started to fall. Edmund seized her and prevented her fall; but she began struggling, wrenched herself free, and fell to the ground. William came running up and helped her to her feet. Elizabeth wiped dirt from her dress. When Elizabeth looked up, she saw Edmund standing unnaturally still with a wild look in his eye. A moment later he bent over, picked up a stone, and threw it violently into the lake. He stood watching the moonlit ripples before turning back to Sophia with an anxious inquiry about her fall. Sophia started walking and suddenly clung to William's arm; the party returned to the Pinney cottage, for Sophia had twisted her ankle.

[19]

AUGUST NIGHT
1843
Oil on canvas, 40 5/8 x 34 1/4 in.

Immediately after completing *Phaedria's Isle* in November 1842, Moorash began a series of sketches for a second Spenser-inspired painting called *The Cave of Despair*, which he worked at through the end of the year; neither the painting nor the sketches have survived. His difficulties continued. In February he traveled to Boston with Elizabeth—his first trip since the move to Saccanaw Falls in 1836. There he looked up old acquaintances whose letters had remained unanswered for seven years, stopped in at the Athenaeum, visited three or four studios, and dined with the Pinneys. Within a week he was restless and fretful, and traveled with Elizabeth to Hartford, where they spent the night with their parents and fled the next morning. They traveled south—Baltimore, Charleston, Richmond—and were back at Stone Hill Cottage on 2 March. A window had broken; snow lay drifted on the kitchen floor. By 4 March Moorash was back at work, on a painting that appears to have been an early version of one of the lost works of 1844. William and Sophia returned to Black Lake at the end of April. Edmund sketched outdoors, took long walks, stayed up all night, and slept till noon. On 31 July he tripped in the barn and cut his forehead. On 2 August, as he and Elizabeth were leaving the Pinney cottage after midnight, he broke away from Elizabeth and returned to the front door, where he said something to Sophia that caused her to step back with a hand raised to her throat. Precisely what he said is unclear, but it appears to have been a declaration of love. The next day he shut himself in his upstairs studio—he had been working in the barn—and began *August Night,* which he completed in two weeks.

It is a remarkable painting, which has retained its power to shock. The startling sky, which appears to crack open and release a violent radiance, is painted with a new freedom of brushstroke, a stroke that makes no attempt to conceal itself, as if the paint and the night it represents are one and the same. The entire picture pulses with a strange, intoxicating energy, as if the hills, the wood, and the swirling night-sky have been swept up into the all-annihilating brilliance of the unseen moon. The picture has been called a celebration, but it evades easy description; it affects the viewer as a release of energy, with the doubleness implied by release: liberation and destruction.

Elizabeth records in her Journal that on the morning of 18 August Edmund called down to her in a "strange, agitated voice." When she entered his workroom she saw two things: the painting, which she calls "a whirlwind," and Edmund, lying on his back on the floor. She cried out and ran to him, but he smiled up at her and said that he had been studying his picture at a new angle. He thought it was done—what did she think? Elizabeth looked at *August Night* "through tears of terror and joy." She never got over the sense that the violent painting had struck him dead.

[20]

ANGER
1843
Oil on canvas, 26 1/4 x 20 1/2 in.

According to Elizabeth's Journal, Moorash rose from the floor, dusted himself off, and immediately began work on another painting, which he completed in the last week of September. *Anger* is unusual in Moorash's oeuvre both for its explicit statement of mood and for its treatment of the small foreground figure: she is drawn in firm outline and heavily stylized—white dress, yellow hair—so that she almost resembles a child's drawing of an angel. She stands with her back to the viewer and is looking out over a red lake. The landscape is sketchy and generalized, suggested in a few bold and flowing lines—shore, lake, hills, sky—and is painted entirely in shades of red, built up with layers of glazes. The red world appears to be streaming out of the little foreground figure, like rays around a sun.

Havemeyer is surely mistaken to attribute the anger of the title to Moorash himself. The evidence of Elizabeth's Journal is decisively against such an interpretation. Moorash reproached himself bitterly for offending Sophia by his words, by his very existence—how dare he sully her purity with his filth? Immediately upon beginning the painting he sent Elizabeth across Black Lake to effect a reconciliation, which she appears to have done; as if nothing had happened, the nightly visits were resumed, even as Moorash painted in red.

[21]

TOTENTANZ
1843?–45
Oil on canvas, 44 1/4 x 52 1/8 in.

The dating of Moorash's final paintings must remain uncertain, for two reasons. First, in the last months of 1843 he began to make a regular habit of putting aside a painting-in-progress and returning to it weeks or months later after having begun a new painting that also would be put aside after an intense bout of work; there is evidence from Elizabeth's Journal that during a single summer month in 1844 he worked on four different paintings (only two of which have survived). Second, the Journal itself becomes spottier in the final years, often omitting whole weeks at a time as Elizabeth becomes increasingly incapacitated by severe headaches and a variety of obscure illnesses that prevent her from making detailed entries. With the possible exception of the final, fatal painting, we have no evidence that any of the last works is complete.

The first definite mention of the *Totentanz (Dance of Death)* occurs in Elizabeth's Journal on 23 June 1844: "A gray day. Edmund has returned to his Death Dance—says he *has* it now." This obscure entry suggests that Moorash was returning to a painting begun earlier, and a number of entries in the fall of 1843 (see Havemeyer for a full account) make it likely that he had begun or was thinking of beginning a painting with a death theme in late October. We last hear of the *Totentanz* in the spring of 1845: "Edmund has put aside his Death Dancers [*sic*] again" (2 May 1845). Whether he took it up again before his death in the summer of 1846 is a matter of speculation; Havemeyer finds some evidence for two periods of work, whereas Sterndale argues that he never returned to it after beginning the final series of portraits.

Moorash possessed engravings of Hans Holbein the Younger's series of drawings *Der Totentanz* (1524) and *Das Todesalphabet* (*The Alphabet of Death*, 1524), as well as engravings from *La grant danse macabre des hommes et des femmes* printed by Nicolas Le Rouge in 1496, but his handling of the subject is so radically his own that the search for a model is surely mistaken: he need have had no more than the broadest sense of a Dance of Death for his imagination to have taken fire. The conception is bold, stark, and disturbing: from a dark ground that at first appears empty and black emerges a line of five milky, transparent figures, who at one moment seem to melt into the darkness and at another to float into a kind of ominous half visibility. The figures, which seem to repel close inspection, appear to be dancing or revel-

ing—they carry sticks, bells, a tambourine—and are oddly distorted, as if displayed in gestures that have been unnaturally arrested. The first figure, with its hollow eyes, snub nose, and
sticklike forearm, emerges after many viewings as a dim, shifting skeleton; the four followers appear to be two men and two
women (with their long, eerily floating smokelike hair). But what
is most striking and uncanny about the *Totentanz* is the way it
continually presents itself as *different* from the way it appeared
a moment before—one is continually stepping closer, and farther back, and to the side, simply in an effort to see what is
there. The background alone is a masterpiece of murk, a tone
poem of dissonant darknesses. Dim forms appear to be visible,
only to reveal themselves as the curves of bold brushstrokes,
which again seem to tease the eye into evoking shapes that may
or may not be there. From Elizabeth's Journal we know something of Moorash's methods: we know, for instance, that over a
ground of white lead and oil he painted a more or less conventional landscape, the sole purpose of which was to be covered
by a layer of black pigment applied in such a way as to permit a
shadowy sense of the obscured landscape to show through at
certain angles or under certain kinds of illumination. We know
that Moorash experimented with scumbles and glazes. We know
that for a while he became obsessed with the literal thickness
of applied pigment and attempted to use that thickness to permit buried images to emerge. It is in this context that we first
hear of a series of paintings, all lost, called variously the Haunted Paintings, the Ghost Paintings, and the Ghost Canvases, to
which it will be useful to turn for a moment.

In addition to the six surviving paintings of 1844–46, there
are an unknown number of paintings now lost—presumably destroyed by Moorash himself—about which we hear from time
to time in Elizabeth's Journal and in occasional letters of Elizabeth and William Pinney to friends. Among the lost paintings,
variously estimated at between seven and fifteen, are a small

number known collectively as the Haunted Paintings, on which Moorash worked from time to time, but especially in the summer and early fall of 1844. There appear to have been at least six of these paintings, several of which are described in some detail in the Journal, for they disturbed and attracted Elizabeth. From her description it appears that all of the Haunted Paintings were characterized by thickly painted dark backgrounds, pale transparent figures that seemed to sink into the thick paint, and an ambiguous manner of impressing themselves on the eye: Elizabeth was never certain exactly what she was seeing. Moorash referred dismissively to the canvases as his "ghost tricks," but kept on painting them. The paintings troubled Elizabeth; she calls them "brilliant but sinister" and begins to feel haunted by them. On 12 August 1844 she records an interesting exchange:

> ELIZABETH: I'm beginning to feel I live in a haunted house!
> EDMUND *(shrugging):* Nothing new here. All paintings are ghosts.

After the concentrated work on the Haunted Paintings of the summer and early fall of 1844, Moorash appears to have dropped them for other projects, returning briefly to them in December; we last hear of a Haunted Painting in March 1845, shortly before his return to the *Totentanz*.

The *Totentanz*, then, may be thought of as the culmination of a particular series of experiments; its uncanny effects derive directly from the "ghost tricks" of the Haunted Paintings. The effect of the *Totentanz* on Elizabeth was extraordinary—she calls it "dangerous to look at" and adds: "Edmund has turned us all into ghosts." There was no doubt in her mind that the four figures led by Death were Edmund, William, Sophia, and herself.

It will be recalled that shortly after Moorash's offending words to Sophia on the night of 2 August 1843, a reconciliation appears to have been effected with the help of Elizabeth; in any case we find the four friends visiting back and forth across Black Lake as if nothing had changed. But everything had changed. From all indications it seems clear that Moorash was now desperately in love with Sophia, but forced to suppress his feelings in her presence. Elizabeth, always keenly sensitive to every nuance of her brother's moods, cannot have felt at ease in her friend's company: she was confused and even frightened by Edmund's passion for another woman, perhaps hurt and jealous, secretly hoping they could all return to a more innocent time— yet even as she suffered his obsession she remained the devoted sister who longed for Edmund to be happy, to have what he wanted. Alongside her jealousy and fear, therefore, another strain sounds in the Journal: her resentment toward Sophia for refusing Edmund. She imagines (4 September 1843) the marriage of Edmund and Sophia: "And why should I not continue to live in the same house with them, loving her as a sister?" She will not have to give up Edmund: she will simply add Sophia to their ménage. What threatens this idyllic vision is not a possible hesitation on the part of Edmund or Sophia to include Elizabeth in their marriage: what threatens it is Sophia's refusal to love and marry Edmund in the first place. But meanwhile new difficulties in friendship had arisen for both Sophia and William. Sophia, who did not return Edmund's passion, was forced to suffer his mute gazes, his pain, his noble suppressions, his deliberate coolnesses; above all she was forced to feel Elizabeth's distraction and unhappiness, for which Sophia felt obscurely responsible. Had she in some way caused Edmund to fall in love with her? (she asks in a letter to her friend Eunice Hamilton). She will not permit him to mistake her feelings a second time; yet she does not relish the role of cruel stony-hearted refuser, and she is aware that, in some way she cannot grasp, her refusal of Edmund has injured her relation to Elizabeth. As for William, his warm friendship for Edmund had already been severely tried during the time of his own unsuccessful suit of Elizabeth—in a sense, he had lost Elizabeth to Edmund—and he cannot have watched calmly his friend's sudden obsession with Sophia. It must at times have seemed to William that Edmund was trying to draw all the women to his side and leave William with no one. In addition, William's own decision not to marry, as well as his decision to live with his sister, was at least in part influenced by Edmund's life with Elizabeth; and now his friend, by throwing himself at Sophia, was rejecting the very world of tidy domestic arrangements that he himself had brought into being and presented to William as a model.

The Pinneys left for Boston in mid-September and did not return to the cottage on Black Lake until the late spring of 1844, when Moorash had almost certainly begun the *Totentanz*. On 8 August 1844, according to Elizabeth's Journal, the four friends were walking in a small wood when Edmund grasped William by the arm and invited him to "come along to the barn," where he still worked during the warm summer months and where the *Totentanz* stood on an easel among bits of straw. When the women returned to Stone Hill Cottage they found William and Edmund in animated discussion in the kitchen-parlor. "Pinney," cried Edmund, springing up from the sofa when Elizabeth and Sophia entered the room, "you're the best friend a raving madman ever had!" William laughed aloud, Sophia looked away with the shadow of a frown, and Elizabeth, who knew that Sophia thought Edmund a little mad, watched the scene tensely. In her Journal she noted that "E never behaves naturally before Sophia." But the elation was genuine: William had been "overwhelmed" by the *Totentanz* and had urged his friend not to abandon it. In doing so he made use of a curious argument that left a strong impression on Moorash. Whether you hate or love the painting, Pinney had argued, makes no difference: you must work on it as if the painting were a destiny, you must work on it as if you were dead.

[22]

DEATH SONATA
1844–45
Oil on canvas, 46 x 54 1/2 in.

The *Death Sonata* is first mentioned by Elizabeth in April 1844, although the entry leaves it uncertain whether Moorash had actually begun the painting or was merely speaking of a possible subject. The picture was definitely in progress by October 1844; there is no mention of it again until June 1845, when he appears to have taken it up for the third or fourth time, after an interval of several months, and we last hear of it in September. Although work on the *Death Sonata* alternated with work on the *Totentanz* (and other paintings), the evidence suggests that the *Totentanz* was begun earlier, and served as an inspiration for or challenge to the *Death Sonata*, which in turn appears to have influenced the earlier painting. The technical relation of the two, although complex, is undeniable; and they are the only two surviving paintings to employ the method of "haunting" a canvas.

The *Death Sonata* is in some respects a more difficult and challenging work than the *Totentanz*, because in it Moorash confined himself almost entirely to black. Indeed the first impression one has is of a uniform black, applied thickly with visible brushwork. The first impression yields to a second, deeper one: barely perceptible black forms are visible in or on or through the blackness. It is tempting to speak of "black on black," but such a description would be misleading: there is properly speaking no background, but rather a thick layer of dark paint (black, purple, burnt sienna) that gradually reveals what might be called "presences." The presences are so elusive, so deeply concealed by the very paint that reveals them, that their precise nature appears to change with different viewings; again as in the *Totentanz*, a deliberately uncanny effect is sought and achieved. Most responsible viewers agree that there is a presiding death-figure, a black-robed faceless figure (Havemeyer detects "an intimation of eyes") who may or may not be seated at a piano. There is a window, with a view of black distances, and perhaps a black moon; in the presumed room, four or more other figures, flowing and shadowy, hover between the visible and the invisible. The effect of the canvas, when it is not merely exasperating, is to haunt the viewer—to draw him or her into its elusive depths with the promise of some dark revelation. The method is in certain respects more radical and mystifying than that of the contemporary *Totentanz;* if it seems less successful, less fully achieved, this may be due not simply to its experimental nature or its state of incompletion, but to our own failure to follow Moorash into the enigma of his art—in other words, our failure to know how to look at it.

The fact that Moorash devoted two of his last paintings to the theme of death should not mislead us into supposing that he had intimations of his untimely end. Quite apart from the attractiveness of Death as a subject for romantic painters, poets, and composers, there were good reasons in 1844 and 1845 for Moorash to be preoccupied with mortality. He was hopelessly in love with a woman who spurned him, and who must at times have made him feel that death was the only way out. He was at the traditional middle of life (his thirty-fifth birthday fell on 16 July 1845), without a shred of worldly success; despite his aggressive self-confidence, he must sometimes have felt himself a failure. His emotional life was entirely bound up in a four-way friendship that had begun to show serious signs of strain—were they not all fools of Death, dancing merrily to the grave? In addition, the Journal makes it clear that he was racked by financial worries, and by guilt over his dependence on his sister's slender annuity. But above all, in these years he witnessed Elizabeth's decline into a disturbing species of illness. By late 1844 the occasional headaches of earlier years had blossomed into crippling two-day or three-day headaches, often accompanied by fits of vomiting. At the same time, Elizabeth begins to record—always very briefly—mysterious "aches" in her legs, as well as occasional attacks of "vertigo." In September 1844 Moorash traveled with her to Boston to consult a specialist in nervous disorders; Elizabeth was placed on a rigorous diet that did not cure her headaches and led swiftly to general weakness and a series of bronchial infections, which ended soon after she returned to her old eating habits. A second specialist, a friend of William Pinney's who traveled up from New York, prescribed pills that contained a mixture of quinine, digitalis, and morphine; the pills had no result other than to dull her pain and make her lethargic, and she began to grow dependent on the soothing effects of morphine. Moorash, who was closer to Elizabeth than to any other human being, and entirely dependent on her, cannot have failed to imagine, during her worst hours, his sister's death and his own death-in-life afterward; and it is possible that the continual, restless turn from painting to painting in these years was a sign of his fear that, once Elizabeth was gone, there would be no reason for him to go on painting.

[23]

WILLIAM PINNEY
1844–46
Oil on canvas, 34 1/8 x 29 1/16 in.

Contemporaneously with the *Totentanz* and *Death Sonata*, as well as with the lost paintings of 1844–46, Moorash turned to portraiture of a startling and original kind. Perhaps it is misleading to speak of these paintings as portraits, although several features of portrait painting remain; rather, they are dream-visions, intimations, soul-studies—what Elizabeth felicitously calls "inner landscapes" (Journal, 4 January 1846). The immense, ethereal figures have the look less of human creatures than of mythic beings; it is as if only by smashing what he once called "the mimetic fetters" that Moorash could release into paint the human mystery.

Moorash appears to have begun a portrait of William Pinney in February 1844, destroyed it or set it aside for the *Totentanz* and later the Haunted Paintings, and returned to it briefly in December. He was at work on it again during the early summer of 1845, at a time when he had taken up the *Death Sonata* after an apparent break; it is unclear whether he laid it aside or proceeded with it intermittently during the next eight months, but he was at work on it once again in March 1846, before abandoning it and all other work in May for what was to prove his final painting.

More than any other painting by Moorash, including *Dornröschen*, the disturbing portrait of William Pinney impresses the viewer as an illustration for a book of fairy tales. A transparent and shadowy giant bestrides a dark lake and rises into the night sky, where his streaming hair forms fiery stars and comets. He is naked and powerful; through his body we see night clouds and a glimmer of moonlit hills. But what is striking is the expression on the face: a doubting, brooding expression, a kind of suspiciousness ready to burst into anger but held in check by uncertainty. His hands are half-clenched beside his sinewy transparent thighs. The giant gives an impression of a great prisoner in chains—of power mysteriously baffled or frustrated. He radiates a peculiar aura of anguish, weakness, and danger. The figure is deliberately a creature of myth or legend, yet a comparison with the conventional chalk sketch of Pinney from 1829 (see [2]) reveals an uncanny kinship. Elizabeth writes on 4 June 1845: "My soul recognized him before my eyes did—in that terrible dream-change—a shudder passed over my body—E has seen into W's very soul—I could not bear to look long, but turned away with a feeling of dread."

Although Pinney remained an unwavering admirer of Moorash's art, and a close friend to the very end—Moorash was to say that Pinney was the only friend he ever had—nevertheless the friendship was subject in an unusual degree to unhealthy strains and tensions. Pinney had courted Elizabeth Moorash and lost; and after a struggle he had resigned himself, with a certain good-natured wistfulness, to the not unattractive role of rejected lover. When Moorash fell violently in love with Sophia Pinney in the summer of 1843, William cannot have been unaware of the almost comical repetition of a pattern, including the rejection of the suitor. But a difference quickly revealed itself. That difference was the difference in temperament between Pinney and Moorash—for Moorash was not a man to resign himself good-naturedly to anything. His passion for Sophia, though he was able to tamp down its outward expression for the sake of being in her company, remained strong, tormenting, and obsessive. Pinney, a sensitive student of Moorash's moods, was therefore forced to endure the continual sense of his friend's suppressed passion, of his suffering and disappointment—and this from the very man whom he partially blamed for his own well-mastered suffering and disappointment. Moreover, Moorash's passion, if successful, would have meant for William the loss of his own sister, so that he was continually threatened by a kind of theft. Meanwhile his relation to Elizabeth was to undergo another change. As her illness became increasingly apparent, William drew closer to her. Often he sat with her for long afternoons while Moorash, deeply grateful to his friend, painted in the barn. But William's new closeness to Elizabeth rekindled his old sense of grievance: in large part he came to blame Moorash for Elizabeth's illness. For, as Sophia put it in a letter to Fanny Cornwall, if Elizabeth had been allowed to flourish as a wife and mother, to establish her own life independent of her brother's, would she not have been far healthier than under the conditions of "an unnatural attachment"? (Sophia appears to be blind to her own life with her brother, but in fact she always insisted on a difference: Elizabeth lived permanently with Edmund in an isolated cottage, whereas Sophia joined her brother only in the warm months and otherwise lived with a maiden aunt in Boston.) But Elizabeth's illness had a further effect. Sophia, despite her apparent insensitivity and even hostility to Moorash himself, was profoundly responsive to Elizabeth's moods; and as Elizabeth's headaches grew more serious, and her health more frail, Sophia herself began to experience sharp, dizzying headaches that left her prostrate for entire afternoons. William, often with two sick women to attend to, could not prevent himself from tracing the harm to his friend. At times he wondered whether his duty lay in protecting Sophia from the ailing Elizabeth; and a desire arose in him to escape from all this, to vanish somewhere into a peaceful place, even as his heart drew him to Elizabeth's side.

Such strains and dangerous tensions do much to account for the darker aspect of the portrait of William Pinney, for Moorash was acutely sensitive to Pinney's moods and cannot have failed to sense his friend's secret doubts and disapprovals. It is not surprising to learn that he showed the portrait to Pinney (on 14 August 1845); Elizabeth witnessed the event. Pinney looked at the painting a long time in silence. He then turned, threw Moorash "such a look as I cannot describe, for it was scarcely a human look," and walked away without a word. It was the only time he had failed to say something about one of his friend's paintings. As for Moorash, he turned to Elizabeth with a look of "angry triumph" and said: "See! He's hit!"

[24]

SOPHIA PINNEY
1844–46?
Oil on canvas, 34 1/2 x 28 in.

The earliest direct mention of a portrait of Sophia is in Elizabeth's Journal for May 1844, although it is not certain that this

is the same canvas as the one Moorash is said to have been working on in December. He appears to have begun two paintings,
abandoning the first in favor of the surviving one, which betrays
a clear kinship with the portrait of William Pinney and may have
been influenced by it. Sophia was shown the painting on 31 August 1845, two and a half weeks after William had viewed his
own portrait; nevertheless, Moorash appears to have continued
working on it during the next few weeks, setting it aside in late
September for the *Death Sonata*. He may have taken it up again
briefly in the early months of 1846; the evidence (see Havemeyer) remains inconclusive.

Again we have the familiar lake and line of hills, this time in
the dwindling light of a summer evening. Brooding over the
scene, like a spirit of the lake, is an elongated and ethereal
Sophia, whose lower body vanishes in the water and whose long
upper body winds serpentlike across the lake and back; her flowing hair continues the liquid lines of her body, and is shown
winding among the hills. The sweeping lines of the creature,
twisting back and forth along the canvas, create a paradoxical
feeling of energy and repose, as of a bird in flight; the barely human face is stricken with grief. Elizabeth, who first saw the portrait in company with Sophia, wrote in the Journal (31 August
1845): "As if struck with lightning. E paints the soul directly,
unencumbered by outward circumstance. Why does S's sorrow
waken in me such a clash and hubbub of feelings? She looks at
me as though I were all princess-white in my coffin. Away! I
crave the physic of laughter. Am I grown so cruel?"

Moorash's vision of a sorrowing Sophia may have been
"prophetic," as Havemeyer puts it, and it may have been a "psy-
chic reversal' (Altdorfer, p. 216) in which Moorash transposed
his own love-sorrow onto the features of the woman who had rejected him, but the facts suggest that Moorash was not making
an imaginative leap in the dark. Sophia Pinney may have lacked
spiritual greatness, but she was by no means the shallow egotist

she has sometimes been made out to be. She did not love Moorash or understand his work, but she behaved admirably in extremely trying circumstances; and in her passionate devotion to Elizabeth she rose above herself to spiritual heights from which she sometimes looked down aghast. Elizabeth was a powerful woman who exercised a kind of spell over Sophia, even more so than Moorash did over William Pinney. Under that spell, Sophia bent her life into a shape that more and more came to resemble the shape of Elizabeth's life; for although she liked to deny it, Sophia's decision to live with her brother on Black Lake was clearly influenced by Elizabeth's decision to live with Edmund. Sophia was as open to Elizabeth as she was closed to Elizabeth's brother, and we have seen that her acute sensitivity took the disturbing form of empathic suffering. In the early days of Elizabeth's illness, Sophia liked nothing better than to sit with Elizabeth in her sickroom for whole afternoons, reading aloud to her or remaining absolutely quiet if necessary, tending to her slightest needs, and passing the long hours by knitting a shawl for Elizabeth or rummaging among the supplies in Elizabeth's sewing table for the thread, thimble, needle, and scissors that she used for mending Elizabeth's frayed clothes. But as her friend's illness worsened, Sophia's own symptoms became more pronounced; and as many letters to Fanny Cornwall and Eunice Hamilton attest, Sophia's suffering was increased by the knowledge that because of her own prostrating headaches she was not always able to come to Elizabeth's side. In any case she felt utterly useless in preventing Elizabeth's decline. She believed passionately that Elizabeth's life with her brother was harming Elizabeth's health; and she never forgave Moorash for keeping his sister, as Sophia saw it, from marrying William. Her desire for Elizabeth's marriage to William appears to have been genuine, although it is difficult to believe she would not have experienced jealousy; it is possible that she desired what she could not permit herself to desire, a life alone with Elizabeth. Certainly, at the very least, she was deeply jealous of Elizabeth's devotion to Edmund. In the summer of 1845 that devotion took a strange turn, which appears to have shocked Sophia.

On an afternoon in late June when the men had walked to Saccanaw Falls to buy a bag of nails and drink a pint of ale at the Cat and Robin, Elizabeth on her sickbed made to Sophia a remarkable proposal. Staring earnestly at Sophia, she offered to marry William if Sophia would marry Edmund. The proposal threw Sophia into confusion and turmoil, as she reports in a letter (unsent) to Fanny Cornwall. She understood immediately that the wild scheme had been hatched for the sake of Edmund: Elizabeth, whose entire life had in Sophia's view been a continual sacrifice to Edmund, was willing to sacrifice herself even further for the sake of giving Edmund what he so desperately wanted: Sophia. Sophia, angry at the proposal's secret cause, nevertheless felt it as a fearful challenge: was she willing to sacrifice her own happiness for the sake of her brother's, and even more for the sake of Elizabeth, who would be delivered from her prison and would regain her health? The thought of moving into Stone Hill Cottage, of, as it were, *replacing* Elizabeth, struck her as strange and dreamlike, and not wholly unpleasing; but to marry Moorash, who made her feel "cold all over," was out of the question. Sophia spent an anguished night and rose at dawn no longer knowing how she felt. After a dreamlike breakfast she rowed across Black Lake with William in the "fierce light" of a cloudless blue day and walked with him the two miles to Stone Hill Cottage, where William left to look for Edmund in the barn. In the dusk of Elizabeth's curtained sickroom Sophia felt dazed; she was on the verge of saying yes, as if acceding to a terrible fatality, when Elizabeth, who was feeling better, immediately retracted her proposal of the other day, calling it "a wild idea bred of illness." Sophia, feeling faint, sat down quickly. The entire episode goes unmentioned in Elizabeth's Journal.

Later that month there occurred another incident that must

be taken into account in any consideration of Moorash's portrait of Sophia. She had spent the morning confined to her room in the cottage on Black Lake, unable to accompany William to Stone Hill Cottage, where he was to read to Elizabeth for an hour before returning to Sophia. In the course of the morning her mood darkened and she experienced a sharp premonition of Elizabeth's death. William returned to find her tense and agitated; after assuring her that Elizabeth was well, he took Sophia with him on horseback to Stone Hill Cottage, where he left her to ride into town. He returned to find her lying with her eyes closed on the sofa in the kitchen, being read to by Elizabeth while Moorash paced anxiously. Elizabeth recorded the incident in her Journal: she had been asleep, and woke to find Sophia sobbing hysterically and shrieking her name. Edmund, hearing the shouts from the barn, hurried to the house, where he discovered Elizabeth attempting to revive Sophia, who had fainted. When Sophia came to, she said that she had entered the darkened sickroom with a feeling of oppression and had been struck by Elizabeth's extreme pallor and stillness. She had spoken to Elizabeth, who lay with closed eyes; she had called out her name and shaken her shoulder, but Elizabeth lay motionless; her cheek felt deathly cold. It had been too much for Sophia, and she had burst into tears—after that, all was darkness. Elizabeth, with her usual sharpness, noted two things about her brother in the doorway: that he had "hesitated, with a kind of modesty, from intruding into the room, as if by coming to Sophia's aid while she was unconscious he would be taking advantage of her—until I summoned him to me," and that he had a spot of red paint on the side of his nose, which at first she had mistaken for blood.

Elizabeth also recorded the viewing of Sophia's portrait, an event arranged for the last day in August. William's absence on this occasion is not explained. It was Elizabeth who persuaded Sophia to walk with her down to the barn, where Edmund had covered the portrait with a white cloth. Was he thinking at that moment of *The Unveiling* [8], his painting of 1837? He stood for a moment staring at the cloth, then crying "So!" removed it with a flourish. Elizabeth, as we have seen, was violently moved: "As if struck with lightning. E paints the soul directly, unencumbered by outward circumstance." Sophia's response, as always, was disappointing. She looked at the portrait with an expression of blank politeness that slowly changed to irritation; and turning to Moorash "with an odd little smile," asked whether her hair was really so much in need of combing as that.

[25]

ELIZABETH MOORASH
1845–46
Oil on canvas, 34 1/2 x 28 1/2 in.

The final portrait of Elizabeth was begun in October 1845. Moorash worked at it continuously for about a month and then fitfully until the following May, when he set aside all his paintings for the ill-fated self-portrait.

Over the dark lake, Elizabeth lies sleeping. So deeply sunk in sleep is she that she appears to be under an enchantment. And indeed there is an air of enchanted stillness in the dark repose of the painting, as of a wildness calmed. It is as if the tension and disturbing energy of the portraits of William and Sophia have been transposed into peace—the same long, flowing lines here resolve into restfulness. The portrait has about it a storybook air: Elizabeth is a princess closed in a tower of sleep, to which no prince will come. Deeply, deeply, Elizabeth lies sleeping, in a spell from which she can never awake. But the world too lies sleeping: the hills, the night sky, the lake, all have fallen asleep beside and beneath and within her. The effect is different from that of *Elizabeth in Dream* [5], for there the world was dissolved by the dreamer, but here there is no dreamer and no dream; rather, there is the vision of an animate universe stilled in sleep. It is, if you like, a childlike vision, but one deepened with adult knowledge—it is such a vision as is possible only after a searing spiritual struggle. For in this portrait Moorash has done nothing less than imagine Elizabeth's death; and by lifting it into a realm beyond grief, he has come out on the other side of anguish.

By the summer of 1845 Elizabeth's headaches and other ailments were causing her to spend more and more time indoors, where she became increasingly dependent on the soothing effects of laudanum, prescribed by a Dr. Long of Strawson and easily obtainable in the two druggist shops of Saccanaw Falls. Only in the remissions of her illness was she able to leave Stone Hill Cottage to take long walks in her beloved woods, along her stream, or in the direction of Black Lake. After a particularly bad attack in late summer William persuaded Moorash to let him hire a housekeeper, a Mrs. Duff from Strawson, who came three times a week and soon became deeply devoted to both Elizabeth and Edmund. Elizabeth at first protested, but she quickly succumbed; there were certain chores she could no longer do.

The absence of Dr. Long's medical records, and the predominance of nonspecific symptoms such as headaches and dizziness, make it impossible to determine the nature of Elizabeth's illness, which may or may not have been psychosomatic. Although a depressive disorder cannot be ruled out, neither the Journal nor the scanty medical records provide conclusive evidence (see Havemeyer, p. 210 ff., for a complete summary). The "vertigo" and headaches suggest the strong possibility of high blood pressure; but since a practical blood-pressure gauge was not invented until the end of the century, all such suggestions must remain entirely speculative. Although hypertension or some related cardiovascular pathology would explain most, if not all, of Elizabeth's symptoms, they can also have resulted from other causes, such as extreme anxiety or excitement. Finally, in any consideration of illness before the mid-nineteenth century—that is, before the discovery of drug-induced poisoning—it must always be kept in mind that the manifestation of new, unexplained symptoms may have been caused by the doctors themselves.

Although the Journal records an increased irritability to certain stimuli, such as the sharp sound of a knife on a plate, the smell of urine, and the sudden dimming and flaring up of a candleflame because of imperfections in the wick, one of the odder manifestations of Elizabeth's illness was heightened sensitivity to literature, music, and art. Certain slow, languorous rhythms in the 1842 *Poems* of Alfred Tennyson, specific hushed, dreamy, drowsily drawn-out effects in Keats, produced by long vowels interwoven with droning *m*'s and *n*'s and softened with sibilants (she records "The maiden's chamber, silken, hushed, and chaste" from *The Eve of St. Agnes*), stray lines suggesting a mysterious vastness ("Noiseless as fear in a wide wilderness") or ringing with a call to some high action ("Say, my heart's sister, wilt thou sail with me?") would bring a quickening of heartbeat and flushed cheeks, so that Elizabeth would be forced to put aside a volume and lie with her hands folded on her collarbone, as if to press down her excitement. Listening to Sophia play Schumann's *In der Nacht* from the *Fantasiestücke*, op. 12, or Chopin's Nocturne in E-flat major, op. 9, no. 2, or the *andante doloroso* of Sonnenstein's Brocken Sonata, op. 16, with its long chains of unresolved harmonic suspensions and its plunging five-note motif, she would be brought to a state of dangerous exaltation, during which a pulse throbbed "visibly" in her neck (did she observe herself in the mirror?) and she felt alternately fiery hot and icy cold. But it was the art of painting that evoked in her the strongest and most disturbing responses. Once when William brought her a book of engravings of medieval German paintings, Elizabeth was gripped by a feverish excitement that kept her from sleep all that night and led the next morning to a fit of such violent coughing that Edmund in alarm had to summon Dr. Long from Strawson. She seemed to take in a picture all at once, like a sudden blow, and to experience it not simply in her nerve endings but in the deepest fibers of her being. It was as though some protective film had been dissolved by her illness, leaving her wide open. But if she was acutely susceptible to painting in general, she was fervently and perhaps unwholesomely sensitive to Edmund's painting in particular, the effect of which she describes in language of increasing intensity: "I turned to look, and lo! it entered me like fire" (2 May 1845); "a blow to the temple was that night sky to me, and I staggered back, gasping for breath" (14 August 1845); "the sweet poison flowed in me, chilling as it warmed" (8 November 1845).

That summer William and Sophia prolonged their stay at Black Lake to mid-September. It was during the second week of September, on a bright and unseasonably warm day, that Elizabeth held an interview with William which she recorded briefly in her Journal, but which Sophia reported at greater length in a letter to Eunice Hamilton (12 September 1845). Lying on her sickbed, her long hair strewn about her, her eyes "glowing with unnatural brightness," Elizabeth asked William to watch over her brother "if he should ever be left alone," for Edmund was "like a child, in some things." William gave his solemn pledge. When he stepped from the room, Sophia noted that his face was wet with tears.

[26]

SELF-PORTRAIT
1845?–46
Oil on canvas, 36 1/4 x 30 3/8 in.

In October 1845 Moorash spoke to Elizabeth of a self-portrait, but it is not clear from the Journal whether he had actually begun it. A self-portrait is mentioned again in December, although in a way that suggests he may still have been only dreaming his way toward it (8 December 1845: "E hard at work on *The Devil's Dream* [a lost painting]. Spoke of paradox of self-portrait: what is a self?") He was clearly at work on a self-portrait by May 1846, and he appears to have worked on it steadily from that time, setting aside all other work, until his death on 27 July.

Elizabeth rallied in the fall of 1845. Despite a small setback in November she had recovered sufficiently by mid-December to enjoy a ten-day Christmas visit from Sophia and William, during which all four took long walks in the wintry woods and fields, went skating on Black Lake, and hired a sleigh with "handsome carvings and cushioned seats, drawn by two horses, a black and a white," in which they took long rides through wild country. She was still well in April, when Sophia and William returned from Boston to their cottage on Black Lake, but in mid-May she took a turn for the worse, staying in bed for three days with headaches and violent vomiting. By June she had returned to her semi-invalid life, receiving visitors in her bedroom or on the sagging sofa in the kitchen-parlor. The Journal entries for June and July are extremely irregular: long, detailed entries on days of relative good health alternate with abrupt, fragmentary notes or utter silence. Despite the gaps, we are able to follow the progress of the *Self-Portrait* in some detail, for Moorash spoke about it to Elizabeth more than he was accustomed to speak of his work in progress; and we can trace the evolution of a strange scheme that quickly became an obsession.

The first mention of the scheme occurs on 6 June, a month after he had begun the *Self-Portrait:* Moorash intends to show the picture to Sophia in order to "open her eyes." The painting is not *for* Sophia; but he intends that she shall "be wakened by it from her slumber." Is he here perhaps thinking of himself as the triumphant prince, climbing to Dornröschen's tower? Elizabeth is skeptical of the plan: apart from Sophia's lack of understanding of Edmund's work, there is the question of the proper *aim* of a work of art. Moorash argues that a painting is intended to "excite feelings"—why then should he not wish to excite the feelings of Sophia? Elizabeth asks if that is all he intends. Moorash laughs harshly and replies that the devil works in mysterious ways—perhaps he'll possess her soul by means of his portrait. Elizabeth, disturbed by his answer, remains silent. On 18 June Moorash is discouraged and thinks of destroying the painting, but on 20 June he is hard at work. On 26 June Elizabeth is attended by Dr. Long after a bad night. The next day Moorash, who has been painting in the barn, moves to his cramped upstairs studio in order to be near Elizabeth. There is a gap of eight days, but on 5 July Elizabeth reports that she has taken a walk with Sophia and William. On 7 July Moorash tells Elizabeth that it's enough for him if Sophia is simply "presented with the evidence." His intention appears to have shifted: he now wishes to address her moral sense. Within a week he is filled with doubts and is on the verge of destroying the picture, but he recovers his enthusiasm and returns to work "with a vengeance." On 17 July Moorash states that "a painting is a dagger aimed at a heart." His intention appears to have changed again: he now wants to *wound* Sophia with his art. On 18 July Elizabeth asks whether he plans to woo Sophia with his portrait. Moorash grows thoughtful and replies: "No, I want her to look at me. She has never seen me." The continual assertion of contradictory intentions during the painting of *Self-Portrait* is perhaps indicative of an overwrought state of mind, but it should be noted that the shifting esthetic positions of June and July are connected by a consistent theme: Moorash is insisting on the power of painting to affect a beholder, to enter another mind. On 22 July he is "almost done with" the portrait. On 23 July he asks Elizabeth if she is willing to look at it and decide its fate. He shuts himself up for three days of feverish work and on the evening of 26 July brings down the canvas, covered with a white cloth, and sets it up on an easel at the foot of her bed. Facing Elizabeth, he watches her closely as he lifts the cloth.

Later that night Elizabeth recorded the events of 26 July in a rapid, excited hand. The painting "thrills and frightens me—pierces me to the very core." It is "dark and terrible—the image of Satan—dark." In the terrible eyes she sees "suffering—and sorrow—and evil unspeakable." She "cannot bear" to look at it "and yet—and yet." She begged Edmund to leave the painting with her for the night, so that she might speak with him about it in the morning.

The events of 27 July are occasionally hazy in detail, although clear enough in outline; there is no reason to doubt the accuracy of Mrs. Duff's *Report*. Edmund rose early and went down to breakfast, which he ate alone in the kitchen-parlor. Elizabeth sometimes slept to mid-morning or later, and he was careful not to disturb her. He returned upstairs to his room, perhaps to work on a painting laid aside months earlier, and was interrupted by Mrs. Duff's cry. He hurried downstairs. Elizabeth was unconscious and breathing erratically. Edmund hesitated for only a moment before leaving Mrs. Duff with Elizabeth and running the half mile into Saccanaw Falls, where he found that the local doctor was out on his rounds. He promptly hired a trap to take him to Strawson, only to discover that Dr. Long was attending a patient six miles away. In Strawson he was able to find a second doctor, a Dr. Parrish, who returned with him to Stone Hill; Dr. Parrish strode into the sickroom, bent over Elizabeth, and pronounced her dead. About fifteen minutes after the doctor left—it is not clear how long he remained—Sophia and William arrived. At the door Mrs. Duff informed them of Elizabeth's death. Sophia rushed wildly into the room, followed by Mrs. Duff, and threw herself to her knees beside Elizabeth. Sobbing hysterically, she seized Elizabeth's hand and began kissing it over and over again and pressing it to her tearstained cheek. William stood for a moment in the doorway, stunned and trembling, before walking into the room and sitting abruptly on the edge of the bed, where he bent his face into his hands. Moorash sat expressionless in a chair on the other side of the bed. Suddenly Sophia stood up, looked wildly about, and stepped over to a small sewing table, where she pulled open a drawer and removed a pair of sharp scissors. Uttering a cry, she ran to the portrait, which still stood on the easel at the foot of the bed, and began slashing at the face with the scissors. During this outburst Moorash stared at her from his chair but did not move. After striking repeated blows, Sophia dropped to her knees, raised her eyes to the ceiling, and with both hands thrust the scissors into her throat. Even as she raised her arms to strike the blow, Moorash leaped from the chair, but he was too late to prevent the scissors from entering with full force. It appears that he next attempted to wrench the weapon from her grasp, but Sophia, though bleeding profusely, struggled violently, as if she were being attacked. It was only now that William, as though startled out of a dream, tore himself from Elizabeth's side and with a "wild look" and "strangled cry" rushed over to the struggling pair. Moorash had succeeded in pulling the bloody scissors from Sophia's throat, and there now took place a fierce struggle between Moorash and William for possession of the scissors, in the course of which Moorash was wounded in the neck—it is not clear how. It is impossible to tell from the *Report* whether William was attempting to prevent a second suicide, or whether, in his half-mad state, he attacked his friend. William suddenly seemed to come to his senses and, holding Edmund gently, laid him on the floor. He became brisk and efficient, tearing strips of cloth to staunch the wounds of Edmund and Sophia, and ordering Mrs. Duff to fetch a doctor. When she returned some twenty minutes later with Dr. Parrish, whom she had overtaken on the road to Strawson, she found William lying on his back on the bed beside Elizabeth, one arm outstretched. She did not know at first that he was dead. On the floor lay one of Moorash's hunting pistols, which William had removed from the small deal table in the upstairs bedroom. Moorash was dead (later it was determined that he had died from a stab wound in the throat). Sophia was alive but unconscious; she died early the next morning.

A tableau of bloody corpses presided over by a mangled painting is an effect that Moorash would have deplored; he detested banal visions of the knife-and-cadaver kind. That his life should have ended as an imitation of a mediocre academic painting would nevertheless, one imagines, have elicited from him a wry smile, for it was his conviction that the contrivances of art were always superior to the accidents of life.

The *Self-Portrait* is badly damaged; despite painstaking restorative efforts, much of the face, including both eyes, is so torn and scratched as to be virtually unseeable. Nevertheless, the design or plan remains clear. Moorash retained the motif of lake, hills, and sky that he used in his three late portraits, as well as the method of mythic representation: the shadows of wings are visible, as if he had intended to portray himself as a great dark angel, a fierce and fallen Lucifer. Although even in its mutilated form the portrait retains a certain power, the damage condemns it to an uneasy place in Moorash's oeuvre, for it seems to hover in a limbo between art and biography, between the realm of imperishable beauty and the world of decay.

Elizabeth and Edmund were buried in the small graveyard in Saccanaw Falls, within sight of Stone Hill. The parents of Sophia and William insisted that they be returned for proper burial in the family plot in Philadelphia.

In October 1846 Charlotte Vail died, after a lingering illness.